In Memoriam

Walter Todds

The Land of the Living

Diffygiaswn pe na chredaswn weled daioni yr Arglwydd yn nhir y rhai byw. ⋆

The seven volumes of this series observe a mainly chronological order. It reads as follows:

⋆ Author's note:
This is the penultimate verse of Psalm 27: '*I had fainted* unless I had believed to see the goodness of the Lord in the land of the living.' It was the word '*diffygiaswn*' that attracted me, and I took it to mean that the poet would give up without the hope of a meaningful destiny for his people. I am aware that the word has been omitted in more recent translations: but it remains apposite to a sequence of stories drawn from the life of a society under siege.

The remaining titles in this series will be reprinted in 2000 and 2001

1

AMY PACED UP AND DOWN IN FRONT OF THE POST OFFICE SECTION of Glanrafon Stores. Behind the grille Nanw More's lips moved silently as she added up the figures in the ledger. The presence of the younger woman made it difficult for her to concentrate. Amy was wearing a fashionable blue dress with a white collar scarf. A box camera in a brand new case made of a brown fabric was suspended from a thin strap over her right shoulder. It bounced against her hip as she moved about in her effort to remain silent. Nanw herself was wearing a faded pinafore and, even as she counted, her hand passed unobtrusively down her front in an unconscious effort to improve her own image.

'His place is here.'

Amy could no longer prevent herself speaking.

'There can be no question about it. Am I disturbing you?'

Nanw smiled wanly and shook her head. Amy walked across the bare floorboards of the shadowy interior of the general store to try and interest herself in the sacks of dried fruit and cereals laid out alongside the grocery counter. She played with a metal scoop with a wooden handle and listened to the voices of workmen across the yard replacing defective sheets in the corrugated iron roofing of the Dutch barn. They were responding as respectfully as they could to the staccato instructions of Mrs Lloyd, Nanw's grandmother and the over-active proprietor of Glanrafon Stores and Glanrafon Farm. Mrs Lloyd's enquiries and instructions did little to facilitate the execution of work in a position that was already difficult enough. Impatiently Amy dropped the scoop and returned to the Post Office section to talk to Nanw.

'I can't see why he went away in the first place,' she said. 'Can you?'

Nanw frowned and held her head to one side as she strained to account for her brother's behaviour. She spoke at last.

'He wouldn't accept anything. Not even death. Especially her death.'

Amy rotated the sole of her shoe against the wooden floorboard.

1

'That's ridiculous,' she said. 'I know he's a poet and all that. But we all have to accept it, don't we?'

Nanw continued to meditate upon her brother's unaccountable behaviour.

'I think there were other things,' she said. 'More general things that disturbed him. He wasn't prepared to accept anything. What I mean is, he wanted to start everything all over again. Even life itself. That's what I think.'

Amy made a great effort to understand the man's distress. He had lost his young wife in childbirth, but the dead girl had also been Amy's closest friend and the bond between them had been just as binding as any marriage, and of longer duration. Impatience welled up again to overwhelm her attempt at empathy.

'She's been dead for almost two years,' Amy said, 'Enid, bless her. It will soon be two years, won't it? And then little Bedwyr will be two years old. A two-year-old boy needs a father. I've never seen anything more obvious in all my life.'

'That's just what I said to him when he was home last,' Nanw said. 'Almost the exact words.'

'And what did he say?'

Amy placed her fingers on the ledge and stared expectantly at Nanw through the wire grid.

'"What's the difference," ' he said. ' "Two minutes or two years." '

Nanw saw the impatience and disapproval on Amy's face. Her inevitable response was to try and construct a better explanation of her brother's behaviour, something that might serve at least as a temporary defence.

'He's trying to forget his sorrow by cultivating these other interests. Play-writing and socialism and so on. In London he can lose himself and forget his pain. That's what I think. And at the same time cultivate these things he's interested in. He meets very interesting people. Outside office hours. And he says by specialising in Company Law he'll understand better the inner workings of the capitalist system and make more money himself in order to contribute more generously to the effort to bring it crashing down.'

2

Nanw's explanation petered out. Amy was looking at her through the grille as if she were some caged curiosity, parroting fragments picked up from her brother essentially without sense because only half understood. It was possible that he too had picked them up to weave them into a sequence of sounds that could bring him some temporary comfort.

'He has a son,' Amy said. 'Doesn't he realise that?'

Nanw sighed deeply. She turned her head to make certain that the cherub in question was still asleep on the mound of cushions in the corner of his playpen that she could see in the side parlour, at the end of the long drapery and haberdashery counter. The door of the room had been removed twenty-five years ago so that her grandfather could keep an eye on the counter while he sat writing at his roll-top desk. The desk still occupied the same position against the parlour wall. Amy leaned over the drapery counter as far forward as she could to catch her own glimpse of the little boy in the pen.

'He doesn't hold that little darling responsible?' she said.

'Oh no. No.'

Nanw was anxious to defend her brother from so brutal an accusation.

'I should think not.'

Amy made no effort to keep her voice down. If it woke him, so much the better.

'The poor little angel. He's so like her. He shouldn't be sleeping really now, should he?'

'It's his teeth,' Nanw said. 'He gets this soaring temperature when he's teething. And then he sleeps it off.'

'He's waking up,' Amy said.

She held her breath like someone about to witness a marvel of nature. The empty stores was filled with a sepulchral hush before they heard the little boy chuckling to himself. The sound drew them like a magnet. Nanw raised a section of the counter so that Amy could join her in the narrow channel between the counters and the shelves. As they tiptoed closer he stood up. He grasped the wooden rails, ready for any joyful encounter. His soft fair hair was damp and flattened against the smoothness of his forehead and the

3

dimples on his cheeks seemed to have broken a delicate sheath of sleep so that he emerged from it as fresh as a newly sprung flower.

'Who's my little lion then?'

Amy murmured ecstatically.

'Who's my little lion in a cage?'

Nanw left Amy's side to pass swiftly between the playpen and the roll-top desk to open the door of the small glass conservatory and reach for a white enamel chamber-pot hidden behind a wilting green palm. She snatched Bedwyr up, removed his trousers and obliged him to sit on the pot. Amy followed the procedure with intense interest.

'Isn't he a good boy?'

She whispered admiringly. She watched Nanw raise a finger to her mouth and then to her ear in order to make the little boy attend to the pleasing sound of his pee pinging against the metal pot. Amy held her own breath ostentatiously to join in the little game.

'Good little boys have good little habits.'

Nanw chanted the refrain. He plodded freely around the pen without his trousers while she moved through the conservatory door to empty the pot down the drain in the paved courtyard. At the end of the yard was a high wall with a green door. This led directly into the front garden of the original eighteenth-century farmhouse to which the stores was a complex extension. Nanw paused briefly in the sunlight. With the pot in her hand she derived momentary pleasure from the open air and the familiar enclosed environment. Amy was talking to her. There was a smile on Nanw's face as she returned to the side parlour.

'Don't you think he should be circumcised?'

The little boy's penis was lost in plump folds of skin.

'I don't know,' Nanw said. 'Should he?'

Aware that the two women were watching him, the little boy began to stamp his feet to invite even closer attention.

'They say it's more hygienic,' Amy said.

Nanw opened the small chest of drawers where she kept changes of clothing for Bedwyr. The understanding between the two

4

women was so complete they could give voice to whatever thoughts passed through their minds or remain comfortably silent.

'He's so like her,' Amy said. 'The living image.'

Nanw's eyes closed as she tested the boy's clothes against her cheek.

'To think he was baptised on his mother's coffin.'

Amy spoke in a trance-like monotone that would make what she was saying unintelligible to the child.

'Every time I see him, I see her. The living image.'

'I wish I'd been kinder to her,' Nanw said.

The confession was blurted out. Absolution came from Amy and it brought immediate relief.

'That's something we all wish,' Amy said. 'She was too good for this world, that was the trouble.'

Nanw was able to smile fondly as she indicated her grandfather's roll-top desk beyond the playpen.

'She used to sit there a lot,' she said. 'When she was pregnant. I could see her from my stool in the Post Office section. Me doing accounts and Enid reading my grandfather's *History of the Presbyteries*. If she wasn't writing.'

'Just like her,' Amy said.

'You can understand it really,' Nanw said. 'Him going away. Not being able to bear it.'

Amy considered the verdict without agreeing. Deftly Nanw shifted the argument to a critical view of the room they were standing in.

'It's so dowdy in here,' she said. 'That's what I said to Nain. "Why can't we do it up? Make it new. Full of bright colours. Make it into his playroom." She wouldn't hear of it. I suppose you can't blame her.'

They both surveyed the contents of the room. The wallpaper was a faded green pattern. The large glass-faced bookcase was tightly packed with sombre-looking tomes. Above it hung a great rectangular wooden frame containing rows of small oval photographs of ministers of religion in their prime at the end of the nineteenth century. As if to match it, above the roll-top desk where Nanw's grandfather had laboured at his two-volume history of the

Presbyteries of Rhosyr and Dinodig, hung an illuminated address to the late William Lloyd JP.

'I suppose for her the room is drenched in memories,' Nanw said. 'I suppose it is for me too.'

They stood in silence, sharing a legacy of things to say and even more to be left unsaid. Amy seized her box camera in both hands and became resolutely cheerful.

'Let's take his picture now,' she said. 'The light in here is just perfect. I'm sure of it. Take all his clothes off, Nanw, and put that cushion on the little table. Over by the window. Take him in the raw, on his little tummy.'

'The shop . . .' Nanw said.

'Bother the shop. This light is perfect.'

'Nain . . .'

Nanw was thinking of her grandmother. Her head stretched back as she strained to catch the sound of Mrs Lloyd's penetrating voice conversing with the two men precariously balanced on the top of the Dutch barn.

'She worries about his chest.'

'There's nothing wrong with his chest,' Amy said. 'If we could move that table against the conservatory . . . with that palm in the background. That would be nice. He'll be as warm as toast in the sun. The light is just perfect.'

Nanw was persuaded by Amy's cheerful confidence. As she undressed him Bedwyr began to wriggle in her grasp and stretch his podgy arms towards Amy. Nanw was prepared to share him.

'He really loves you, doesn't he?' Nanw said. 'It's as if he knew. How close you two were.'

She pressed the little naked boy into Amy's arms. He had to be held firmly. It became an act of presentation. Amy pressed her lips into his neck and murmured her urgent affection close to his cheek. In her embrace he was reduced to a condition of warm docility. Amy handed him back to Nanw so that she could take his photograph. They both maintained a chorus of soft reassuring sound as Nanw determined to follow Amy's instructions closely. The little boy's eyes moved from one to the other as his emotional state vacillated between trust and fear.

'On his little belly,' Amy said. 'Maybe he'll kick his little legs in the air.'

The tip of Amy's tongue peered out of the corner of her mouth as she gazed intently into the convex viewfinder of her box camera. She bent her knees in an attempt to improve the composition of the picture.

'If this doesn't bring him running home . . .' Amy muttered to herself and Nanw listened to her intently.

'How any father could live without seeing such a beautiful son every day of his life, I cannot imagine . . . I'll take one with you afterwards Nanw . . . bother . . . this is a cheap camera. It isn't really good enough. Neither am I really. But we've got to try. You don't get anywhere in this world without trying, do you?'

Everything about Amy seemed to impress Nanw. Here was a County schoolteacher with a salary of her own, her own camera and her own little car, dressed in the latest fashion, able to make decisions (great and small), to take initiatives and even capable of bringing some pressure to bear on the relentless course of events. Nanw herself was obliged to perch all day behind the grille of the Post Office section, keeping careful accounts and yet receiving no monies for herself except by her grandmother's grace and favour, and able to derive a mild form of excitement if a customer should arrive at the drapery and haberdashery counter and require her attention. She and little Bedwyr watched Amy with the same concentrated admiration as she tilted the mysterious black box and wound the film on to the next number in the tiny red window.

'Let's try another,' Amy said. 'Turn him a fraction to the left, Nanw, would you? It's all right. He won't fall off.'

Bedwyr was beginning to tire. His head was still turned towards Amy, his mouth and eyes open with curiosity, but his wrists were sagging under the weight of his body.

'That's it!' Amy said. 'Keep quite still.'

Mrs Lloyd's voice echoed through the shop as she called out Nanw's name. The lens shutter clicked as Bedwyr began to cry.

'Bother,' Amy said. 'Did I get him in time do you think?'

Nanw was listening nervously to the sound of her grandmother's heavy tread on the bare boards of the deserted shop. Her nervousness transferred itself to the child in her arms. He began crying more lustily.

'Here,' Amy said briskly, 'Let me hold him. I'll rub his back. He likes that!'

Indeed once Bedwyr was in Amy's arms, he did calm down. Like a frightened subordinate Nanw waited for her grandmother to negotiate the two steps into the side parlour. Her penetrating voice preceded her.

'There's a green motor car standing where I park the trap,' Mrs Lloyd said. 'It's blocking the entrance to the carthouse. It should be moved.'

She stood in the arched doorway and stared at the naked child in Amy's arms.

'What is that boy doing undressed?' she said.

'It's my car,' Amy said. 'I'm sorry. I'll move it right away.'

'He'll catch his death of cold,' Mrs Lloyd said. 'Get him dressed at once. And who's looking after the shop, may I ask?'

'It's my fault, Mrs Lloyd,' Amy said. 'I wanted to take his photo. The light was just right.'

'There's a place for that sort of thing,' Mrs Lloyd said. 'And a time.'

She reinforced the irrefutable correctness of her observation by ramming the palm of her right hand down on the crown of the black felt hat she was wearing. Her russet hair was thick and in an apparent state of untameable disorder. Her day was too full to find the time to comb it. She had few white hairs, but it was late afternoon and lines of fatigue were showing on her face. Under her ripe apple cheeks lay an abiding yellow pallor: resentment at the prospect of failing physical prowess made her permanently irritable.

'A stores should never be left unattended,' Mrs Lloyd said. 'I should have thought that was obvious to everybody.'

'Blame me, Mrs Lloyd,' Amy said. 'Don't blame Nanw. I was so keen on getting a picture of little Bedwyr.'

'What for?'

Mrs Lloyd gazed at Amy suspiciously. The box camera and its case also came in for her disapproval.

'For his father, for one thing.'

Amy spoke calmly as she handed Bedwyr back to Nanw.

'And for his grandmother. Enid's mother. After all, she's never seen him.'

Mrs Lloyd's nostrils widened as she detected a note of criticism. 'Is that my fault?' she said. 'Am I responsible for that woman's condition?'

'Not at all.'

Amy resolved to be cheerful and at the same time unstintingly frank.

'But it is sad. She just sits in front of the fire all day, staring into the flames. She's never got over losing her only daughter.'

'And blaming me, I suppose? Is that what you mean?'

'Of course not,' Amy said. 'Enid thought the world of you. She admired you no end.'

A hint of flattery was even less acceptable to Mrs Lloyd than an undertone of criticism.

'We've all had our tragedies,' she said. 'I can't help it if the woman can't pull herself together.'

She stared critically at Nanw pulling a jersey over Bedwyr's large head.

'Why on earth did you take his clothes off?' she said. 'I can't understand some people. The boy could have caught his death of cold.'

'It was the sun,' Amy said. 'Sunlight is good for him.'

'A cough in the sun is worse than a cough in the rain,' Mrs Lloyd said grimly. 'Colds at this age and he'll have a weak chest for life.'

Bedwyr's mouth was open and his eyes watching the adult faces towering above his head. Nanw raised a quick finger to her lips in an effort to calm them both.

'Little ears are listening,' she said.

Her grandmother ignored her. Her target was Amy and she was resolved to strike.

'You have no rights here, Miss Parry,' she said. 'I think you should remember that.'

'Nain.'

Nanw was desperate to divert her grandmother's attention from

9

Amy. The attack was enough to make her more acutely aware of how much she had begun to value the schoolteacher's friendship.

'Nain,' she said. 'Please. Babes should be fed with milk not gall.'

Such gnomic utterance only served to incense Mrs Lloyd.

'You may have been his mother's best friend,' she said aggressively. 'But that doesn't give you any rights over him. Any rights at all.'

'Thank you.'

It was all that Amy could think of saying, but she felt obliged to repeat it as she snatched up her camera.

'Thank you very much indeed.'

She marched out of the side parlour and down the narrow corridor between the shelves and the counter. It was not an easy exit. Nanw caught up with her as she tugged the door open and the shop bell tinkled urgently over their heads.

'She's not well,' Nanw said.

She whispered the information urgently as she followed Amy outside.

'It makes her irritable. She resents growing old.'

Amy opened the door of her little car. Sitting at the wheel seemed to calm her a little. Nanw placed her hand admiringly on the hood.

'She likes you really,' she said. 'She really does.'

'She has a funny way of showing it,' Amy said.

Nanw stared at the box camera on the passenger seat. The car was second-hand and the green leather seat had faded. The two men were still working in the roof of the barn. The sound of their hob-nailed boots grating against the corrugated iron reverberated in the silence of late afternoon.

'What will you do with the photographs?' Nanw said.

She spoke at random to delay Amy's departure.

'Send them to John Cilydd if they're any good,' Amy said.

Her hands gripped the steering wheel. She wrinkled up her nose and grinned mischievously at Nanw.

'See if they'll prick his conscience,' she said. 'If he's got one left.'

Nanw did not take the remark lightly. Her face looked pale and tense with concern for her brother. As she spoke, the words spilled out with an increasingly incoherent urgency.

10

'The last time he was home we were all ready to go to chapel in his car. He didn't want to go, of course, he just wanted to please Nain. But he was late. Or she thought he was late. That made her cross. And she has no idea how quickly you can get from one place to another in a motor car. And she always wants to be first in chapel, sitting there in her pew, eyeing the congregation as they come in. She's so keen on punctuality. He turned up late as she saw it, and before he could open his mouth she was pointing at his neck and saying, "John Cilydd, you're never going to chapel in a soft collar?" And that was the end of it. We never went. The next day he was on his way back to London.'

Amy could not help smiling.

'Well, I must say, who could blame him?'

Nanw was anxious to enlarge upon the deeper significance of what could appear to be a trivial incident.

'I know it sounds ridiculous. Everything means so much to her. As if the past was a great haystack that would fall over the minute she moved her back away from it. That's what John Cilydd says. We can provide all sorts of explanations. We can talk about it for ever and a day. But meanwhile, little Bedwyr is growing up. Every day there's something new. And John Cilydd is missing all of it. A little boy needs a father anyhow for a thousand reasons.'

Amy was nodding solemnly.

'But I don't need to tell you all this,' Nanw said. 'Won't you stay to tea?'

Amy smiled, patted the back of Nanw's hand on the car door and shook her head.

2

MRS PRYDDERCH STARED WITHOUT SPEAKING INTO THE FLAMES OF the kitchen fire. They seemed to interest her more than the photograph of her grandson. The print lay so loosely between her fingers it could easily have slipped to the floor. Amy shifted closer to Mrs Prydderch's chair. If the photograph fell she would have to pick it up. It was a sunlit afternoon. The back door was open. Beyond the gloom of the scullery Amy could see the side garden in a bright rectangle of light. In the dry weather, grass grown through the gravel had withered in untidy tufts. The leaves of the unclipped privet were coming out in yellow patches.

'You keep it,' Amy said.

She tried not to sound anxious.

'I can always have some more done.'

Mrs Prydderch's mouth barely moved in response. Sweat gleamed like a heavy coat of varnish on her face. The kitchen at Ivydene was her chosen domain. From her basket chair by the fire she could glower resentfully at any intruder. Elsewhere in the large red-brick house her husband could compose music that nobody played; his uncle could write endless letters in a shaking hand to the press on the subject of world peace and disarmament; her sister-in-law, the inspector of schools, could write her interminable reports on school visits and indulge in sporadic bouts of secret drinking, and the rooms of her children could remain empty. It was impossible for Amy to judge at that moment who or what was the current object of Mrs Prydderch's resentment. It could have been her sister-in-law. Sali Prydderch HMI was standing in the middle of the kitchen as though she needed the maximum space to remove her wide-brimmed hat. She stood behind the table in a manner that suggested she was the only member of the extended family left to sally forth from the fastness of Ivydene to keep in touch with the outside world and bring back with her a current of fresh air and some relief from the constant uncomfortable heat of the kitchen.

'I think it's a lovely snap,' Sali Prydderch said. 'I really do.'

Without her hat she looked older, smaller, more vulnerable. Her fingers trembled as they sought uncertainly to fluff out her flattened hair. The silver coins of the bracelet of her thin arm clattered with a hollow gaiety to supplement the smile she was directing towards Amy.

'I think Amy is a marvel,' she said. 'Bringing us such a sweet picture of our little Bedwyr. We are truly grateful, aren't we, Mamie?'

It was obvious that Mrs Prydderch had no wish to be told by her sister-in-law how she felt. Her fingernails tapped the photograph

12

with a determined lack of reverence for a piece of paper. No more than a few years older than the inspector of schools, Mrs Prydderch had allowed herself to lapse into premature old age. Her back was bent. In the middle of the afternoon, the coarse apron she had put on in the morning to make the fire was still tied round her bulging waist.

'It's a lovely snap,' Sali Prydderch said. 'It really is.'

'It may be,' Mrs Prydderch said. 'I can barely see it.'

Amy stared anxiously at Mrs Prydderch's glaucous eyes. This was Enid's mother and her sole remaining source of comfort seemed to be feeding the fire. There was a smear of coal dust on the fingers that held the photograph. The fire was the dominant source of light in the room. The lace-curtained window faced north and the walls and ceiling of the kitchen had been painted shades of brown a long time ago. Their surfaces were unresponsive to light from the outside.

'Really, Mamie,' Sali Prydderch said. 'You should have your eyesight seen to. You really should.'

For the first time Mrs Prydderch gave the photograph close attention.

'Does it look like him? I suppose it does.'

Mrs Prydderch answered her own question. There was some-thing more important she had to ask. The firelight illuminated her challenging stare. Even the skin that sagged at the corners of her mouth seemed to resent putting a question she, of all people, should never have been obliged to ask.

'She should never have married him,' she said. 'If she hadn't married him, she would be alive today.'

The stare she gave Amy demanded unqualified assent.

'I warned her. She wouldn't listen. And why I wonder? Because in this house my opinion was never worth listening to.'

Amy could not move a muscle. Enid's mother was prepared to go on addressing her indefinitely in her droning monotone. In some sense it would bring her daughter back if only to make her stand where Amy now stood so that she could reproach her and fill her with something of her own remorse.

'She wouldn't listen,' Mrs Prydderch said. 'I tried to tell her. She was much too young. He was much too old for her. I knew all about it. The man was absorbed in himself and all that poetry. Just like her father with his music. I told her straight out. I said, "Is this a case of history repeating itself?" I said, "If you want my opinion, a bit of poetry is no basis for a successful marriage. Your John Cilydd More may be a national eisteddfod winner but that doesn't make him another John Masefield." I didn't know whether she was going to laugh or cry, but I could see I'd upset her. But I had to speak. I couldn't sit here all day swallowing my saliva.'

'Mamie dear.'

Sali Prydderch picked up her hat from the oilcloth-covered table and ran the rim through her fingers.

'Don't upset yourself,' she said as tenderly as she could.

'Who says I'm upsetting myself?'

Mrs Prydderch stared obstinately into the fire.

'Upsetting you, more like. And we must never do that, must we?'

'Why go over it?' Sali Prydderch said.

She seemed inclined to put her hat back on her head.

'We must look to the future,' she said. 'If only for the little boy's sake. We really must. We can't go on living in the past.'

She raised her arm towards Amy in a mute gesture of appeal. Mrs Prydderch made a fresh attempt to scrutinise the photograph before stuffing it into her pinafore pocket under her apron.

'Where else is there for me to live,' she said. 'If it comes to that.'

Amy took the opportunity to shift her position in the wide space between the kitchen range and the table so as to bring herself closer to the open door. Mrs Prydderch was loath to let her go.

'Does he look like her?' she said.

'Oh yes,' Amy said.

At least this was a simple fact that could provide Enid's mother with some degree of pleasure.

'He's gorgeous,' Amy said. 'Really gorgeous. And he turns his little mouth in just the way Enid used to do. He's beautiful.'

For a moment it seemed as though Mrs Prydderch was about to smile. Instead she addressed a murmuring protest to the fire.

'His place is here,' she said. 'This is where he ought to be.'

Her basket chair creaked as she adjusted her position inside it. Sali Prydderch was moved to raise her voice.

'Oh no,' she said.

Mrs Prydderch allowed herself the ghost of a grim smile.

'Of course, nothing I say counts in this place,' she said. 'Never did.'

'The child is better off where he is. Isn't that so, Amy?'

Amy's upper lip tightened with embarrassment. She glanced longingly in the direction of the open door.

'As if this house wasn't big enough,' Mrs Prydderch said.

She leaned forward in her chair to detach a hearth-brush from its iron hook.

'Well of course it is.'

Sali Prydderch forced a laugh out of herself.

'Much too big. And rapidly becoming a Home for the Aged. And I count myself in the vanguard of decrepitude.'

Mrs Prydderch had begun to brush the bars of the fireplace bringing the black bristles perilously close to the red coals.

'Always enough money for some things.'

She was muttering loudly enough for Amy to hear.

'That's how it's always been in this house. Wasn't the place filled to overflowing with clever people. Degrees all over the place. Certificates in every room. And where is my eldest son? Educating Southern Rhodesia and still biting his nails longing to get back. And where is Ifor? You remember Ifor? The great revolutionary?'

'Of course Amy remembers Ifor,' Sali Prydderch said.

Mrs Prydderch ignored her sister-in-law's attempt to respond light-heartedly to what she was saying. Her remarks were addressed pointedly at Amy, but the questions were rhetorical and required no answer.

'In the Home Office, if you please. A London gentleman. Wears a bowler hat and makes excuses for not coming home to see me. I'm not clever enough for him to talk to. I suppose that's the answer. She would have been a comfort. I know that. And she was taken from me. And nobody did anything to stop her.'

'Mamie . . .'

Sali Prydderch pleaded with her sister-in-law to stop. Mrs Prydderch raised the hearth-brush and sat with graven stillness peering into the fire.

15

'All that was needed was one brief letter of apology. And she could have gone back to the academic world where she belonged. Don't think I wanted to keep her here. I would never stand in her way. She was the really bright one. She could read in both languages before she was five. More in her little head than Emrys and Ifor put together. Even my sister-in-law agrees with that. Instead she went and married that so-called poet and self-centred man. And where is he now? In London if you please. And what is he doing there may I ask, and leaving his little son to be brought up by relatives and not once has it crossed his mind in the space of two years to bring that child to see his mother's mother and be where he belongs.'

'Oh, Mamie.'

For the first time Mrs Prydderch turned in her chair to eye her sister-in-law with cold contempt.

'You're dressed to kill,' she said. 'Important meeting no doubt.'

Sali was driven to raise her voice in protest.

'Let's be honest about it,' she said. 'The little thing is better off where he is. It's where Enid would have wanted him brought up, I'm sure of it. She idolised the place. She always talked about Glanrafon as if it were the earthly paradise. Didn't she, Amy?'

Amy was watching Mrs Prydderch as though she were waiting for yet another disquieting revelation.

'He is better off where he is,' Sali Prydderch said. 'We must accept that. We could almost say it was providential that little Bedwyr went straight into the care of his great-grandmother and his aunt at Glanrafon.'

It appeared an argument she had won many times before. Silence descended in the kitchen. It was Mrs Prydderch's domain and no temporary victory in debate could ever impinge upon her sovereignty.

'I don't know whether you are still slimming.'

Mrs Prydderch spoke sardonically in the direction of the fire.

'In any case Martha Roberts will leave a Cornish pasty in the oven.'

She sank into her chair, a mother permanently bereaved who wished to be left alone to age in peace by herself. With an

16

expression of exasperated despair Sali picked up her hat and beckoned Amy to follow her into the house. They both trod lightly on the patterned tiles in the passage. Sali paused at the bottom of the wide staircase.

'My room is in such a mess,' she said. 'Do you mind if we go in the dining-room? It's one of the less oppressive rooms in this house.'

The dining-room smelt damp from lack of use. Sali stood in front of the mirror of the cumbersome Victorian sideboard. It was a chance to do something about her hair. Her face was glistening. She rummaged in her large handbag for a powder-puff.

'She's impossible,' Sali said.

She could speak freely once Amy had closed the dining-room door. At the end of the room there were french windows which had not been opened for years and beyond them cast-iron pillars of a veranda which bordered the south side of the house. Out in the garden Amy could see an ancient swing and beyond it an unkempt wisteria drooped along a high brick wall. Sali finished powdering her nose and pulled open the top drawer of the sideboard. A framed photograph lay face downwards on the table linen. Sali pressed her hand against it.

'I'm sorry for her,' she said. 'Of course I am. But she was always jealous of me. Heaven knows why. She had three children. My brother was devoted to her. He still is. Closes his eyes to all her faults. I lost my lover. He was killed in the war. On the other side. He was a German. She taunted me about that for years. Indirectly of course. Always indirectly. I told you about Werner?'

Amy nodded sympathetically. Sali searched in her handbag for a handkerchief ready to apply to her eyes.

'Terrible, isn't it? The way an old maid will go on about her lost love.'

She held the framed photograph towards Amy. It was an enlarged snapshot encased in an elegant silver frame. It was Enid as a schoolgirl, sitting on the seashore, leaning on a taut right arm and smiling whole-heartedly at the camera.

'She was closer to me than to her mother,' Sali said. 'You know that don't you? I used to keep a record of the things she used to say. She was such a brilliant child. You know that too, don't you? She's gone for ever and yet I want to please her more than ever. Is that ridiculous? The dead are dead, aren't they? And nothing can bring them back. And that makes the little boy all the more important. He's our only hope. That's what I mean, isn't it? He's our future and he keeps us going.'

Tenderly she raised the white tablecloth and hid Enid's photograph in it. She closed the drawer and sat down at the polished dining-table.

'I'm a mess, aren't I?'

She seemed to be referring to what she had seen in the sideboard mirror.

'I've arrived at middle age. It's like sitting on the platform at Afonwen station waiting for a train that never arrives.'

She wanted to laugh but tears were assembling in the corners of her eyes.

'That's a silly way of putting it,' she said. 'I'm trapped in this house and there's not much point in chatting to empty chairs. Anyway I have my independence and an interesting job. And I'll always be ready to help you, Amy. Whenever you feel you need me.'

Amy sat down in the chair next to her like a young woman who feels obliged to make a sympathetic response.

'There are always things I want to tell you,' Sali said. 'When you're not here. I think a lot about you. But I just don't want you to think I'm trespassing too far or anything like that. Into your private life and so on. But I'd like to say this. As a friend, although there are so many years between us. If I were in your place, if I were as beautiful as you are, if I had a choice between a fine independent career like mine, or some reasonably tolerable form of marriage, I would choose marriage every time.'

Briefly she rested a hand on Amy's arm. She felt it stiffen and the young woman's face flushing as though she resented the intrusion. Sali Prydderch hastened to generalise.

'No two cases are the same of course,' she said. 'I quite realise that. I just wanted to give you the benefit of my experience, but the moment I did so I could see quite clearly how little benefit it could possibly be to anyone. And perhaps particularly to you, my dear.'

Amy began to apologise for her attitude.

'I didn't mean that,' she said. 'I've always wanted to be independent like you.'

Sali Prydderch straightened her back and gave Amy her most dazzling smile.

'That's wonderful,' she said.

Her voice was warm and grateful as though Amy had presented her with an expensive gift.

'Amy. Could I ask you the most enormous favour?'

'Yes of course, Miss Prydderch.'

'Do call me Sali. I won't feel so ancient. You'll tell me, won't you, if I'm asking too much?'

Amy had to nod before she would continue.

'Do you think your wonderful Aunt Esther would come and keep house for us?'

Amy could not conceal her surprise.

'Oh, I know it's asking a great deal,' Sali Prydderch said hurriedly. 'But she was so marvellous to us when Mamie took to her bed when Enid died. What I'm asking is really the greatest favour. But the place is getting more hopeless by the day. Martha Roberts is no good. No good at all. She's dirty and she's lazy and she can't see dust when it's right in front of her nose. Life is quite impossible sometimes. Mamie doesn't do anything. My brother John is shrinking into nothing inside those thick tweed suits of his. And my poor dear old Uncle Peter is living on apples and nuts most days of the week. I'm lucky. I get out and about of course, and I can eat in hotels. But Ivydene would be so different if there were a competent housekeeper in charge. Like your dear Aunt Esther. I know she has your Uncle Lucas to look after and he's not the easiest of persons, but I promise you I'd pay her well. And it would cement the link between our two families, Amy, in a practical way, if you know what I mean?'

She paused briefly to give Amy a chance to speak and then plunged on.

'It's not my house of course,' she said. 'Legally it's John's, but I contribute more than my share to household expenses. Don't think I want to take advantage of your aunt or of our friendship or

19

anything you might think you owe me because of the past or anything like that. It ought to be on a business footing. But it's part of the link between us. I mean anything I leave will be between you, my dear, and little Bedwyr. Let me put it no more precisely than that. Which in any case is completely by the way. All I want to ask you really is whether you think your aunt would consider the request. I can hardly call it an offer. And whether you, my dear, would have any objection.'

Amy shook her head to demonstrate that she would have no objection on social grounds or personal pride. She would give the proposal the most sympathetic consideration.

'I'll ask her,' Amy said. 'I'll certainly ask her.'

Sali Prydderch snatched her hand and squeezed it with uninhibited enthusiasm.

3

AMY'S TWO-SEATER CAR WAS PARKED JUST INSIDE THE GATEWAY TO the private sanatorium. It was dwarfed by the ornate pillars and the wrought-iron gates still embellished with the arms of the original lords of the manor-house. Val Gwyn was smiling down at the little green motor car. Amy's hand was thrust into the jacket pocket of her knitted suit. She was observing his reactions closely.

'It's not much of a thing,' she said. 'But at least it allows me to come and see you.'

She waited for him to react. Defensively he pushed back a lock of black hair that hung over his pale forehead. The gateway was the limit imposed on his afternoon walk.

'You don't mind me coming?'

Amy was insisting on frankness. He smiled at her fondly.

'Of course I don't.'

'I just have to sit in it,' Amy said. 'And it bowls along. Thirty miles an hour. Trouble-free motoring. So far anyway. I'm not a bad driver. Better than Sali Prydderch anyway.'

She tapped the bonnet of the car affectionately. Together they strolled down the drive towards the sanatorium buildings. Val's manner was polite and attentive and yet remote. He seemed to have a special concern for the landscape around them. He frowned as he studied the condition of the trees. He stood still to observe a red squirrel scurry up an elm and leap with amazing agility from one branch to another. He gazed upward with a smile on his worn face as though he were witnessing the feat for the very first time. Amy made a bid for his undivided attention.

'So you're glad to see me?'

He did not immediately sense the teasing note in Amy's voice.

'You aren't scared that I'm going to ask you to marry me again?'

They laughed together as she took his arm without weighing on it. He was a man who spent most of his time resting in bed. The first stage thoracoplasty had not been a success. Bed rest was the current treatment, with limited exercise and graded walks. At each stage of a measured walk, the world was capable of renewing its freshness. If it was given the proper degree of study it possessed a capacity for continuous revelation. Amy shuffled her shoes in the gravel as she held herself back from impinging too forcefully on his consciousness. She had to restrain herself from plying him with questions. She removed her arm from his so that they could walk further apart. But the trees did not provide her with adequate compensation and within a short time her fingers began to stroke the sleeve of his jacket. She sighed aloud in spite of her effort at restraint. It sounded like a profound longing to return to a time when they had both been in perfect health walking happily together in their own untroubled world.

'Tell me what you're thinking.'

She seemed to disapprove of the pleading note she heard in her own voice. She spoke more purposefully.

'I've been looking at some of the letters you and Enid used to write to each other. I felt such an ignorant fool. I was jealous to tell you the truth. Not jealous that you were writing to each other or anything like that. Just resentful of my own ignorance. I just don't have the knack for philosophic thought or whatever you call it. Appearance and Reality. What's the difference? And the way that

21

poor sweet darling went on about it. And the things you used to write her, Val! "Tuberculosis is like Unemployment: incurable but capable of temporary arrest." You never wrote things like that to me.'

Val smiled at her gently.

'I didn't want to worry you,' he said.

'Did you think I was a backward child or something?'

Even as he shook his head he was grimacing in a way that suggested he was having difficulty in reading what exactly he had thought or felt.

'Well perhaps I was,' Amy said. 'But I'm not any more. You can say whatever you like to me now. Absolutely anything.'

She waited patiently for him to speak. She stood a little apart from him, an alert figure between the trees, ready for any revelation.

'This place is too expensive.'

This seemed to be what was chiefly on his mind. It was a practical problem and Amy could address herself to it with vigour.

'Of course it isn't,' she said. 'If it does you good. You should have the very best, no question of it.'

'I'm only paying half the fees,' Val said. 'And even then it's too much. He says he wishes he could afford to pay me, since I'm such a satisfactory guinea-pig.'

'Well, there you are!'

'He insists on passivity,' Val said. 'Physical and mental. And it creeps over you, like a habit of mind. I could never get excited about anything. Just lie back and let it all wash over me like water in a thermal bath.'

'And that's not what you want?'

A shrewd note in Amy's voice made him more acutely aware both of her presence and of the problem.

'I don't want passivity to become indifference,' he said.

Amy clasped her hands behind her back. Her forehead furrowed as she tried to comprehend the complexity of the problem behind such a bald statement.

'He doesn't know everything,' she said. 'Why don't you let me look after you?'

22

'Amy.'

The way he spoke her name suggested the depth of his abiding affection for her. It was also clearly intended to restrain her impulsive generosity.

'You wouldn't have to marry me,' she said. 'I don't mean that at all. But the terrace house in Pendraw is empty since Enid died. You could rest there as much as you like, with that glorious view of the mountains and the bay. It's just the kind of thing Enid would have approved of. I could organise it. You could write a bit and I could keep my job in the County School.'

She fell silent when she saw she had not succeeded in making him share her enthusiasm for the idea. She assumed he was feeling tired and looked around for somewhere they could sit.

'Just think of it as a serious possibility,' she said. 'Whenever you feel this place isn't making you better. That's all I ask. It would cost you nothing.'

Val led the way towards the terraced gardens that lay on the west side of the house. On a lawn in front of a row of connected chalets a group of well-dressed patients were playing clock golf. Their movements were so deliberate they could have been figures in a slowed-down film. When Amy and Val settled on one of the benches, they became spectators. The players began to raise their voices. Amy did not approve of the sound they made.

'Just listen,' she said. 'Liverpool shopkeepers trying to make an upper-class noise. Ready to lay the law down on any subject you care to mention: the Manchester ship canal, the rules of clock golf, home rule for India. I don't know how you can stand it. They don't even know they're in someone else's country.'

She studied Val's appearance. Parallel lines ran down his cheeks, visible evidence of the treatments he had endured. They did not impair his good looks. His brown eyes were larger and although he was trained in patience, they were still filled with a mysterious intensity that could trouble and disturb. Amy bent down to pick up a fuchsia flower that had been brought down from its bush by the breeze. She contemplated it on the stretched palm of her hand. The calyx was undamaged and a vivid purple colour. The four petals of the corolla curved outwards in perfect symmetry as if they

23

had been moulded in pink wax. Val was watching her. Briefly she held up the flower below the lobe of her left ear.

'Should I wear ear-rings?' she said. 'Or a ring through my nose?'

Val smiled at her fondly.

'I had an unexpected visitor,' he said.

Amy's eyes widened with curiosity.

'Oh? Who?'

'Pen Lewis.'

Amy's mouth tightened. In spite of herself the colour began to drain from her cheeks. She swept the fuchsia flower off her lap.

'What did he want?'

Her hostility seemed so intense she could not bring herself to utter his name.

'He came in a borrowed butcher's van,' Val said. 'There were three other men with him. It must have been a very uncomfortable journey. They'd heard the Home Secretary was on holiday near by so they formed themselves into a deputation about the Means Test. They didn't get near him.'

'He's got some cheek,' Amy said.

The colour was flooding back into her face.

'He's a brave man,' Val said. 'That's something to admire.'

'I didn't mean that. I meant coming here to see you. Barging in here with his butcher's van and his deputation. Just like him. No consideration.'

'I was glad to see him,' Val said. 'Really I was.'

'He's got no respect for anybody. Certainly not for anything you stand for.'

'I was sorry for him,' he said.

Amy was surprised by the gentleness in Val's voice.

'He still loves you, Amy. That's why he came here. He thinks I still have some lingering influence over you. It was the last thing he said before leaving. He was standing on the running board giving me his clenched fist salute. "If you see Amy Parry," he said, "will you tell her my offer still stands?"'

'Offer indeed.' Amy was indignant. 'What's he got to offer?'

'He wants to marry you,' Val said.

'What he wants is a slave to scrub his back,' Amy said. 'He talks

24

glibly enough about communism and freedom and whatever but that doesn't really include women. Well I've got other plans, thank you very much.'

She was already regretting the violence of her outburst. She held out her hand for Val to take. When she found his hand cold, like an anxious mother, she moved closer to him on the seat to do her best to warm it.

'Would you like to see the photos I took of little Bedwyr?'

She searched eagerly in her handbag for the yellow Kodak paper wallet that contained her snapshots.

'They're not very good,' she said. 'I want to try again and get some better ones. Isn't he just like her? Can you see the likeness?'

Val studied the photographs closely.

'He's so good,' Amy said. 'Just like her. A little angel. I wish you could see him, Val. It would do you good.'

He handed the pictures back. She continued to look at them herself.

'Shall I tell you what I think I ought to do?' Amy said.

There was a challenge in her voice. The expression on his face showed his concern for her future.

'I think I ought to ask John Cilydd to marry me.'

She stared at Val defiantly.

'I've asked you,' she said. 'So why shouldn't I ask him? I'd make this little darling an excellent mother. I know that's what Enid would have wanted.'

She lay back on the wooden seat and listened resentfully to the high-pitched voices of the patients playing clock golf with restrained gaiety.

'You think I'm wrong, I suppose.'

Val had said nothing. Amy could no longer preserve her sullen silence. She had to justify herself.

'The boy needs a mother. And John Cilydd should be living here in Wales, not fooling about in London. You must agree with that, surely? I'm not a philosopher. But it seems to me that if the world is in a mess we should do something about it and make a start on the personal level. I'm only trying to put into practice all the things we learnt from you, Enid and I. We have to do something about preserving the values we cherish. We have to act to save our language, our identity, our culture and what have you. You're the one that said it.'

Val closed his eyes. The question he wanted to ask seemed to cause him some embarrassment.

'Do you love him?'

'I adore him.'

Amy was staring at her snapshot of Bedwyr.

'When he puts his little arms around my neck I never want to let him go.'

'I meant Cilydd.'

Amy grinned at Val mischievously.

'Not as much as I used to love you, Val Gwyn. But you wouldn't have me at any price, would you?'

'I'm serious,' Val said.

'So am I.'

'And what about Pen?'

'It doesn't matter about Pen.'

'But you loved him once.'

'That was only a physical thing.'

Amy spoke with stern disapproval.

'Nothing more than self-indulgence. No basis for marriage. I mean that. In any case, he's a man that lives for his own way. If he's married to anything he's married to his politics. I'm not blaming him for that.'

Amy sounded as though she was struggling to be fair and objective.

'But I can't let him drag me down into it. I just can't. The "Class War" isn't the answer. It isn't the answer, is it?'

She raised her voice so loudly that some of the players turned to look at her. Val was obliged to speak.

'There are economic remedies to social injustice that don't involve violence,' he said.

Amy had barely heard him.

'Well, there you are then,' she said. 'Why should I allow him to drag me down into it? And what would it amount to? Poverty, that's all. And all the sweat and tears and misery that go with it.

26

I'm not a philosopher, but I know what I'm talking about. I want this little darling to have a proper future and a proper inheritance and that's what his father should want. I want John Cilydd to come home and accept his responsibilities and write whatever he has to write in decent Welsh and accept his destiny and pass it on to the next generation. Isn't that exactly what you kept telling us?'

'Well of course . . .'

Val was finding it difficult to fault her argument.

'If you believe it,' he said.

'Of course I believe it.'

Amy's voice rang out defiantly.

'Am I embarrassing you?'

Val seemed sensitive about the attention they were receiving from the players on the 'clock golf course.

'Our identity, our language, our culture, our this and our that,' Amy said. 'We have to fight to keep them. Fundamental rights and fundamental freedoms and all that. I'm only quoting you, Val Gwyn. I'm only putting what you preach into practice.'

'So long as you know what you're doing.'

In the wake of her enthusiasm his hesitancy sounded dispiritingly feeble.

'Of course I do.'

Val gazed across the lawn to the veranda of an isolated chalet. There a nurse in uniform sat rigidly upright next to a patient who seemed to be lounging back in a deck-chair under a thick travelling rug.

'You see those two,' he said.

Discreetly he drew Amy's attention to the motionless figures of the patient and the nurse.

'He is a rich man,' Val said. 'The patient. Very rich. He inherited a fortune in South American hardwoods. A family of Liverpool merchants. He is dying.'

Amy stared across the lawn. The monotone in which Val announced the rich man's fate caused her to shiver inside her knitted suit.

'His wife's a doctor. She knew how bad his case was. So she

27

dumped him here. She never comes to see him. Scared of catching it, they say. But that nurse is devoted to him. Never leaves his side.'

Amy looked pleadingly at Val, her lips parted and ready to speak. But he had more to say.

'She's in disgrace,' Val said.

Amy stared more intently across the lawn. The nurse was young. The relaxed way the patient lay back in his chair was in fact a condition of final helplessness. Alongside him the nurse looked a figure of rude peasant health. Her hands as red as her face were folded neatly in the lap of her white apron.

'She's under notice of dismissal,' Val said. 'They say he means to marry her before he dies. That's why management leaves them alone. It's against the rules for nurses to associate with individual patients. You can see them there every day. Like graven images. Waiting for the end.'

Amy jumped to her feet.

'This place,' she said. 'It isn't good for you. Isn't there somewhere else we could sit?'

They passed through an ornamental gate into a rose-garden below the open window of the library. He pointed out the elegant proportions of the original house, but Amy took little pleasure in them.

'I'm right you know,' she said. 'I ought to take you away.'

Val smiled at her. He contemplated her changes of mood with the same affectionate attention he gave to the landscape and the weather.

'You've got enough commitments already, Miss Parry,' he said.

'No Val, I mean it. You should take me seriously you know. I'm a very practical person. And very determined.'

'Oh, I know. I know.'

'Well, there you are then,' Amy said. 'What about it?'

A figure in the window of the library waved at him. Briefly Val waved back, before turning away from the house and taking a path which led back to the trees and the drive. He folded his arms as he walked and lowered his head to share his most intimate thoughts with her.

'I must get away,' he said. 'Everything must die. Of course it must. That chap on the veranda will die in the arms of his nurse.

28

That's how he wants it. I've got more life in me but what I want is to understand why I was given TB. Is it supposed to be some strange gift that I have no idea what to do with?'

'That's cruel,' Amy said sharply. 'And it's rubbish too if you ask me.'

'Is it?'

He continued to smile at her.

'Yes it is,' Amy said. 'The next thing you'll be saying is that Enid died for a reason.'

'Perhaps she did.'

'Rubbish.'

Amy dismissed the notion angrily. Val looked apologetic.

'I'm not expressing myself very well,' he said.

'If you ask me you are just talking yourself into a frame of mind,' Amy said. 'If you ask me it's no way at all to talk.'

'Words.'

Val sighed heavily.

'Millions of them. Billions of words. Billions of people. All yearning for expression, all yearning for survival. And yet in each a destructive element. Lingering bacilli. And in each a yearning beyond the yearning for survival. The yearning for incomprehensible love that will at least commend the fact of our existence, accept and even cherish the mystery of our individual consciousnesses.'

'Well, well,' Amy said. 'Our dear old friends Appearance and Reality, all over again.'

The remark seemed to deflate him. He looked around for somewhere to sit. They found a bench under the trees that gave them a view of the slow curve of the driveway.

'That's the trouble with my disease,' Val said. 'Your mental knees give way after the smallest effort. And then the patient longs to burrow back into the comforts of hibernation and routine oblivion. Blanket bath. Bed rest. Medications. Shaving water. Back rubbed and watching the orderlies troop in like a different species designed to dust and polish.'

'Oh, Val.'

Amy became restless with the desire to embrace him. The presence of visitors in the gardens restrained her.

'I can do all that for you,' she said. 'And more.'

He shook his head.

'You've got your baby,' he said. 'You don't need another. In any case I'm not fit for public circulation any more. What I need is somewhere where I could be a sort of out-patient monk.'

'Oh, Good Lord!'

Amy sounded uncertain whether to be cross or amused.

'I'm serious. What I need is some kind of hospice for invalids who want to learn about and practice the contemplative life.'

'Val.'

'I mean it. There are such places. In France certainly. If they're Catholic I can't help it. I don't mind. It's what I need. So that I can exist in the present, learn to pray even, and still have my hand within touching distance of the latch on death's door.'

Amy's eyes were beginning to fill with tears born of frustration rather than sorrow. She searched in her handbag for a handkerchief to blow her nose.

'Val,' she said. 'I can't bear to hear you talk like this.'

'Of course not,' he said. 'Why should you?'

'I don't know how you can be so cold,' Amy said. 'You know how much I love and admire you.'

He stretched his hand to touch her back but the gesture appeared remote, almost impersonal. They both sat still, uncertain what to say next.

'There are things to be done,' she said. 'Things you have to do.'

Under her breath she repeated the words like a litany. Val responded in the same tone.

'No one is indispensable,' he said.

Amy gazed down the drive. She saw Sali Prydderch in the distance. She was dressed in bright green and accompanied by Professor Gwilym who had already spotted Amy and was raising his hat and his pipe in a florid gesture of greeting.

'Goodness,' Amy said. 'Sali P. and Professor Gwilym. They did say something about wanting to speak to you and I quite forgot to tell you. I didn't think they'd turn up here this afternoon. He says he wants to interview you for his magazine or something. I hope you don't mind.'

Val stood up. He began to walk in the direction of the new chalets. Amy had to run to catch up with him.

'What's the matter?' she said. 'Have I done something wrong?'

'No of course not,' Val said. 'But I don't want to speak to them.'

'I said you would speak to him,' Amy said. 'Sometime or other. Something for his magazine. He's on our side Val. It doesn't have to be now of course. If you just said "Hello" and say it's time for your rest or something.'

'You can say that,' Val said.

Amy was hurt.

'I know he's pompous and pipe-sucking and full of himself, but at least he's on our side,' she said. 'And we need all the help we can get, you said that yourself. They're both of them very good to me and they do a great deal of good for the cause in their own quiet way.'

They had passed behind the rose-garden. The drive and the unexpected visitors were no longer in view. Val's face was white and sweat had begun to break out on his forehead.

'Amy,' he said. 'I'm sorry if I sound hysterical, because that's the last thing I want to sound, but he's the kind of man that brings out a horror of humans in me. I wish I could explain it. I don't like him. But it's worse than that. My dislike for him closes up my throat. It chokes me.'

She was slow to appreciate the extent of his desperation.

'You were quite willing to receive Pen Lewis and his silly deputation,' she said.

'I want to explain. A horror of people precludes me from loving them which I want to do more than anything, so that means I have to keep my distance to keep my sanity.'

She looked nervously over her shoulder.

'What am I going to say to them?' Amy said. 'What am I going to say?'

She sighed with relief. She was willing to release him.

'Tell them I'm ill,' he said with a rueful smile. 'God knows that's true enough.'

4

'NOW CLOSE YOUR EYES, AMY! CLOSE YOUR EYES.'
Sali Prydderch stood with her hands clasped together in front of the dining-room door. When Amy's eyes were closed she flung open the door with a dramatic flourish.

'Behold!'

Her bracelet of silver coins clattered gaily about her wrist. Obligingly Amy opened her eyes. The dining-room at Ivydene had been completely redecorated and refurnished. The massive Victorian sideboard had gone. In its place, with an eighteenth-century arcadian landscape above it, stood a bow-fronted side-table with a long shallow drawer across the front. A wallpaper with a faint strip of alternating pink and silver on a white ground had transformed the whole atmosphere. In this setting an oval regency dining-table surrounded by ten sabre-legged chairs took on a fresh elegance.

'Isn't it marvellous?'

Amy looked around with particular care, smiling and nodding her approval.

'Do you know what I used to abhor most of all?' Sali Prydderch said. 'The smell.'

She held back her head, wrinkled her nose and gestured as she sought out precise definition.

'You know what it was like? It was like a musty lifetime of disappointments.'

She sniffed and breathed in the smell of fresh paint and furniture polish.

'And now it's all gone. Thanks to your wonderful Aunt Esther. Was there ever such a woman? She's rescued me from the slough of despond. I'd never have got round to having this done without her. I can't tell you the difference she's made. The men, of course. "The boys", as she and I call them. She handles them like a trained nurse. But the real miracle is Mamie, my sister-in-law. I've never seen anything like it! I'm not going to claim that she can twist that woman around her little finger. I don't think even your aunt, bless her, could quite do that. But she can handle her. Do you know, I just stand there with my mouth wide open and wonder how in the name of heaven and earth she does it.'

Sali Prydderch waited for Amy to share her admiration to the full.

'It's my uncle,' Amy said. 'If you can handle Lucas Parry you can handle anybody. She's had a lifetime's practice.'

Amy touched the polished surface of the dining-room table with the tips of her fingers before moving to the french window. Out in the garden she could see Nanw More pushing little Bedwyr to and fro on the ancient swing. Nanw was wearing a new outfit of matching grey hat and coat specially bought for her first visit to Ivydene. Amy's aunt, Esther Parry, stood near by, taking pleasure in watching the little boy enjoy himself. Her sleeves were rolled up above her elbows and even the way she stood suggested that her visit to the garden was not a waste of time. She had tied a cushion to the wooden seat so that the rotten edges would not endanger the little boy's flesh with a splinter. Her pinafore had been washed so often the flowered pattern had almost disappeared. The smile on her thin face stretched as tightly as the hair drawn back into a bun which was streaked with white. For Esther Parry there was never time enough to spare: brief intervals between prolonged bouts of domestic labour. Sali Prydderch stood alongside Amy to admire the garden scene.

'At last he's here!'

Reverently, Sali Prydderch murmured her gratitude into the window.

'Thanks to you again, Amy. You've put us so much in your debt.'

She had a range of delicate feelings to express and she licked her lips repeatedly as she sought for the precise phrases that would reveal the depth of her appreciation and gratitude.

'It's like watching a new flower grow,' Sali said.

The simile seemed inadequate the moment she began to use it.

'To replace the old one is what I mean,' she said. 'Oh, just look at him. Isn't he a little darling? And so manly too.'

Bedwyr's back stiffened. He was resisting the efforts of Nanw to seat him more securely on the cushion. Esther came closer and her right arm was stretched forward indicating both her desire to help and hesitation to intervene.

'He needs a firm hand,' Amy said.

She was visibly restraining herself from going out and taking charge.

'He's very affectionate, but he needs a firm hand.'

'Oh dear . . .'

Sali excused herself.

'It's just as well he's not living here. I would spoil him outrageously. I know I would.'

Bedwyr had stopped wriggling in his seat. Nanw More had drawn his attention to the single plum tree and its higher branches loaded with fruit ripening in the afternoon sun. Beyond the swing the wisteria sagged against the high brick wall. Each forward swing gave him a better view of the fruit on the plum tree. Through the window they could hear the faint noise of Nanw and Esther reciting a nursery rhyme.

'I'm a little worried about her, to tell you the truth,' Amy said.

She was talking about her aunt. Sali Prydderch was instantly sensitive to a possible criticism.

'I hope you don't think it's too much for her, coming here?'

'She loves it,' Amy said. 'It gives her a chance to get out of that pokey little number three Harris Street. And to get away from my uncle. No, it's her health I'm thinking about. If only they lived in a more convenient house it would be something.'

'Would you like them to move in here?' Sali Prydderch said.

She made the offer eagerly. The notion seemed an ideal way of shifting the balance of debt between them. Regretfully, Amy shook her head.

'Uncle likes being near the Public Library and the bowling green. Because of his bad leg. He would never agree to moving. And she is devoted to letting him have what he wants.'

Sali Prydderch touched Amy's arm lightly to comfort her. It was a signal of sympathy and understanding. Whatever the difference in age and situation, they were both professional women with family problems and so far as possible they should support and help each other. Amy drew her attention to the figure of Professor Gwilym

34

treading lightly but purposefully across the lawn in the direction of the swing. There was an ingratiating smile on his face. He was carrying a briefcase and he raised his grey Homburg hat politely as he addressed Esther Parry. She introduced him to Nanw More and to the little boy on the swing. The professor snapped a jovial finger and thumb over Bedwyr's head before returning his earnest attention to Esther.

'What on earth does he want with your aunt?'

Sali Prydderch voiced the question on her own behalf and on Amy's.

'He's taken to calling here quite regularly since we've put the place in better order,' Sali said. 'And his wife's an invalid, of course. He's taken a great fancy to your Aunt Esther's sponge cakes. I must say they are delicious. How is Val Gwyn by the way? In all the excitement I quite forgot to ask.'

Amy bit her lower lip. She avoided looking Sali in the eye.

'It's difficult to tell,' she said.

'I know how you must feel,' Sali said. 'I don't want to pry but I want you to know how much I sympathise.'

'We're not engaged or anything like that,' Amy said.

She looked as though she had had to steel herself to make the revelation.

'Everything like that has been over between us for quite a long time. But I don't admire him any the less. More, if anything. He's the finest man I've ever known. I know that much.'

'Ah, my dear . . .'

Sali was prepared to demonstrate more intense sympathy until she saw that the professor was approaching across the lawn. Her attention was taken by the satisfied smile on his wide mouth. He had not seen them watching through the window. He continued to tread with the delicate step of the privileged visitor towards the front door.

'Bother,' Sali said. 'Now he'll pull that front door bell and the noise will be enough to waken the dead.'

She looked around for a mirror to check her appearance before hurrying to answer the door. The peremptory clang rang out before she could prevent it. Amy smiled to herself as she heard the professor's nasal voice apologise for the noise. Miss Prydderch was steering him as fast as she could towards the comparative privacy of the redecorated dining-room. Once in the doorway he impeded Sali's efforts to close the door by striking a posture to express his extreme pleasure at having discovered first one nymph and then another. To close the door she was obliged to push him forward gently even as he was explaining his presence for Amy's benefit.

'I hope you don't mind, Miss Parry,' he said. 'But I felt I had to speak to your aunt. Ask her advice you see. I don't know whether Miss Prydderch has told you, but my poor wife is crippled with arthritis. She has other ailments as well. A complete invalid. So at last I have been able to persuade her to agree to our looking for a full-time live-in housekeeper. I thought your good aunt would be able to advise me.'

'I hope you weren't trying to tempt her away from Ivydene!' Sali said.

Her playful smile did not altogether conceal a real anxiety.

'Oh goodness no,' Professor Gwilym said. 'Desperate as my situation is I would never dream of betraying you in such a fashion, dear lady. What Mrs Esther Parry did say was that she had a cousin who kept house for the aristocracy in London. Mrs Connie Clayton, to give her her courtesy title. She was careful to point that out. She also told me that this Mrs Connie Clayton thought the world of Miss Amy Parry and was always saying how much she would like to come back to a position in Wales if only for the pleasure of seeing more of her.'

Professor Gwilym was smiling broadly at Amy to show how easy it was to understand the housekeeper's desire to see more of such a beautiful young lady.

'Seeing the grouse train off to Scotland and goodness knows what else. But too much responsibility, if I understood Mrs Esther Parry correctly. And not all that splendid remuneration. Do you think you could offer yourself as bait, dear Miss Parry, to lure this domestic paragon back to the land of her fathers?'

'She adores them,' Amy said. 'The aristocracy. Almost as much as they adore themselves. She won't hear a word said against them.'

36

'A fluent Welsh speaker,' Professor Gwilyn said. 'Even after passing Shrewsbury clocktower. A devout church-goer. An excellent cook. My mouth waters at the mention of her virtues.'

'She looks down on non-conformists,' Amy said. 'She hasn't much time for people without titles.'

'Isn't "professor" a title?'

Professor Gwilym smiled winningly at Amy.

'She is the most awful snob.'

Amy looked apologetic.

'I'm sorry to have to say it. But you ought to know the truth.'

'Ah well . . .'

Professor Gwilym made a gesture to show he was prepared to leave the problem of a housekeeper a little while longer in the lap of the gods. He looked around the room appreciatively.

'You know this is a room which could become the birthplace of a new movement.'

He moved about to familiarise himself with the refurbished room and calculate its possibilities.

'I'm perfectly serious about this. I know Val Gwyn is unwell and I sympathise from the bottom of my heart. Of course I do. But sooner or later there must be a synthesis of points of view. A meeting of minds. And where better than in a room like this? An informal conference and then a council of action. If we don't act, who else will to save what little we have left. I'm writing a piece about it you know for the next issue. It's time to list the essentials, draw a firm line and build our defences along it. I thought of calling it "The New Dyke", but I'm not certain about that. We have to be fluid, don't we, and we can't always think in terms of outworn military strategy. Our problems are cultural. But they are closely bound up with social, economic and political factors.'

He paused to give Miss Prydderch and Amy a chance to demonstrate their approval. Outside the little boy was crying. Amy looked anxiously through the window.

'Take that little fellow's father,' Professor Gwilym said. 'I'm going to speak quite frankly. I wrote to him urgently for a contribution on poetry and politics. Something right up his street, and do you know I haven't had a reply? Not a single word. One of my most faithful contributors and now not even bothering to answer my letters. It's a symptom, you see. Things are falling apart. What is he doing up there and who are the set he's mixing with? From what I've heard, rich dilettantes with more money than sense dabbling in left-wing politics. His place is here.'

Sali Prydderch was watching Amy nervously from the corner of her eye.

'Don't think I'm unaware of his personal tragedy,' Professor Gwilym said. 'But as I see the world, that kind of blow either demoralises an artist for ever or transforms his work to an altogether higher level.'

Amy remained silent. In the garden her Aunt Esther had gone down on one knee to draw little Bedwyr's attention to the fruit on the plum tree. She looked as if she were offering him one of the treasures of the earth. Nanw More stood by, her hands holding down her coat, clearly impressed by the way Esther was able to pacify the child.

'A general agreement on the minimum action required to safeguard the well-being of a small nationality among all the storms and stresses of the twentieth century,' Professor Gwilym said. 'That's all that is necessary. I say that's all and it sounds quite simple. But we have to take into account the deplorable tendency of our society to get bogged down in nineteenth-century habits of mind. And of course that fissiparous nature that seems endemic among the inhabitants of mountainous regions.'

The professor closed his eyes tightly as he concentrated on elaborating his thesis. Sali Prydderch was nodding happily and glancing at Amy from time to time. This was a perfect opportunity for the younger woman to appreciate why the inspector of schools spent so much time in the professor's company. His shortcomings were more immediately apparent than his virtues. He had to be given the proper ambience before he could begin to demonstrate the better qualities of a thoughtful mind.

The professor's discourse was interrupted by a screech from the garden. It was an alarming sound, suspended briefly in the air like the cry of an unfamiliar species, followed by a breathless silence.

'Bother,' Amy said.

She could see her aunt stretched out on the ground under the plum tree. A moss-covered branch had broken under her weight. Amy shook the handles of the french windows angrily. They refused to open.

'It's the paint,' Sali Prydderch said.

The professor tried to be helpful. Attempting to open the windows allowed him to press himself against Amy. She could see her aunt was not moving.

'Oh, do get out of the way,' she said.

Sali Prydderch tried to calm her as she followed close on her heels through the front door and across the lawn. Her own mounting concern was difficult enough to control. The woman whose tireless labour and efficiency had transformed the life of Ivydene lay like a wounded body under the plum tree.

'Auntie! What on earth are you trying to do?'

Amy was already scolding her aunt before reaching her side. Esther Parry was winded and still could not speak. She held up a plum in her hand. She wanted Bedwyr to take it. He backed away against the skirt of Nanw More's grey coat, bewildered at the figure of a woman trapped like a bee on its back in her horizontal position.

'Now you keep quiet,' Amy said crossly. 'You've caused enough trouble already!'

She picked the plum from Esther's cold fingers and thrust it into the little boy's open mouth. It slipped out of his mouth as he began to cry more vociferously.

'Don't move, Auntie,' Amy said. 'And don't try to speak. Don't touch her anybody.'

There was no one who proposed to do so. Sali folded her arms tightly around her waist and paced around the site of the accident as if she were measuring it for some obscure official purpose. With his hat on and his briefcase in his hand, ready for a stealthy departure, Professor Gwilym moved restlessly between the lawn and the shade of the veranda.

'We need a board,' Amy said. 'To act as a stretcher.'

She looked back at the house. In the first-floor window she could see the thin figure of John Prydderch, Enid's father, in his brown tweed suit, anxiously gnawing his moustache, the sunlight glittering on his gold watch-chain as his fingers fiddled with it. His concern was apparent enough, but he showed no inclination to act. On the floor above, his Uncle Peter had heard nothing. It could only be assumed he was at his small desk composing letters in a large flowing hand, his boots at the side of his chair and his stockinged feet deep in the warmth of a cardboard box half-filled with hay.

'She mustn't be moved. Not on any account,' Amy said.

She ran to the dilapidated garden shed and began to tug violently at a trestle top leaning against the cobwebbed wall. A stack of earthenware plant pots tumbled over. The dust made her cough. Nanw arrived at the door calling excitedly.

'Amy,' she said. 'Esther Parry's sitting up!'

They ran back and found Esther struggling with her breath in an effort to recite a nursery rhyme that would put Bedwyr at his ease.

'Down, down, down . . . we both fell . . .'

'Keep quiet, Auntie,' Amy said. 'Save your breath. And keep still.'

Esther drew up her knees and turned her body in an attempt to breathe more easily. She was smiling in a way that only intensified Amy's concern.

'I can tell you one way,' Esther said, 'one sure way to find out how old you are . . . fall out of a tree!'

5

JOHN CILYDD MORE STOOD CLOSE TO THE WINDOW OVERLOOKING THE inner quadrangle of the college. Beams of light from other windows penetrated a mist that rose from the lawn and swirled in ghostly fashion around the isolated shape of a sundial. In a bell tower somewhere beyond the college walls a team of ringers was practising. Peals jangled into one another and in the intervals reverberations hung in the moist Oxford air like the tense silences that can fill a house during a prolonged domestic quarrel. At the window Cilydd looked like a caller who was uncertain whether to stay or leave. His long grey scarf still hung around his neck. Smoking a cigarette was a way of postponing the decision. The room was comfortable. Firelight flickered among the shadows on the ceiling and the panelled walls.

His head turned to listen to the sound of voices on the stairs. A hectic outburst of laughter could have been intended to disturb the solid calm of the sixteenth-century building. A wry smile appeared on Cilydd's face. He recognised the laugh. Eddie Meredith burst into the college guest room, his face glowing with excitement. He switched on the pale centre light and stretched out his arms in triumph.

'We're in!'

He banged the door behind him.

'Isn't that really something?'

From a wall-cupboard he extracted a half-bottle of whisky and glasses which he held up briefly to the light to see if they were clean.

'You should have seen me, JC. You should have seen me. I've got a gift for it you know. I really have.'

Eddie was eager to celebrate his victory by going over the tortuous committee process in detail. He sank into a leather armchair and unlaced his shoes so that he could warm his feet by wriggling his toes close to the fire.

'I shall never lose my taste for attacking the bastions of privilege,' Eddie said. 'Never. It's the supreme pleasure of being a rank outsider. Childe Eddie to the Dark Tower came for the umpteenth time. Ollie Petrie was against it. Would you believe it? Our one and only fox-hunting Marxist. Said he felt an extra responsibility in his role as honorary treasurer. Played right into my hands really. JC, why the hell don't you come and sit down? You look as if you're waiting for a train or something.'

It seemed an effort for Cilydd to relax his statuesque position by the window. Eddie needed a sympathetic and attentive listener. The least he could do was respond.

' "You want to deny me my chance, Ollie", I said. "That's what it amounts to. And I'll tell you why: because I'm a working-class lad from a Welsh workhouse. Down on two counts. You can't have a rank outsider like me making use of the Oxford seal of cultural rectitude!" That made him splutter. I wish you could have seen it.'

Eddie sipped his whisky. There was a smile of roguish pleasure on his face that brought out the dimples on his cheeks. His black curls tumbled around his forehead.

'Then he shifted his ground,' Eddie said. 'Nobody wanted to see Eddie Meredith get his chance more than the Honourable Oliver Petrie. The play might very well turn out to be a revolutionary sensation but who was this J. C. More and so on. He was never at Oxford, and if there was going to be music and dancing and spectacular sets and so on where was the extra cash going to come from? I had him on the hop, I can tell you. By the end he was talking about Meredith and More as if they were the biggest thing since Beaumont and Fletcher and Gilbert and Sullivan! And when I said Hetty Remington and Margot Gromont were standing by with a guarantee against loss he caved in completely. And then, of course, all the young things did too.'

Eddie began to frown. There was much else to recall and celebrate but Cilydd's response was lacking in enthusiasm.

'I'm not suggesting the world is already at our feet,' Eddie said. 'There's a great deal of work still to be done. I admit it. But the chance is there. The opening. It's there.'

Cilydd sighed and stared into the fire.

'The allegory is too obscure,' he said.

Eddie brushed this difficulty aside.

'Allegories are meant to be obscure,' he said. 'That's the least of our worries. It's the sensation that matters. Honestly. With a number like "There's war in the workhouse of this world" you can't miss. That's the trick really. Big ambiguous themes and then the production number that hits them between the eyes.'

Eddie gave a sudden leap in his stockinged feet. He pushed his chair back and began to sing and dance.

> ' "Oh my crutches, yes, my crutches, both are broken,
> And my feet com-ple-he-tly free! . . ."

Impact, JC. There's always got to be impact. Impact and fun. The first principles of entertainment.'

He pranced about determinedly until he saw an expansive smile on Cilydd's face.

'I'm not saying we can do without the touch of poetry. And the solemn undertones. And the intellectual teasers to keep them guessing. We need them all. That's the secret of the recipe. And that's where you come in, comrade. The magic ingredients from those tender Welsh hands.'

Carried away by his own eloquence Eddie was slow to observe the increasingly anxious expression on Cilydd's face.

'I don't think I've got the right kind of talent for this kind of thing,' he said.

Eddie emptied his glass and waved his hand in the air.

'Now don't let's have North Wales humility slopping all over the place. Be arrogant, JC. *Il faut s'imposer!* It's the only thing to be among the English. Otherwise they put you down and tread all over you. By the way, did I hear you say you needed a cigarette-case?'

Eddie felt in his inside pocket and extracted a flat silver case. He tossed it across so that it fell into Cilydd's lap.

'It's got my name engraved inside it. I hope you won't mind that!'

Cilydd opened the case and looked inside it.

'Who gave you this?'

'Old Dowser,' Eddie said. 'Poor old sod. Not that he's much use to man or beast any more. I told you about him. Sherry and tutorials and mumbling away about *amor intellectualis.*'

Eddie stood up and stretched himself.

'I think I ought to take a bath,' he said. 'Committees make me sweat with excitement. How about the George for dinner? Nigel's invited me, but I know he'd be glad to pay for us both.'

'I should be starting back.'

Cilydd stood up and reached for his overcoat and hat.

'You have your bath,' he said. 'I'll be off.'

'No.'

From the door of the bedroom Eddie shouted out the monosyllable.

'We've got things to discuss.'

43

He came down the single step into the room.

'There's a time-scale we've got to work to,' Eddie said. 'What I suggest is we book rooms in that place in the Cotswolds for three nights and really get down to revising *The Workhouse*. Everybody thinks it's a marvellous script.'

'Who's everybody?'

Cilydd grinned at the urgently gesticulating figure.

'Everybody that matters, of course. But there ought to be more songs and we ought to think of something more spectacular for the workhouse rebellion in the second act. We've got to snatch at every chance to exploit the material. You can see that as well as I can.'

Cilydd was morosely thoughtful.

'You don't really need me,' he said.

'God, you get on my nerves sometimes.'

Eddie began to undress.

'I'm as honest as I can be with you, John Cilydd, and yet you never seem to believe me. It's *your* imagination. I just feed on it. You are the host. I am the parasite. Understand? I plug into your music and out comes a more vulgar noise. It's not perfect, of course, but why should it be? Imperfect art is a better reflection of an imperfect world. Do you fancy a bath?'

Cilydd shook his head. Eddie moved about the bedroom. In the bathroom beyond he began to run the bath. He burst out singing another impromptu song.

> ' "Life is for living, flesh and all,
>   Rich and poor, come to the ball . . ." '

Briefly he appeared in the doorway to display his half-naked body.

'You know the trouble with you, JC, is you are the victim of your residual puritanical restraints. It's like the grip of childhood guilt. It never, never lets you go.'

Cilydd adjusted his spectacles and stared with controlled appreciation at Eddie's athletic young figure.

'Poetry is not as important as politics,' he said.

Eddie took in the solemn announcement before beginning to splutter with laughter.

'What the hell has that got to do with my beautiful body,' Eddie said. 'Honestly, JC, you never cease to amaze me.'

'There's only one task that matters,' Cilydd said. 'I'm absolutely clear about that. To create a public conscience. To make the people wake up to what's happening in the world. That can only be done by direct political action. Everything else is literally a waste of time.'

Eddie bounded back to the bathroom to turn off the hot water tap. He came back tying the cord of his dressing-gown.

'Who's been getting at you?' he said. 'Now come on, JC. Come clean, as they say at the pictures.'

'Every sane man should take up political action. That's all I'm saying. Look around you. Reactionary governments everywhere supporting Fascism. Including the government here. The only answer is to put socialists in power. It's so obvious. And yet all the means of communication in these islands, all controlled from London, are geared to pull the wool over the eyes of the entire population!'

'And what about your little Wales?'

Eddie grinned mischievously, but Cilydd took the question seriously.

'Everything else must wait. The struggle comes first, otherwise everything will be lost. Everything.'

Eddie raised both his fists and shook them angrily.

'What else is our play for, except to open people's eyes?' he said. 'To open people's eyes, damn it. I can't for the life of me see your difficulty.'

'My poetry doesn't add one ounce to the play's message, not one dram,' Cilydd said. 'If anything it only serves to obscure it. Anyway, my poetry is not English. It doesn't work. It piles up a new linguistic barrier instead of breaking through it. My mind is made up, Eddie. You can make use of whatever I've given you: but don't expect me to spend any more time working on it.'

For once Eddie seemed at a loss for something to say. He sat in front of the fire with his jaw sunk on his chest.

'This is a bit of a blow,' he said.

Cilydd made an apologetic noise.

'The end of our collaboration,' Eddie said. 'Even before it got properly going. We were good, you know. A terrific combination. What is this political action anyway?'

'There's the ward committee of the Labour Party,' Cilydd said.

Eddie groaned melodramatically.

'One of a team,' Cilydd said. 'You can't ask for anything more. We've started the society of socialist lawyers, on a broad front. It includes Fabians and Marxists. There are pamphlets to write. Statistics to collect. Elections to fight. It's a massive task. And there's so little time. What energy I have I'm going to direct right into it.'

'What about Hetty?'

'What about her?'

A faint blush appeared in Cilydd's cheeks. He picked up the whisky glass and drained the last drops a second time.

'She thinks you're the biggest thing since T. S. Eliot stopped parting his hair in the middle.'

'Rot.'

Cilydd's face was red. Eddie was delighted to provoke him further.

'I'm in the know,' he said. 'Margot's mouth is like a sieve. The poor little rich girl is crazy about her Welsh poet. She thinks you're inscrutable, like the Sphinx. And a tragic figure to boot who lost his young wife in childbirth and never talks about it. She has plans for you. Vienna, Venice, Rome. She wants to show you the kingdoms of the earth and bring you back a sophisticated tom-cat with his whiskers dipped in gold! My God!'

Eddie was overwhelmed by a terrible realisation.

'If you back out she'll never back the show. Have you thought of that, my bardic friend? Hells bells, this could be a major disaster!'

Cilydd smiled at him calmly.

'There's no need to worry,' he said. 'Now you've got the Oxford Society behind you. You can go on using whatever stuff of mine you need. And I'm sure Hetty would never let you down.'

'I wish I could believe that.'

Eddie tugged viciously at the cord of his dressing-gown.

'Rich people are notoriously fickle. I know that from experience, my friend. Look! You've got to get hold of them tonight. Bring them both to the George. Wine and dine them. Cement the deal before Hetty tumbles to the fact her bard has backed out. Come on now. It's the least you can do for me.'

'You don't even know if they're here,' Cilydd said. 'In any case you don't have to worry.'

'We can try,' Eddie said. 'And you can stay the night. Golly! At last I'll be able to entice you into my bed. Think of this beautiful body of mine going to waste. And think of all the gossip I still haven't passed on to you. Fascinating stuff.'

'I've got to get back to London!'

Eddie leaned forward with a great show of confidentiality.

'Have you heard the latest about the delectable Amy Parry?'

He smiled when he saw Cilydd swallow in an obvious attempt to appear only mildly interested.

'You won't believe it when I tell you.'

Eddie held him in deliberate suspense.

'Info,' he said. 'You can never tell when it comes in useful. Not to be confused with gossip which is just frothy. Info is useful.'

He waited for Cilydd to react and smiled at the effort of his restraint.

'Info is the mortar that holds the bricks of history together,' Eddie said. 'What about 43 Culpepper Place?'

'What about it?'

'Nigel's aunt. Her London house.'

'So.'

'The housekeeper at that august establishment is Amy Parry's auntie!'

'How do you know?'

Eddie tapped the side of his nose and then adopted an airily objective tone.

'Fascinating sociological study,' he said. 'If all else fails I'll write a thesis about it. "Nationality and Class: an analysis in depth by E. V. Meredith." The impoverished Celts obliged to fill all the servile roles in the Anglo-Norman hegemony. Irish at the bottom, Welsh non-coms and the Scots scratching away to scramble into

47

the top layer. Maybe I should abandon my theatrical dreams and settle for the academic life. There's a big future for working-class dons, don't you think?'

Eddie abandoned his line of thought when he saw Cilydd had stopped listening.

'Are you still keen on her?'

He put his question in an insinuating tone.

'Come on, JC, you'll have to talk about it sooner or later. Even a solicitor can't wrap himself up and sleep in a deed box with his lips sealed for ever. It's not good for you.'

Eddie waved his arms in triumph when he saw the beginnings of a smile on Cilydd's face.

'Sometimes you look just like a cross between Harold Lloyd and Buster Keaton,' Eddie said. 'The old stone sphinx himself. No wonder women like Hetty get seized with Cilydditis. Curiosity is the most easily roused of all the female instincts. Come on now, JC, as between friends and erstwhile collaborators.'

'I don't think Amy approves of me,' Cilydd said at last.

'Oh.'

Eddie held his head to one side to show how intrigued he was.

'She thinks I'm avoiding my responsibilities.'

'That's a good one.'

Eddie slapped his knee appreciatively.

'She thinks I'm irresponsible and frivolous!'

The incongruity of the misconception struck them both as extremely funny. When they had finished laughing Eddie was eager to include his own estimate of Amy.

'Would you like to know what I think? She's nice to look at,' he said. 'Of course she is. A positive jewel set in the toad's head of Pendraw. But as a person she has no sense of adventure and she's completely lacking in vision.'

He was encouraged by the intense attention Cilydd was paying him.

'You just compare her to Hetty, for instance. Or to Margot, for heaven's sake. They're not nearly so pretty. There's something distinctly horsey about old Margot, bless her. But they're game for anything. That makes them so much more exciting to be with. They have that touch of arrogance, that confidence, that touch of effort-less superiority that comes with their wealth and upbringing. Do you know what I mean? The trouble with Amy is that she's a born provincial. In the end nothing but the humdrum will satisfy her.'

He paused in a way that suggested there was more he could say. Cilydd already appeared to be pondering his judgement in complex depth.

'That's what I find about people,' Eddie said airily. 'They impose their own limitations on themselves. You could say they were the warders of their own prisons. It's fascinating, really. Are you going to soap my back?'

Eddie pointed authoritatively towards the bathroom.

'It's the least you can do, you know,' he said. 'After letting me down so dreadfully.'

Cilydd looked ruefully apologetic.

'What difference is your socialist lawyers' society likely to make to the course of history? A bloody good play would be far more effective. Can't we talk about it seriously, JC? You can't go back tonight surely. Sleep here. There'll be the most bloody awful fog in London.'

Cilydd was determined to leave.

'I must get back tonight,' he said. 'There's a lot to do.'

6

THE HOUSEKEEPER HAD A LIMP WHICH SHE TRIED TO MINIMISE WITH A sideways movement as she led the way to the orangery extension built along the east side of the enclosed London garden. The bunch of keys attached to the belt of her long black dress proclaimed her status. They jingled obediently each time Connie Clayton adjusted her stance to smile at Amy.

'You are looking so well Amy, my dear! And so beautiful, if I may say so.'

She paused in the high-ceilinged corridor as if to give Amy the opportunity of taking her into her confidence.

'I'm sure all the young men of that place where you're teaching must be running after you.'

Her toothy smile suggested it was an experience she herself might have enjoyed in the past. Amy frowned as she shook her head, her mind clearly too preoccupied to entertain such frivolities. Connie Clayton continued with the conducted tour.

'I'm afraid Lady Violet has a passion for changing things around. We had the most dreadful time when she decided to switch Sir John's library to the Chinese room. Or where the Chinese room used to be, I should say.'

Their footsteps echoed in the orangery. There were neo-classical statues in every niche. Amy looked at each one in turn with reluctant curiosity. At the end of their walk they were confronted with a large bust of a male with a thick neck and a frowning face, mounted in an alcove like a Roman emperor on a coin.

'That's Sir Alton Duff Plunkett. He was Governor of Madras. Lady Violet's grandfather. She was devoted to him. They had so much in common. Very artistic he was. And a great builder. He sketched his design for the orangery on the back of an envelope before going up to Scotland for the Twelfth. He said he wanted it ready by the time he got back. And it was.'

Connie's speech took on a pronounced lisp as she tried to reflect something of the grandeur and elegance of the family that employed her. Amy sighed quietly as she moved out to the terrace to examine the enclosed garden. All sight of other habitations had been blocked out by a high wall mantled with ivy. The noise of traffic was reduced to a persistent hum. The leaves of the ornamental trees on either side of the fountain were mostly fallen. A marble statue of a naked hunter with his dog at his heels leaned forward with ponderous eagerness in the late afternoon light. The flower-beds were crowded with gold and red chrysanthemum and dahlia blooms still struggling to display what was left of their splendour.

'Would you like to see some more, Amy?'

Connie Clayton was standing close behind her.

'All the treasures here are in my care. It's a responsibility of course. But I enjoy it!'

Her voice was full of the pride of a trusted servant. Even when so much of the furniture was under dust-covers, it was clear that she felt the entire contents of the elegant town house were in some mystical sense an essential part of her being and more important to her than her own personal belongings could ever be.

'Connie,' Amy said authoritatively. 'They make use of you.'

It was the only approach she could take. A flush of resentment crept up Connie Clayton's pale, powdered cheeks.

'I wouldn't say that at all,' she said. 'I've never had such considerate employers.'

She saw Amy raise her eyebrows.

'Lady Violet keeps me in constant touch with her movements. And she insists on the family treating me with every respect and consideration. "Don't impose yourselves on Mrs Clayton, children, whatever you do." And I must say they don't.'

Eager to convince Amy of the benevolence of her employer, Connie took out a postcard she was carrying in the pocket of her black apron. She handed it to Amy so that she could look at the picture and read the hurried scrawl on the back. It was a blue tinted picture of a massive Victorian gothic hotel situated in splendid isolation between a lake and a range of snow-capped mountains.

'Those are the Rockies,' Connie said. 'Canada. Lady Violet always sends me a card from wherever they go.'

Amy handed the card back.

'You are wearing yourself out in their service,' she said. 'And what will you have at the end of it all? A collection of postcards?'

Connie Clayton was hurt. Without speaking she turned to limp back into the house. Amy caught up with her in the semi-darkness of the arched passage that led to the orangery. Her urgent apology echoed in the silence.

'I didn't mean it Connie. Honestly. It's just that I want you to think seriously about Professor Gwilym's offer. I know Aunty would love to have you nearer home. And so would I.'

Connie continued to move forward in silence until she reached the electric light switch outside the library door. She turned to Amy to address her with a forgiving smile.

51

'I do want you to enjoy a little holiday in London,' she said.

A pool of light from a table lamp already lit was lost when Connie switched on the central chandelier.

'I appreciate your thinking about me,' Connie said. 'I really do. And it would be ever so nice to be near Esther, even though your uncle can be very trying at times. He never loses a chance to take a dig against the aristocracy when I'm around. But I could never let Lady Violet down. She really depends on me.'

Amy restrained herself from comment. She frowned at the luxurious oriental rugs and carpets that covered the library floor in some profusion.

'I know you have been through a trying time,' Connie said.

She spoke in a low voice that invited Amy's confidence.

'Esther has told me a great deal about it,' she said. 'Your young man in the sanatorium. And losing your best friend, the poor girl. So young in childbirth.'

Amy's lips were shut tight.

'When one has been through a trying time, a change of air is bound to do the world of good,' Connie said.

With a graceful gesture she invited Amy to sit.

'It's such a restful room, I always think. Lady Violet insists when the family is away I should come upstairs of an evening and enjoy the library. I never do, mind you. I like my own little room. And I would never want them to think I was taking some advantage. But you can sit here, Amy dear, any time you like.'

An emotion welled up in Amy that she could not suppress. She pointed indignantly at the massive white fireplace.

'Just look at that!'

Connie looked around unable to discover the source of Amy's indignation.

'Make-believe,' Amy said. 'Play-acting. You've only got to look.'

The chimney breast was outlined in fluted marble and surmounted with a broken pediment in imitation of a doric temple.

'Nothing but a charade,' Amy said. 'A large-scale pretence. Empty people just stuffed up with their own importance. That's what they are.'

Connie Clayton was too shocked to speak.

'The place is stuffed with books they never open and pictures they never look at and treasures that are mostly plunder. One is forced to ask, can they be human beings at all?'

'Oh Amy . . .'

At last Connie Clayton found her voice.

'The Duffs and the Plunketts are a most distinguished family,' she said. 'They are related to some of the best families in the land. I've heard Lady Violet say herself that she could count fourteen cousins and second cousins in the last parliament. And I can tell you this, they are generally acknowledged to be very clever. And very able. Sir John's uncle was Governor-General of New Zealand.'

Everything Connie said only served to fuel a further outburst from Amy.

'All this tommy-rot about serving the Empire. I'm sorry Connie, but it's nothing but a cover for exploitation and hypocritical English imperialism. Everybody knows that.'

'Well, I never.'

The onslaught had left the housekeeper short of breath and speechless.

'Look, Connie, you're not English, any more than I am. What on earth have you got to gain from all this? One way or another? Absolutely nothing. If you came home at least you would be with your own people.'

Amy continued to look as calm as a doctor who has made a diagnosis and was recommending a course of treatment she knew the patient would find unpalatable. Connie struggled to stiffen her back and raise her head high.

'It's the British Empire,' she said. 'And we're all British after all. Especially the Welsh people. Especially us.'

'There you are,' Amy said. 'Isn't that exactly it? We pull the wool over our own eyes and sleep-walk towards the abyss.'

'Abyss?'

Both the word and the context clearly mystified Connie.

'What abyss?'

They eyed each other in uncomprehending silence. The desire to understand each other seemed hopelessly insufficient to bridge the gulf between them. The quiet of the square outside was broken by an untuneful blast on a trumpet. They were both startled by the noise. They moved to the long window and looked down into the street. A young man sat at the wheel of a taxi-cab wearing evening dress under his leather flying-jacket. He waved the brass trumpet up at the window.

'That's Master Nigel,' Connie Clayton said. 'What on earth is he doing driving a taxi? And who are those people with him?'

A working man in a cloth cap with a scarf folded across his chest emerged from the taxi and claimed his trumpet from the young driver. He had a knapsack slung over his shoulder and his ancient tweed overcoat reached almost to his ankles.

'Pen.'

Amy muttered his name to herself.

'Pen Lewis.'

'They're all coming here.'

Connie Clayton was alarmed.

'That's Miss Margot, Master Nigel's cousin. Master Nigel is rather wild, I'm afraid. Lady Violet feels responsible for him. His mother and father were killed in a motoring accident in the South of France. A terrible tragedy.'

Eddie Meredith and Margot Gromont stood on either side of Pen Lewis like a guard of honour. Margot's hair and her jaw hung down as she smiled self-consciously while Eddie kept waving at Amy standing in the light of the library window, expecting her to share his pleasure in such a surprise encounter.

'I don't know, I'm sure . . .'

Connie Clayton was muttering to herself, acutely conscious of her responsibilities. Without switching off the engine, Nigel had descended from the taxi and dashed up the steps to tug at the door bell. Like a nervous mare Connie's nostrils quivered as she raised her head to listen to the clang of the bell reverberate through the house.

'I shall have to answer it myself,' she said. 'I'm not at all sure that Lady Violet would want them to come in. Master Nigel can be very noisy. Like his sister, Cecily. There was one occasion during the season in 1928 when she had the scent of a treasure hunt going right through the kitchen and into the bins in the back. Lady Violet was furious with her.'

Amy waited at the top of the staircase to watch Connie Clayton open the doors. This was in itself a performance. Her keys jingled as she knelt unsteadily to reach the lower bolt. As soon as the catch was released the door was pushed open by the impatient Nigel.

'What's up, Connie,' he said. 'Are you under siege?'

He tossed back his head and stared at her with a fixed grin on his red face. Connie bobbed her head and held a protective palm against her grey hair.

'This is a hunger marcher,' he said blithely. 'You've heard of the hunger marchers, Connie?'

Connie took a step back and nodded nervously.

'Mad keen to meet you.'

Nigel strode possessively towards the middle of the hall. He raised his arms in rhetorical gesture.

'Workers of the world unite!' he said. 'I've put my taxi at the disposal of the hunger marchers and the TUC. And in that order. God, I'm starving. Is there anything to eat, Connie?'

Connie's mouth was open as she watched the stalwart figure of Pen Lewis enter the house, followed by Eddie and Margot. His hob-nailed boots scraped the polished tiles like chalk on a blackboard and set her teeth on edge.

'There she is.'

Eddie Meredith pointed triumphantly towards Amy standing in the shadow at the top of the stairs.

'The princess of Pendraw! Amy! Isn't this marvellous?'

Margot stood at Eddie's side prepared to display unstinting friendliness. Nigel demanded Connie Clayton's undivided attention.

'Look, Connie,' he said. 'The thing about hunger marchers is that they're hungry. How about a piece of your marvellous game pie? Shall we all troop down to the kitchen?'

Nigel was prepared to lead the way himself. Connie still hesitated. Her eyes was fixed on the strangely military nature of Pen Lewis's tattered accoutrement: the soiled khaki pack, the heavy boots, the brass trumpet. Even the cloth cap which he had not removed seemed part of a uniform.

'Don't worry, Connie dear,' Nigel said. 'This is Mr Lewis from

Wales. A very responsible fellow. He has no intention of stealing the silver.'

Pen showed no sign of being amused by Nigel's remarks or even listening to them. He marched towards the staircase obviously intent on speaking to Amy. Eddie was ready to follow him but Margot held on to him by his sleeve. They followed Nigel downstairs to the kitchens and the servants' quarters.

'Nice place.'

Pen smiled at Amy and removed his cap. He followed her to the library. He pursed his lips and raised his eyebrows as he looked around the room.

'Very nice,' he said. 'Make a nice holiday home for collier's kids after the Revolution.'

Amy looked pale and temporarily hypnotised by the cheerful huskiness of his voice and his muscular presence. He felt his unshaven cheek and then grinned at her like a man resolved above everything to maintain his self-possession.

'How did you know I was here?'

Amy was frowning.

'That Eddie chap,' Pen said. 'He was with those college kids giving us a feed and cheering us along, first thing in the morning. We needed a bit of cheering too. Wet through we were. He recognised me from Coleg y Castell. Remember those half-baked courses for the unemployed? Economics for five-year-olds, the scientific method for retired methodist ministers and old Tasker Thomas's endless lectures on Affirmative Living. He was one of Tasker's boys. A bit of a creep I'd call him, but it turns out he's on the right side. Or maybe he just knows on what side his bread is buttered.'

Amy was staring at him resentfully. Pen began to chuckle.

'I don't know what it is,' he said. 'That look you've got on your face when you're cross. I find it irresistible.'

Amy moved towards the door. She seemed determined to leave the library. Pen barred her way, holding out an arm to restrain her.

'Hold on, girl,' he said. 'Just give me a chance to state my case.'

'Don't you dare touch me,' Amy said threateningly.

'Just let me say my say, damn it. Then you can do what you like.

There's a job in Hendrerhys. It includes teaching Welsh, for God's sake. It's yours, kid, if you want it. I really mean it. We could get married and I could carry on my organising work. I don't want to go on my knees, Amy. If I did, I'd be too bloody tired to get up. You know how much I love you, for God's sake. If I could have stopped I would have done so long ago. But why should I? Why should I?'

Her stillness as she listened to him did nothing to help his resolve to remain self-possessed. He turned his anger and frustration against the room in which they stood like alien intruders.

'Look at this,' he said. 'It's worse than the bloody Winter Palace. We've got to overthrow all this. You know that as well as I do. You mustn't let them make you feel included and accepted.'

'My aunt is their servant,' Amy said. 'Not that she's my real aunt. She was adopted by my mother's uncle. Not that that matters either. She's my family. I belong down there in the servants' hall.'

She smiled wanly and he was immediately encouraged.

'That's my girl,' he said. 'The only war that counts is the class war. You know which side you are on.'

He was close enough to attempt to embrace her. Angrily she knocked his arm away.

'You just think you can impose your will by physical force,' she said. 'Not with me, Pen Lewis.'

'Amy.'

A note of pleading entered his voice for the first time.

'Amy. My girl.'

'Just bearing down,' she said. 'Just trying to overpower me.'

'Amy,' Pen said. 'Why not? You belong to me. I belong to you. You know it as well as I do.'

She struggled out of his embrace.

'I don't,' she said. 'I don't, Pen Lewis. If you want to know, I'm engaged. I'm going to marry someone else.'

Pen's arms fell to his side. He was suddenly overwhelmed with tiredness. He sank down on the nearest settee. His old clothes grimy with marching contrasted with the soft velvet of the upholstery.

'Who?'

'Never you mind who,' she said.

57

She was at last able to view him with sympathetic detachment.
'Wouldn't you like something to eat?' she said. 'That other lot
are liable to wolf every morsel left in the kitchen.'

Pen shook his head. Enveloped in weariness and a rising tide of
misery he was unable to move.

'Who?'

What animation remained in him was encapsulated in the single
syllable. He kept repeating the question like a groan.

'Who? Who?'

'It's a secret,' Amy said. 'Nobody knows yet.'

'Some bloody lord or other.'

He looked around resentfully at their surroundings. Amy was
able to smile but that brought him no comfort.

'Who?' he said hoarsely. 'I have a right to know. You've been with
me. We were lovers or whatever the bloody word is in this day and
age. That gives me some right to know.'

She stood in front of him and stretched out a hand to help him
to his feet.

'You'll be the first to know,' she said. 'Before anyone else, Pen
Lewis. Come and get something to eat. Where will you sleep tonight?'

Pen's head was lowered as he struggled to cope with his misery.

'In some bloody chapel vestry,' he said. 'On the floor. Like a
bloody dog.'

7

NIGEL WAS IN HIGH SPIRITS AS HE STEERED AMY SKILFULLY AROUND
the dance floor. The band was playing a tango and Nigel was
determined to demonstrate his virtuosity: in spite of his solid bulk
he would execute the swaying motions with all the feline supple-
ness the music demanded. He concentrated hard, but once it was
achieved, it became a joke they could also share.

'I'm a Dutchman pretending to be a dago!'

He shouted the remark when his mouth was reasonably close to
Amy's left ear. Amy was already laughing. In a white evening dress

with bold sleeves and a frilled skirt hemmed with blue, she was a strikingly lithe and attractive figure.

'D'you know, I like dancing with you even better than driving my taxi.'

They executed a sequence of intricate steps in full view of the table on the fringe of the dance floor where the rest of their party sat. Eddie Meredith raised both hands to clap. Margot did the same, smiling shyly behind her long hair. Amy gave a quick glance to see whether John Cilydd was watching. His head was turned the other way. He had his elbow on the table and he was listening intently to Hetty Remington. Whatever she was saying was of far greater importance than anything occurring on the dance floor. Hetty had an ice-cream spoon dangling between her white fingers. She caused the spoon to tremble between two empty wine bottles on the table as she struggled to express herself.

'I'm twenty-five next week,' Nigel said.

Amy made an effort to show polite interest.

'Then I more or less inherit. My grandfather tied everything up so that I wouldn't get my greedy fingers on anything until I was twenty-five. Sorry!'

He stumbled as they moved through an obscure area beyond the raked bandstand.

'I'm a clumsy sod at heart. I do beg your pardon.'

A cruising motion made it easier to talk.

'What do you think I should do?'

Nigel's question sounded quite urgent.

'I'm torn, you see. This hunger march business and all this political stuff makes you think, doesn't it? But at heart you know I'm a terribly frivolous person. Eddie says I'm something the dog brought in left over from the naughty nineties.'

'You don't want to take too much notice of what Eddie says,' Amy said.

'It's a weakness, you know, in our family,' Nigel said. 'I had a great-uncle who devoted his whole life to enjoying himself. My Aunt Violet says I'm just like him.'

'What happened to him?'

Nigel grinned.

'Apoplexy,' he said. 'He had a stroke on his fiftieth birthday. From then on he lived in Rapallo and spent the rest of his life cursing his slut of a housekeeper out of the corner of his mouth. There's a lesson there somewhere!'

The insistent rhythm of the tango was a form of consolation. It brought Nigel back to the tip of his toes and Amy was equal to the challenge. With sure-footed ease they swept once more past their table. Cilydd was still deep in conversation with Hetty. Eddie had a hand raised as he ordered another bottle of wine.

'The thing is.'

Nigel held Amy more tightly as he prepared to ask her advice.

'Should I join the Communist Party or take my taxi on a tour of European capitals?'

With the palm of his hand pressed into her back he could sense her amused response. He smiled himself before resuming his solemn discourse.

'I'm bloody serious actually,' he said. 'You are dancing with a man at the crossroads. That sounds silly, but it's true. You know I would absolutely love to be able to boast that I drove my taxi in every single European capital before I was thirty. Can you imagine anything sillier. More socially irresponsible, as my cousin Margot would say. My God, she'd have a fit if she heard me, I can tell you.'

Amy eased herself from his excited grip.

'She may look shy and harmless,' Nigel said. 'But, my God, that girl is all steel inside I can tell you. The fact is I'm quite scared of her.'

Nigel became temporarily absorbed in the execution of a sequence of complex steps. When it was over he resumed his attempt to arouse Amy's interest in his problems.

'I think women are frightfully mysterious creatures, don't you?'

Amy leaned back to smile at him.

'I mean, you can never tell what they're thinking. Or what the hell they'll do next. They're even worse than politics really. Maybe I ought to devote myself to enjoying myself after all. I'm too damned stupid to do anything else.'

The tango came to an end. The dancers stood still on the floor to reward the band with polite applause before returning to their tables.

'You should ask Margot to dance,' Amy said.

Nigel was surprised.

'Should I? I don't think she can, anyway. All she can do is plot revolutions. She was terribly impressed with that hunger march chap. I couldn't understand it really. She is a strange girl. Mind you, I know how bad it is down there. All of those blighted valleys. Of course, it's where you come from isn't it?'

'No. I'm from the North,' Amy said.

'Of course you are. The fact is I'm pig-ignorant about Wales.'

Nigel grinned happily. When they returned to the table there was momentary confusion since Cilydd had occupied Amy's chair in order to confer more closely with Hetty. Amy insisted that he should not move. She took a chair with its back to the dance floor so that she could face the others across the table. The wine-waiter arrived with a bottle of white wine and twirled it in the ice-bucket. Eddie made a fresh attempt to engage the attention of the whole party with an anecdote he had tried more than once to finish.

'I just told him, "Look, Bertie, I am a past-President of the Mermaid Society so don't try and tell me how to speak English blank verse."'

Hetty stretched her arm across the table towards Amy. Her dark hair rose in waves from her high forehead. She spoke with a faint American accent. The tense earnestness of her manner made Amy lean back in her chair as if to make herself that much less accessible.

'We were discussing whether John should make this trip to Vienna or not,' she said. 'I honestly don't think he should go. I realise it's important. It's a terrible situation out there and the people need help. But for a start he doesn't speak German. There must be legal people on the socialist side who speak fluent German. That's my point. There are other ways in which a poet can serve the cause. Don't you think so?'

Amy looked at the young woman and at Cilydd who was fumbling nervously in his pocket for a packet of cigarettes. She took so long to speak she could have been making a rapid sequence of guesses as to the exact nature of the relationship between them. Her face had gone paler and as though to avoid looking at either

61

one or the other, she fixed her gaze on a group of opulently dressed middle-aged people occupying a table in her direct line of vision.

'What do you think?'

Hetty pressed the question. Amy continued to avoid looking at her.

'I don't know anything about it,' she said. 'In any case he's a grown man. He has to make his own mind up.'

The band struck up a popular fox-trot and the noise allowed Amy to give up talking across the table. Nigel was humming the tune as he insisted on Margot accepting his abrupt invitation to dance. Eddie attempted to mime an inebriated blessing. The thin vocalist with the band placed himself in front of the microphone, fingering his white tie before he began to sing in a reedy tenor. Hetty resumed her attempt to dissuade John Cilydd from his proposed mission to Vienna. Amy could hear the more emphatically pronounced words, but the German and Hungarian names meant nothing to her. The earnest discussion was plainly something she wanted to avoid looking at and she was in no mood to listen to Eddie. She fixed her gazing on the middle distance, staring apparently at nothing until a blonde woman in a fur-trimmed gold lamé evening dress suddenly loomed up into the space between Hetty and Cilydd. She jabbed a finger in Amy's direction. The rings flashed on her plump fingers.

'You've been staring at me all evening,' she said. 'And I'll not have any more of it.'

Amy put her hand to her bare throat as though to protect herself from such an unexpected attack. Hetty and Cilydd were so intent on their discussion that they did not become aware of what was happening until the woman began tapping nervously on Cilydd's shoulder. He looked up and his mouth hung open with amazement.

'Staring at me as if I was dirt. Who do you think you are? I have as much right to be in this place as you have, my girl.'

Amy was shaking her head helplessly.

'Looking at me as if I was dirt.'

'I wasn't looking at you,' Amy said. 'Really I wasn't.'

The woman was not appeased.

'Seeing through me I suppose,' she said. 'As if I wasn't there. As if I didn't exist.'

One of her companions came to persuade her to return to her table. The deep voice that emerged from under his heavy moustache and the soothing tone reduced the blonde woman to tears. He led her gently back to the table. Eddie turned to observe their departure.

'What was all that about?' he said.

His voice was querulous with a need for attention. He was tired of being ignored.

'My God,' he said. 'Did you see her backside. Bigger than the Queen Mary. Look at her blubbing into her whisky.'

Hetty and Cilydd were showing their concern for Amy. The blonde woman's outburst had upset her.

'I wasn't looking at her,' Amy said. 'I didn't even see her.'

She was no longer comfortable in her chair. Hetty and Cilydd's concern did not console her. She resented their gaze as much as the strange woman had objected to her stare.

'I'm going,' she said defiantly.

Cilydd attempted a soothing smile before looking at his watch.

'Amy,' he said. 'It's only half past nine.'

'There's no point at all in me being here,' she said. Her cheeks were beginning to redden.

'I'll leave you to carry on your conversation in peace.'

It was only then that Hetty began to assume that her guest had been offended.

'Oh, my dear,' she said, stretching her hand once more across the table in an oddly muted gesture of reconciliation. 'Don't go. I was just obsessed with this business about Vienna. I'm sure it's not right for John. And I'm sure you agree with me.'

'It's none of my business,' Amy said.

She was on her feet, her bag in her hand and her wrap on her arm ready to depart. The music had stopped. The dancers were clapping. Nigel and Margot were ready to return to their table. The absence of background noise would make whatever was said more clear and decisive.

'I'm sorry,' Amy said. 'I should never have come. I don't want to spoil your evening.'

She had to squeeze past the blonde woman's table as she made her exit. The woman raised her hand to demand her attention. It was possible she wanted to apologise. The man with a heavy moustache continued to comfort and restrain her. Cilydd caught up with Amy in the dimly lit area by the cloakroom counter.

'Amy,' he said. 'Wait. Wait will you? What's the matter?'

She looked at him. Her eyes filled with tears that obstinately refused to fall.

'I wanted to talk to you,' she said. 'That's why I came.'

'They think you're marvellous,' he said urgently. 'Honestly.'

'I don't care what they think,' Amy said. 'Who are they anyway? Just a bunch of rich children who think it's their job to put the world to rights. Who do they think they are? A man of your age, John Cilydd, being carried away by whatever it is you think they've got. And I can't stand the sound of Eddie Meredith's made-up Oxford accent.'

Cilydd smiled to show that he could sympathise with her objections.

'What was it you wanted to talk to me about?'

'Little Bedwyr of course. What else?'

He frowned as though he had to make an effort to focus his mind on the change of subject.

'You didn't even show them his photograph,' Amy said. 'If you want to know what I think, you're behaving like a man who wants to pretend he's much younger than he is.'

Cilydd struggled to keep the smile on his face.

'Fair play, Amy,' he said. 'I'm not all that old.'

'And you sat there listening to Eddie Meredith making fun of Tasker Thomas and you didn't say a word. After all Tasker has done for him. Him and his wider world. Wider world! He would never have got near that horrible Berlin of his if Tasker hadn't fixed it up for him. He does nothing but show off. And I can't bear people who have no respect for their origins.'

'Amy . . .'

Cilydd's gestures implied that he did not know where to begin justifying his friends and, by association, arranging his own defence.

'They are young,' he said. 'They belong to the privileged class. I admit that. But they are conscious of what's wrong with the world just as much as we are. But they're realists as well as idealists. That may be because they've been born into the governing classes. But all I can say is that their analysis of the situation is a good deal less blurred than dear old Tasker's. He's so emotional and simplistic. You know yourself, Amy, I admire him as much as you do, but half the time his feet aren't even touching the ground. His sermons are so naïve.'

'Enid believed he was right.'

Cilydd received the mention of his dead wife's name like a blow on the chest which had left him temporarily speechless. Amy recovered her umbrella and Cilydd covered up his confusion by giving the cloakroom girl a large tip. Amy paused in front of the revolving door. Outside it was beginning to rain.

'I'll leave you to your friends,' Amy said.

She could not resist a parting shot.

'I'm sure they are much better than anything you could find at home.'

He watched her push her way determinedly through the revolving door. After a moment's hesitation he followed her, turning up the collar of his dinner jacket in the street. He caught up with her on the street corner, raising the hem of her ball-dress in a vain attempt to avoid being splashed by the passing traffic. He took hold of her umbrella so that both her hands were free to cope with her dress. He steered her into the shelter of the nearest café.

'We've got to talk,' he said. 'You've got to tell me what you came to talk about.'

The brightly lit café was almost empty. Cilydd pointed their way to a deserted corner. He ordered coffee and cakes to justify their possession of the table and leaned across the table ready to listen to the slightest thing Amy might have to say. She stared unhappily at the view of the wet street through the plate-glass window.

'I expect I'm jealous,' Amy said at last.

'Jealous.'

The word puzzled him. He seemed unable to connect it with Amy as he shifted in his chair to study her face more closely.

65

'She's keen on you.'

Amy spoke in a sulky voice in spite of her visible effort to remain calm and objective.

'Hetty? But there's nothing of that sort between us. We just have a common interest and concern with the political scene. All of us!'

'She thinks you're a poet of great promise and all that sort of thing. She's rich. She can help you.'

Cilydd shook his head.

'Politics,' he said. 'They're more important than poetry. That's what I keep telling them.'

The waitress brought them coffee and cakes. As soon as she had left them Amy said:

'What about little Bedwyr?'

Cilydd stirred his coffee and sighed.

'I want you of all people to understand, Amy,' he said. 'God knows how I can explain the complexity of my own motives. But I thought when he was older, old enough to go to school, say, there is a very nice little private school just around the corner from Margot's mother's house. In a year or two I shall be doing quite well, concentrating on Company Law. It's a possibility.'

'Bring him up to be a little English gentleman,' Amy said. 'An imitation Nigel.'

Cilydd began to laugh until he saw how serious she was.

'You don't approve,' he said. 'Just like Nain.'

He made a poor attempt to imitate his grandmother's tone of voice.

' "Nothing will come of you, my boy, until you get back to your roots." '

He had still not succeeded in bringing a smile to her face. He could see she was steeling herself to say something.

'Have you ever thought of asking me to marry you?' Amy said.

It took time for the significance of her question to sink in.

'Thought?'

He repeated the word to himself.

'There was a time when I thought of nothing else,' he said. Having made her statement, Amy chose to remain silent. She kept her eyes on his face like a gambler who has made her last throw and has nothing in the world left to do except wait for the wheel to stop rotating.

'There was Val,' he said. 'There was Val, of course. Poor Val. How can one understand oneself? You remember how we were. When Enid was alive. How she wanted us to be: the four of us close together. I thought I was the odd man out. She used to write those long letters to Val and you never minded it. I think it was because of you as much as anything I went away. I was confusing my memory of her with you.'

They could hear their own voices whispering urgently in the isolation of their corner of the deserted café. The sound was printing the silence with words that would stay in their memory for ever.

'I was guilty about you,' Cilydd said.

He reached out and took her hand as though the action would give him courage to make his confession.

'I think Enid knew,' he said. 'She understood so much. From that day I first saw you, I think. Walking up the school hill carrying a haversack. You couldn't have been more than eighteen. She knew. But she loved you even more than I did, so she didn't mind.'

'That's all over now.'

Amy spoke in a gentle comforting voice.

'That's all in the past. We're here now. What are you going to do?'

His face was transformed with joy. He began to mutter incoherently.

'I can't believe it,' he said. 'I can't believe it.'

'You won't have the best of both worlds,' Amy said, smiling at him. 'Maybe only the worst of one.'

'To think you are willing to marry me,' Cilydd said. 'I'm drunk with the idea. How can I keep still? I want to dance in the streets.'

Suddenly he pushed back his chair, clasped her shoulders and kissed her squarely on the mouth.

'John Cilydd.'

Amy reproved him mildly.

'That woman at the pay-desk is watching.'

'Let's go back and tell them.'

Cilydd was too excited to sit.

'Let's go back and dance. Dance!'

Amy shook her head.

'You are a lawyer, Mr More,' she said. 'So sit still and think it all out.'

'Think?'

'There's a lot we can do together,' Amy said calmly. 'Make a proper home for little Bedwyr, for a start. That's what Enid would have wanted.'

He looked at her as though for the first time he had realised how much thought she had already given the subject. He took her hand, kissed it gently and showed how willing he was to fall in with every detail of her plans.

'You go back to Fralino's now,' Amy said. 'But don't tell them our secret. Tell them I was ill or something and that you put me in a taxi and packed me off to Culpepper Place. Start thinking about our marriage. Will you go to Vienna?'

Cilydd shook his head fervently.

'Not if you don't want me to. No!'

'If we married quietly in a registry office,' Amy said, 'we'd only need two witnesses. Is that true, Mr More? You're the lawyer, you should know.'

They both began to shiver slightly with the excitement of conspiracy. He ventured to touch her face with the tips of his fingers and when she kissed them hurriedly he was overcome with emotion.

'You are perfect,' he said. 'The perfect flower of womanhood. The perfect flower.'

'We'd better leave,' Amy said. 'That woman at the pay-desk is dying of curiosity.'

Outside in the street, close together under her umbrella, she allowed him to kiss her on the lips again.

'I'm drunk,' he said in a whisper. 'Absolutely drunk.'

'What a pity,' Amy said mischievously. 'I hoped it was me.'

A taxi was difficult to come by. He clung to her side reluctant to leave her.

'No. You go back,' she said. 'Your coat is in the cloakroom. But keep our secret. Promise.'

Under the umbrella it was easy to giggle.

'Eddie,' Cilydd said. 'I can't wait to see his face when I tell him.'

'You keep our secret.'

'He told me that hunger marcher chap, Pen Lewis, was keen on you.'

'I can't help that,' Amy said.

She held out an arm to stop a taxi. Her signal was ignored.

'He told me this Pen chap had told him there were only two things he wanted to do in London. Strangle the Prime Minister and kidnap Amy Parry.'

'Well, the poor man didn't do either, did he?'

Amy turned to face Cilydd so that he was obliged to raise the umbrella high over her head. Suddenly he grasped her around the waist with his free arm and pressed her as hard as he could against his loins.

'To think you're going to marry me,' he said. 'I'll do anything for you. Anything. Don't take any notice of this living in London business. Company Law and all that rot. I'll live wherever you want, do you hear me? On the top of a tree if you like.'

She made him relax his grasp so that her feet were back on the pavement.

'A home,' she said. 'A home. That's what we'll make together.'

8

IN THE PASSENGER SEAT, AMY SANK HER CHIN FURTHER INTO THE FUR collar of her overcoat and thrust her hands deeper into the wide pockets. Through the windscreen she could see the vast storm clouds gathered in the west. Cilydd wanted to talk to her. He smiled at her more than once in the hope of gaining her attention. Her troubled gaze was difficult to interpret: equally it could mean the desire to arrive at their destination before the storm broke or a deep reluctance at having to make the journey at all. He was also inhibited by the presence of Reverend Tasker Thomas who spread himself generously over the back seat. Tasker was taking a boyish delight in the ride as if he had never ridden in a motor car before. He was liable to bring his bulk to bear on the backs of their seats in order to share the thoughts that occurred to him with his travelling companions, but for the moment he was content to let himself ride with the movement of the vehicle.

'What do you find so amusing?'

Amy had caught a glimpse of Cilydd's smile from the corner of her eye. She murmured her question into her collar so that Tasker would not hear.

'You look just like that painting,' Cilydd said. 'What's it called, "The Last of England". Only like the man, not the woman. And we're not holding hands.'

Behind them Tasker started singing. He rolled about on the back seat as Cilydd swerved to avoid a sequence of water-logged pot-holes. When he regained his equilibrium Tasker placed his forearms securely on the backs of their seats. He relished this posture since it gave him equal access to both their ears and he had several points to make.

'They are the salt of the earth, you know,' Tasker said. 'We mustn't forget that. The old Glanrafon family. The salt of the earth.'

He waited for some sound of agreement from either of them. It was not forthcoming.

'You can analyse it, you see,' he said. 'It's not the shop, delightful as it is. It's what lies behind it. The economic base as they say. There you have the earth and there you have the salt which gives it savour. Two farms. Ponciau and Glanrafon. And the stores. The "general" stores. But man does not live by bread alone. Then you examine the family and its dependants. All equal in the eyes of the Lord. There's the salt for you. The basis of any depth of civilisation. It's what we believe, isn't it? Poetry needs roots in a community. It's what I mean you see, John Cilydd, by that phrase "the poet's cradle".'

Cilydd smiled at the wintry view through the windscreen.

'Or his prison,' Cilydd said.

Tasker chose to ignore the comment. He had many more observations to make and they were nearing the end of the journey.

'Don't underrate any of them!'

A note of exhortation crept into his voice.

'Not even your Uncle Simon. I know he treated you roughly when you were a boy. A sensitive youth. But the art of maturity is to stand back and see such figures and their compulsions in perspective. What kind of a world would it be if it were filled with human beings we had to look at with contempt instead of respect?'

Tasker tapped Cilydd repeatedly on his left shoulder until he was obliged to nod in order to get him to desist.

'I have to admire them all you see,' Tasker said. 'Your three uncles. And your Aunt Bessie, bless her. Blessed among women. Seeing it as a privilege to serve in the humblest capacity. Have you noticed her hands?'

Tasker held out his own hand for their inspection.

'Yes, I've noticed them,' Cilydd said.

'Cracked and scarred with years of service. The stigmata of devotion. And your grandmother of course. I see her as a grand matriarchal figure. And your good sister Nanw.'

Tasker's large head waggled with the pleasurable contemplation of such a choice array of family characters and connections.

'But do you know what gives me pleasure? Passing the time of day with your Uncle Tryfan in his cobbler's workshop! Now there's a man for you. A human gem. There are smart and would-be-sophisticated persons who ignore him as being a simple creature if not a simpleton. But do you know, I can listen to him for hours on end. And as I sit there I just wait until I see an aura of innocence shine like a halo about his head.'

Tasker paused to rein in his own eloquence. He was quick to interpret Cilydd's unresponsive silence as scepticism. It moved him to tap Cilydd's shoulder again.

'And I can tell you who else sees it. Little Bedwyr. He will sit in his little chair there just inside the door and watch your Uncle Tryfan repairing boots by the hour. Did you see those perfect little boots he made for him? Now there's a subject for a poem for you.'

Cilydd squinted up at the great black cloud approaching overhead.

'People are forever suggesting subjects for poems I could write,' he said.

'A new tale of the golden shoemaker,' Tasker said. 'But this time the gold is the nobility of the essential wisdom in his possession. But I suppose you would find that too moralistic for the modern style?'

The downpour of rain and hail struck the hood of the tourer like a fist. Cilydd changed gear and weighed over the steering wheel to bring his face nearer to the brief arc of vision provided by the busy windscreen-wiper. Tasker sprawled back in his seat, eyeing the hood. With his sleeve he tried to clear the celluloid side window to gain a better view of the submerged world outside. He began a nasal chant of the words of a hymn.

' "... yet in the storm I sing, God will forgive my flaw"!'

At the crossroads, visibility was so bad, Cilydd drew to the side, waiting for the storm to pass. With the engine still running, the blue tourer seemed to be cringing under the impact of the rain. The three sat in silence listening to the downpour. They smiled with relief when it was over. The sun low on the horizon burst through with unexpected power filling the road ahead with an atmosphere of bright haze. Tasker opened the rear door and emerged as eagerly as a naturalist from a hide. He was unaware that the car was about to move off. Amy and Cilydd watched him with detached curiosity as he stretched out his arms to take in the steaming hedgerows.

'The greatness of nature! The world after the flood! Isn't it amazing. You know I never cease to marvel.'

The car was moving off with the rear door open when he climbed back in.

'We mustn't be late,' Cilydd said.

He murmured the statement like an apology over his shoulder. Tasker leaned forward to address them both confidentially.

'Have you thought of what you are going to say?' he said.

Cilydd glanced at Amy. She was not prepared to speak.

'Just tell them we're married,' he said. 'There isn't much else one can say, is there?'

Tasker's face creased up with the effort of deep thought. The black clouds were gathering again, more powerful than the setting sun. Cilydd was accelerating and the car was moving too quickly for Tasker to gather any fresh inspiration from the landscape.

'Let me tell you how I see their old-fashionedness,' Tasker said. 'It's not fossil. Not at all. It's like a tough seed. Hiding in the dark ground ready to bloom again for the benefit of generations yet unborn. Does that sound too fanciful?'

Tasker's eyebrows quivered anxiously. He thrust forward his head to smile at Amy and attempted a gentle tap on her shoulder.

'Now then Amy, Mrs More. You are the one to puncture these bubbles of speculation. Put me in my place.'

Amy shook her head.

'I'm only too glad you are with us,' she said.

He patted her back consolingly before leaning back in his seat and contemplating his folded hands.

'What I hope they will see, as a family, is the sheer courage of your decision. Two adults facing the world responsibly. Two ordering their lives for the benefit of others as well as fulfilling themselves.'

'I shall keep my mouth shut,' Amy said. 'It's about the only way I can avoid saying the wrong thing.'

She smiled weakly when she heard Cilydd laugh with uncharacteristic heartiness. Tasker continued with his train of thought, rehearsing arguments that could be put forward if the need arose.

'It's your nature to be loyal,' he said. 'Of course it is. They must be made to see that. You could so easily have settled in Chelsea or Dulwich or somewhere like that. But you put your traditional obligations first. You thought of that little boy. These things are instinctive. Of course they are. But there are moments in the lives of individuals, in the life of a nation indeed, when they have to be spelt out.'

What he had said brought him evident comfort. He was able to relax in his seat and observe the rays of the sun make a last effort to penetrate a mass of trees at the end of an expanse of low fields. A flock of crows exploded in the pale light and tossed themselves about, wild with resentment at some disturbance. As the car advanced they watched the crows sweep across the road, blown as

73

well as flying, unexpectedly large and black, driven by a wind that preceded a fresh onslaught of sleet. Their hoarse cries as they rocked about were momentarily louder than the noise of the engine.

'There is nothing that calm and patience and understanding cannot overcome,' Tasker said. 'We have to believe that. And if families cannot live together in harmony, then who on earth can? They must see you as harbingers of a new age. Sometimes you know I see my ministry as a balancing act. My job is to guide people across the gulf, the great divide, between the generations. Between what was and what is to come.'

Nanw was waiting for them in the shop doorway. Cilydd brought the car as close as he could over the cobbles, but she still had to open the large black umbrella as they came out of the car. Tasker stamped his feet appreciatively on the dry floorboards of the shop as the shower of hailstones bounced on the cobbles outside.

'Isn't it terrible weather?' Nanw said.

She looked pale and strained and unwilling to face her brother as he stared at her challengingly.

'Have you told them?'

Nanw nodded briefly. There was no means by which she could protect herself from their intense scrutiny as they attempted to fathom the nature of the family reaction to the news. Her pale cheeks flushed bright red.

'How did they take it?'

Cilydd was impatient for an answer. Amy placed a restraining hand on his arm.

'Where's little Bedwyr?' she said.

Nanw was grateful for the understanding note in her voice.

'He's got a bit of a cough,' Nanw said. 'Nothing serious. But Nain said he should go to bed early.'

Cilydd's face darkened with anger.

'Didn't you tell them he would be coming back with us?'

'Well I did mention it,' Nanw said. 'But she didn't seem to take it in. She was so worried about his cough. She made me make a fire in the bedroom. Mind you, it isn't as bad as all that.'

Cilydd's jaw stretched aggressively. In a deliberately jocular manner, Tasker paced about from one counter to the other.

'Aladdin's cave!' he said. 'Do you know when I was a boy it was my heart's ambition to own a country store? Now wait a minute!'

He paused in front of them to crave their indulgence with a raised finger.

'How does it go? Tryfan taught me the chorus last time I was here. "Pitch, honey and relish and furniture polish" . . .'

He burst out laughing at the words and his inability to remember them or the tune. Nanw listened to him patiently. He stretched an arm towards her.

'It all brings back memories you know,' he said. 'Shops were part of my childhood.'

'She's done it quite deliberately,' Cilydd said.

He was muttering angrily to himself about his grandmother. Tasker stretched himself to his full height and placed his hands soothingly on Cilydd's shoulders.

'Wasn't this once the centre of your little universe, John Cilydd?'

His gesture conveyed the astonishing variety of the premises. Cilydd looked up at the shadowy coils of rope, the buckets, milking-stools and brush-heads hanging from the ceiling.

'I used to have a nightmare,' he said. 'I can remember that much. Spending the night up there, hanging like a bat from the ceiling. I could squeal away for ever and nobody would hear me.'

In the kitchen the lamps were already lit and the table laid for high-tea. Members of the family occupied their positions with a formal stillness almost as inanimate as the plates of the home-made bread and cakes. Mrs Lloyd wore a black bonnet instead of her customary black felt working cap and her faded red hair was brushed and tied back with unaccustomed neatness. This made her face look thinner and older. She sat in her high-backed chair with a rug over her knees, fingering an old Christmas card with the last vestiges of disdainful curiosity. Uncle Gwilym stood behind his mother's chair like an heir-apparent posing for a photograph with one hand resting lightly on the back of the throne. His obedient wife sat in the corner behind him, protected by his stiff back and the comforting shadow of the grandfather clock. His elder brother, Uncle Simon, sat in mock humility on the stool he was accustomed to occupy on the opposite side of the fireplace. When Cilydd escorted Amy into their view from the dim passage between the kitchen and the shop, Simon was engaged in nibbling the calloused skin established on the side of his index finger by the same unremitting toil on Ponciau fields that had stiffened all his joints. He was uncertain how to react to the long awaited arrival. His narrowed eyes were fixed on his brother Gwilym. Sibling rivalry had settled deeper into his bones than the arthritis. As the elder son he had the stronger claim to the throne and could afford to bide his time. But his brother Gwilym was a weekly columnist with a bardic pseudonym and therefore better placed to understand the ways of an increasingly confusing world.

The moment Gwilym began to finger the right end of a moustache that had once been waxed, and bowed in Amy's direction, Simon lumbered to his feet and bent his elbow in preparation of offering his solidly calloused hand. But his youngest brother, Tryfan, whose words and movements he was in the habit of dismissing or ignoring, already held both of Amy's hands in his, shaking them repeatedly and beaming at her his own unstinting welcome.

Tryfan was the only member of the family entirely at his ease and free from restraint. While his brothers were immobilised by their own dignity and their unceasing competition for their mother's approval, he bustled about to find Amy somewhere to sit and thumped his nephew enthusiastically on the back, at the same time muffling the impact by using the heel of his hand. Tasker stood by, very ready to encourage any tilt towards cheerfulness. Nanw slipped away to join her Aunt Bessie in the smaller kitchen. There was more food to be carried in: tinned peaches and cream in glass dishes, salmon sandwiches, sponge cakes and hot scones direct from the oven. Tryfan clapped his hands and started for his usual place at the bottom of the table. His best boots squeaked as he stole back to poke Cilydd playfully in the ribs.

'If you hadn't come,' Tryfan said, 'we would have had to go out into the highways and the hedges. Isn't that so Nanw? Bid them all to the feast!'

Tasker pointed at Tryfan admiringly.

'Listen to that man,' he said. 'How wise he is.'

The lilt of adulation in his voice was sufficient to irritate Mrs Lloyd. With an impatient gesture she tossed the old Christmas card into the fire and watched it curl as it turned black in the flames.

'From what I hear,' she said, 'there are fifty Welsh chapels in London. I don't know whether or not that is the case.'

She turned in her chair to fix her grandson firmly in her line of vision.

'Wasn't any one of them good enough for you to get married in?'

Nanw and Auntie Bessie moved on tiptoe as they ferried more plates to the already loaded table. No one spoke as Mrs Lloyd waited for her grandson's answer to her question. Cilydd's mouth closed in a tight line with the effort of restraint he was imposing on himself. It was Amy who brought relief to everyone by breaking the silence.

'We were hoping to have Mr Thomas officiate,' she said.

Amy gave Tasker a smile of such warmth that no one who saw it could doubt the admirable fitness of her choice. She called him Mr Thomas with obvious respect. For her he represented the highest values. She and Cilydd were not to be censured if the great press of humanitarian business had somehow prevented him from conducting their wedding service. A hasty ceremony in a registry office had been perhaps Amy's loss more than anyone else's. Tryfan saw a fresh chance to be jovial. He slapped his thigh and piped out in his highest tenor voice.

'If ever I venture into matrimony, dear friends and family, he would be my first choice of conductor too!'

Tryfan's confirmed bachelor status was an approved topic of light-hearted comment at any loitering time, whether around the table or the fire. Even Mrs Lloyd allowed herself a faint smile. Tasker quickly abandoned any attempt to account for his absence from the quiet wedding in a London registry office in order to join in the outburst of merriment. The older men were hungry and they approached the table, ready to eat. Mrs Lloyd folded her rug and moved stiffly to her place at the head of the table. When she was seated, the merriment subsided. She invited Tasker Thomas to say grace. His eyes were screwed up tight as he composed an extempore variation on the theme.

'Our Father which art in Heaven, we meet again around this old table on a special occasion. An occasion for gratitude and rejoicing. Let us begin by acknowledging our daily debt for our daily bread. We remember that this earth is wrapped in the envelope of Thy love. From the bountiful and unsparing hand of a loving Father flow all our blessings, temporal and spiritual. Show us once more that the debt can only be paid in Thy currency, Thy coinage of loving kindness and sacrifice which was struck for us here on earth by Thine only son, Jesus Christ. May he live and reign in our hearts for ever more, Amen.'

Cilydd's old place under the framed aquatint of *The Broad and Narrow Way* was occupied by his sister Nanw. She had arranged for Cilydd and Amy to sit with Tasker on the other side of the table in places usually taken by visitors and guests where they were plied with food by Auntie Bessie until they were obliged to refuse it. 'Come now, come now,' she would say at regular intervals and only rarely make any other contribution to the conversation.

Uncle Gwilym raised a moot point from a sermon that had caused something of a stir at their recent denominational Preaching Festival.

'Wasn't he going a bit far?' Uncle Gwilym said.

He touched his moustache with a cautious gesture. He was aware his mother was listening.

'Let me put it like this,' Uncle Gwilym said. 'How far can we loosen the nuts and bolts of Dogma, before the whole edifice of our Faith collapses. Falls apart?'

He spoke as a man content to formulate intelligent questions. His wife was watching him admiringly and he had said nothing his mother could easily fault.

'It's not simply a case of less Christian doctrine and more Christian behaviour,' Tasker said.

Both Uncle Simon and Uncle Gwilym were now competing with each other in giving him their critical attention. Uncle Gwilym's wife was slipping her food unobtrusively into her mouth and keeping a wary eye on her mother-in-law.

'The whole emphasis of the Gospel for this day and age must be on Love and Reconciliation,' Tasker said. 'I'm quite convinced of

78

that. We are faced with a warring world. An unending struggle for power. Everywhere. What else can our message be? And where else can it begin, this mission of peace, but in our Christian churches.'

'Yes, well . . .'

Uncle Gwilym nodded and his brother quickly followed. No church member could dissent from the expression of such impeccable sentiments. But they found the enthusiasm of their younger brother somewhat excessive. He had begun to thump the table. His mouth was full, but as soon as he had swallowed the contents he shouted merrily.

'That's the spirit! Ever faithful, ever forward.'

Tasker leaned over to squeeze his arm gratefully and almost knocked over a milk jug.

'Witnesses for Peace!' Tasker said. 'Right across the denominations. Bring the old barriers down. Everybody seems to be marching these days. Now why shouldn't Christians be marching for Peace? Displaying courage for peace!'

Tryfan waved his fist.

'That's the message!' he said.

'Yes, it is a message and a mission,' Tasker said. 'And the mission is to carry the message, like a serum into the darkest recesses of the secular world. Right into the heart of the enemy camp.'

Mrs Lloyd held out her large cup so that her daughter Bessie could refill it from the tea-urn.

'Don't you think that is asking a lot from an assembly of sinners, Mr Thomas?' she said.

Tasker wagged his finger at her as if she had been indulging in one of the characteristic outbursts of frankness that had made her a figure both feared and respected in the life of the surrounding district.

'That's what a church is, is it not?' Mrs Lloyd said. 'That's what I was brought up to believe. And I must say I have the evidence of a long life to support it.'

'Oh yes.'

Tasker laughed out loud.

'I know what you mean, my dear Mrs Lloyd! "How these

Christians love one another." Umm? A very valid criticism. But it doesn't exempt us from trying.'

Amy's eyes were raised to the row of salted hams which hung from the beams. Tryfan grinned at her and pointed upwards with his spoon.

'You shall have one of those,' he said. 'As a wedding present.'

Amy showed that she was listening to a sound coming from one of the bedrooms.

'I think I can hear little Bedwyr crying,' she said.

Instinctively Nanw looked at her grandmother before finding the strength to stand on her feet. It was dark outside. As the people around the table strained to listen, the wind whistled in the chimney and hurled squalls of sleet against the window panes. The crackle of the fire and the ponderous tick of the grandfather clock were more comforting sounds.

'If he's awake he may as well be down here,' Cilydd said. 'We shall be taking him anyway as soon as we are ready.'

Uncle Gwilym's wife clutched both her hands together under her heart. Mrs Lloyd stared at her grandson as though he were still a headstrong and irrational youth who had to be firmly handled.

'We have to think of the child's health,' Mrs Lloyd said. 'He has a cough. A nasty little cough.'

'That's no reason for leaving him upstairs crying,' Cilydd said.

He shifted his chair to look sternly at Amy. He was plainly suggesting she should undertake the role of a mother and see to the child upstairs. Amy smiled across the table at Nanw.

'Shall we go and see?' she said.

Mrs Lloyd could not resist a final word of instruction as Nanw took a small lamp from the window-sill and held it high so that Amy could follow her up the stairs.

'Don't pick him up if you can help it,' she said. 'Just put another pillow under his head.'

When they had gone it was Gwilym's wife who found the strain of silence most difficult to bear.

'Is it his teeth, do you think?' she said helpfully.

Mrs Lloyd gazed down the table at the childless woman with a tolerant contempt. Her eldest son Simon was still hungry. His bald head creased as he resumed eating with concentrated effort. The Reverend Tasker Thomas was no longer engaged in the kind of theological speculation to which a responsible deacon should give his undivided attention.

'We have a room ready for him,' Cilydd said. 'It's much better three doors up the terrace. No flooding trouble in the basement. When are you going to come and see it, Nain?'

Cilydd was making an effort to be amiable with his grandmother. She shook her head with an uncharacteristically fatalistic gesture.

'I'm not sure that I haven't seen enough of this old planet,' she said. 'Enough changes anyway.'

Cilydd tried to treat her remark as a joke. Tasker smiled at him encouragingly and Tryfan gave the table another thump that was still sufficient to make the crockery at his end rattle.

'You are as fit as a nut,' he said to his mother.

'I wish you would try and get out of that habit of bumping the table,' Mrs Lloyd said. 'It can be most nerve-wracking.'

'It's a pretty room,' Cilydd said. 'Painted in bright colours. We painted it ourselves. It was my hope to have bought a more modern house in a better part of the town. But moving back has been a bit of a loss for me financially.'

Both Simon and Gwilym pricked up their ears. This was the kind of information about their nephew that was not easy to come by. They tried to disguise their interest: but their reaction had been sufficient to dry up the source. Tasker was ready to bridge a gap of uneasy silence with a rapid deployment of general principle.

'We have to understand these young people,' Tasker said. 'I can tell you I am full of admiration for them. It's not easy is it, to come back from a life of ease and comfort and success to what is after all a life of continuous struggle and protest!'

'I suppose I must be too old to understand these things,' Mrs Lloyd said. 'First you insist on going. Going away is the most important thing in the world. Then you insist on coming back. It costs you something. That is obvious. You must forgive me for asking such a question, but can you tell me in a few plain words what good can come of such inconsistency?'

Cilydd grinned cheerfully at his grandmother.

'Well you know what the American said. "Consistency is the hobgoblin of small minds",' he said.

Mrs Lloyd was not in the mood to share a joke.

'I suppose that means I've got a small mind,' she said. 'It always gives you pleasure to humiliate me.'

Cilydd pushed back his chair angrily.

'Nain! You know that isn't true. I'm grateful for everything. Right up to this very moment.'

Mrs Lloyd sat back in her chair with her fist under her chin. She ignored Cilydd's restless movements around the kitchen. Her remarks as they occurred were addressed to an invisible jury that could decide the issue between them. The rest seated around the table stopped eating to listen.

'I am a very simple person,' Mrs Lloyd said. 'Uneducated and so on. All I ever tried to do was work hard and live by the rules. Simple people need simple rules. Perhaps even clever people do. Perhaps they need even simpler rules, stronger and simpler, so they can't use their cleverness to bend them.'

Cilydd wrung his hands, indifferent as to whether or not there were witnesses to his exasperation.

'I keep saying I'm grateful. What more can I say?'

'There's no need to say anything,' Mrs Lloyd said.

'Nain! I don't want to quarrel . . .'

'Who said I did? I'm only concerned with speaking the truth. It's right for us to face the truth. I'm sure Mr Thomas would agree with that?'

Tasker had been suddenly included in the narrowed field of her displeasure. He smiled uncomfortably and his arms wavered like unsupported tendrils in the lamplight.

'Beauty and Truth are one and the same,' he said. 'We should believe that. And look for them together. It is a wonderful wife who brings her husband back to where he belongs. We could look at it like that. And then find it beautiful.'

'Beautiful . . .'

Mrs Lloyd repeated the word as though it had become an indecipherable fragment long detached from any language that could give it meaning.

' "Whatsoever things are lovely, whatsoever things are of good report . . .",' she said, screwing up her eyes as she dredged up the verse for fresh consideration.

Tasker waved his arms at her encouragingly.

'That's it!' he said. 'That's it exactly.'

Her eyes opened to stare at him dolefully. If he had glimpsed the meaning she would be grateful to be allowed to share the revelation.

'Good old Paul,' Tasker said. 'He had a special affection for the Philippians. And why? Because they were generous.'

Tasker had made a broad gesture to indicate the table before him.

'Now that's beautiful,' he said.

Nanw opened the door and Amy came in carrying the little boy in a heavy woollen blanket. He was dressed in a red tunic with a yellow halter and shoulder buttons. His gaiters, coat and cap, Amy was carrying in her right hand. He was already smiling shyly in anticipation of the volume of approving notice he was bound to receive.

'Here he is,' Amy said. 'Little master plump cheeks himself. Doesn't he look well?'

Uncle Gwilym's wife stood up smiling ecstatically and plainly longing to embrace the child.

'Peaches and cream? Do you think he could have some?'

She seemed uncertain whether to address her request to Amy or to Mrs Lloyd.

'A special treat?' Gwilym's wife said.

Her voice had already begun to tremble under the impact of her mother-in-law's withering stare. Mrs Lloyd rose from the table and made her way back to her fireside chair. When she was seated and her rug was in place Amy moved across and planted little Bedwyr firmly on her lap. The little boy gazed apprehensively at his great-grandmother. Her stiff arm held him in a grip that was secure but not constricting.

'He had a cough,' Mrs Lloyd said. 'A nasty little cough.'

'Well, he's better now,' Amy said. 'Thanks to the care you've taken.'

Mrs Lloyd's head jerked towards the window.

'Listen to it,' she said. 'I wouldn't put a dog out on a night like this.'

Amy laughed happily as if Cilydd's grandmother had made one of her dry jokes. She moved a stool so that she could feed Bedwyr with peaches and cream while he sat in the old woman's lap. Everyone seemed entranced by the pleasure of watching him eat. Nothing they could say could equal the eloquent way in which the glistening fruit slipped into his mouth and rolled about inside his cheeks. When he chuckled everyone laughed. Uncle Tryfan thumped the table without any fear of rebuke: his mother was too preoccupied with noting the smallest details of the behaviour of the child on her knees. She stared at him with an intensity that memorised every gesture.

When he had finished eating Amy began to dress him with methodical efficiency in front of the fire. Cilydd stood behind his grandmother's chair to watch her. Mrs Lloyd folded her hands in her empty lap.

'He'll never remember me,' she said.

Her voice was calm and unemotional.

'Nain,' Cilydd said. 'Don't talk so foolishly.'

'It's the truth,' Mrs Lloyd said. 'I'm only telling the truth. When I'm gone he won't remember anything about me.'

Gwilym's wife fluttered about in an effort to hold back the threat of a prolonged silence.

'Isn't he good?' she said. 'Isn't he a good little boy? A little angel.'

'That's because he's been well brought up,' Amy said. 'Haven't you, my darling? Been well brought up. By Nain. And Auntie Nanw. And Auntie Bessie.'

'Yes,' said the little boy.

Everybody present heard his reply and marvelled at it. The mere sound of his voice seemed to manœuvre them about until they had taken their appropriate postures in a tableau of adoration. Cilydd restrained his own impatience to be gone, as Amy guided the little boy around his relatives, urging him to kiss each one in turn. In the case of Uncle Simon the kiss landed on his bald pate. This did not seem to matter. All was cheerfulness and goodwill until he came to kiss his great-grandmother. For a moment he appeared to hover between two persons who would otherwise prefer to keep their distance. Amy held him out so far she was in danger of losing her balance. Mrs Lloyd was slow to present her cheek for a kiss and before it was completed Amy had to snatch little Bedwyr back to save him and herself from tumbling into the fire. She could not present him for a kiss a second time because Mrs Lloyd had turned away and seemed to be sulking as she stared at the flames. Cilydd relieved his sister Nanw of the suitcase of Bedwyr's things she was carrying.

'We'll have to go I'm afraid,' he said. 'We shall have to put the young man to bed. Twice in one day. But that can't be helped.'

Tasker spoke in hushed tones.

'Unobtrusive transitions,' he said. 'Those are always best. Like Mother Nature herself. If only we could take the time to observe her more closely, how much easier human life would be. How much greater our capacity for happiness.'

His glance happened to be on Uncle Simon's weathered face as he finished speaking. In spite of his frown of incomprehension, Simon nodded dutifully as if he were sitting in the deacon's pew listening to a sermon.

'Say good-night to Nain, Bedwyr,' Amy said.

Mrs Lloyd turned to transfix Amy with a deliberate stare.

'You've got what you wanted,' she said.

Cilydd's face was bright with anger.

'Nain!' he said. 'You are being deliberately difficult. And offensive . . .'

Amy reached out to squeeze his arm.

'John,' she said. 'There are little ears listening.'

Nanw held the lamp above her head as she escorted them through the shop. Auntie Bessie managed the door and the large black umbrella. Tryfan was there too, to see them off. He made jokes about the wind and about the weather and tickled little Bedwyr under his chin. The little boy looked at him solemnly as though he found his behaviour mysterious and difficult to account for. Tryfan was trying to address Amy in a comforting sotto-voce.

'Don't take too much notice of her,' he said. 'She hasn't been well lately. And she dotes on this one only she won't let herself admit it.'

He spoke as a connoisseur of the vagaries of his mother's conduct. Amy smiled at him forgivingly before Cilydd ushered her into the back seat of the car. She sat in the corner so that Bedwyr could be as comfortable as possible in her lap. Tasker sat in front. He was loud in his praises of everyone within earshot. As the car moved off the weather seemed to improve. He expressed his gratitude for this also. When they had settled down to the journey he seemed glad of the opportunity of a quiet chat with Cilydd.

'Your uncles,' he said. 'Simon and Gwilym. They could be more sympathetic towards the cause than we give them credit, you know. Gwilym particularly. He has reserves of real intelligence. He asked me to give him some material on the Peace Movement for his weekly piece in *The Herald*. "Gwilym Glaslyn's Column".'

Tasker smiled fondly as he quoted the heading.

'He was our leading jingo,' Cilydd said. 'During the war. Right up to the end. Very keen on hanging the Kaiser.'

Tasker caught his breath and inhaled deeply. He was appalled by his own thoughts.

'That was a terrible time,' he said. 'Mangled bodies and mangled minds. Wholesale massacre. We must never let it happen again.'

'Some people you can't change,' Cilydd said grimly.

They travelled on through the darkness in silence. In the back Bedwyr curled up in Amy's lap ready to sleep under the mesmeric hum of the engine. His father swung round to catch a brief glimpse of the shadowed outline of his wife and son in the dark interior. He and Amy smiled triumphantly at each other.

'It was like robbing a bank,' Cilydd said. 'Or a waxworks. A museum of methodistical miseries.'

Amy was more responsive to Tasker's presence.

'Now then,' she said. 'We must be fair.'

'Can you imagine,' Cilydd said. 'She wouldn't allow my sister to paper that old side-parlour to make some kind of a playroom for the poor kid.'

'Never mind,' Amy said. 'It doesn't matter now.'

Cilydd took no notice of the restraining note in Amy's voice as it floated softly from the darkness in the back of the car. He was intent on expressing the way he saw his family and the society they belonged to.

'It's a system of iron masks,' he said. 'Iron masks and corsets. Fearfully uncomfortable to wear. But much to be preferred to any form of freedom. They are terrified of freedom. Nothing alarms them more. Why else should they have embraced the religion of serfs?'

His voice grew more bold as he made Tasker a direct challenge.

'It is the nature of the serf to lick and love his chains,' he said.

'Cilydd,' Amy said. 'Keep your voice down. He's nearly asleep.'

Tasker leaned closer to Cilydd so that he could put in his counter-argument with quiet but intense sincerity.

'Let us begin by expecting the best of people,' he said. 'Looking out for the best in people. Whoever they are. But particularly those most closely related to us. Our own folk.'

'Then you can expect to be disappointed,' Cilydd said.

Tasker's fingers grappled with the air as he cast about for a fresh approach.

'Do you know, I sometimes believe the external world is only a reflection of our inner condition,' he said. 'Do you know what I mean? If the sun is out in your heart you are bound to catch a glimpse of the reflection in the sky.'

Tasker was pleased with the figure as it came to him. He smiled patiently, waiting for Cilydd to appreciate it.

'I'm sorry to have to say this,' Cilydd said. 'But I wouldn't count on either of them. Uncle Gwilym or Uncle Simon. When it comes to a vote in the open, they become strangely unavailable. Hence their devotion to the secret ballot.'

Tasker turned to appeal to Amy.

'He's not listening to a word I say, this husband of yours. Now tell me, Amy, what do you think?'

Amy whispered so softly they could barely hear what she was saying.

'I have to be quiet,' she said. 'My baby is asleep.'

87

9

CILYDD REVERSED HIS MOTOR CAR INTO THE LANE OFF THE NARROW country road. He seemed determined to be cheerful and to execute the manœuvre with a speed and expertise that might impress Amy as she watched him with her hands in the pockets of her belted mackintosh. He left the car and joined her in the road where she stood to survey their surroundings. The slate roof of Cae Golau was visible through the belt of trees that had been planted for its protection at least two generations ago. The place and the landscape were dwarfed by the movement of cloud in the sky. Sullen towers threatening rain were massed on the northern horizon above the ridge which formed the geological backbone of the peninsula. More directly above them, cloud levels of varying density drifted at different speeds across a benevolent expanse of blue sky. In the two fields between the road and the isolated house, the fleeting sunlight made the grass of the aftermath glitter in its own uniform shade of emerald. Cilydd touched Amy's arm to encourage her to walk confidently at his side towards the house.

'Let's see what you think, my dearest,' he said. 'See how you react to it.'

He sounded resolutely reasonable.

'Things have to change,' he said. 'That's obvious enough. The trick is to make them change the way we want. I don't know. Basic principles are so devastatingly obvious: but the minute you try and put them into practice they get to be more complex than the Creation.'

They stepped carefully between broad patches of mud fringed with soft untrampled grass. In some places they could not walk side by side between the overgrown hedgerows and the brambles. Cilydd stopped at one point to stretch out his arms to estimate the width of the lane and calculate how much it would need to be widened when it became necessary to establish a road surface capable of taking vehicular traffic.

'Change and decay in all around I see.'

He held out his hand so that Amy could take it.

'My goodness, it doesn't take long, does it? Two seasons of

neglect, three at the most and it all returns to the jungle. Civilisation is fifty percent wear and tear and fifty percent regular upkeep.'

Amy was so deeply thoughtful that he lapsed into silence himself. Whatever he had to say would take second place to how she felt: it was his intention also to demonstrate the full extent of his faith in her judgement. In a marriage of true minds seniority counted for nothing. Amy reached out to touch a spray of early blackberries protruding temptingly from a mass of bramble. Cilydd relaxed sufficiently to allow himself to go on speaking.

'I don't think you ever saw him,' he said. 'My great-uncle Ezra. For some reason I always called him Uncle Lloyd. Past President of the North Wales Temperance League and very widely respected.'

They both laughed.

'That's what Nain used to say. She thought the world of him. For her he represented the best of what was left of the Old Dispensation. There it is.'

Cilydd placed both his arms on top of the rusty gate. The laurel hedge had shot up out of control and mingled on both sides of the gate into a tangled mass of overgrown rhododendron and azalea bushes. A pair of monkey-puzzle trees grew in the centre of what had been a circular lawn in front of the house. In between them there was a view of an ill-proportioned portico made entirely of slate.

'She used to send me here at least twice a week with delicacies and messages. Fresh butter, buttermilk, blackcurrant jelly, that sort of thing. Awkward stuff to carry. I hated it. For one thing his housekeeper hated the sight of me. I think she must have known he was going to leave it all to me. I represented the blasting of all her cherished hopes. Nain was convinced the old dragon was scheming to trap poor old Uncle Lloyd into matrimony. So the oftener I came here the more the housekeeper disliked the sight of me. Jet-black hair she had and blood-red cheeks. I used to be really scared of her. He always asked me the same questions when I eventually penetrated what she was pleased to call his study-parlour. He used to sit at the table as if he was waiting to have his photograph taken, with one hand tucked inside his waistcoat and wearing a high white cravat to hide the hole in his neck.'

Cilydd squeezed his own throat with his right hand to give an imitation of his great-uncle's hoarse constricted speech.

' "Do they ask about me?" and, "Have you heard the Call?" You could say those were the parallel lines between which I was brought up. Like the blinkers on a horse's harness. "They" were the all important Nonconformist public and "The Call" was what I was supposed to hear before being conscripted into the ministerial apostolic succession. Sometimes I think my grandmother has never forgiven me for not becoming a minister.'

'It's a very odd family you belong to,' Amy said.

He looked at her with a whimsical smile on his face.

'It's your family now too,' he said.

'There's nothing odd about me,' Amy said.

She pushed at the gate. Cilydd had to lift it so that she could squeeze her way through. They advanced across the soft gravel to the house.

'Here we are,' Cilydd said. 'Temperance Towers. Nain used to get so annoyed when I called it that.'

He took out a large iron key from his pocket.

'I can tell you one thing, it made me think. It still does.'

'What?'

Amy was curious and yet impatient to inspect the house.

'The life of Great-Uncle Ezra. All that effort. Wearing himself out four or five times a day for the sacred cause and churning out all those pamphlets written in laborious longhand far into the night. Even as a boy it made me think. All that devotion. And what was his reward? Instead of wetting his whistle all the poor chap got was a hole stuck in the side of it.'

'That's not funny,' Amy said.

'Oh I know it isn't. Any more than Job's boils. But it shook my faith, as they used to say. In the ways of providence and so on. At the ripe old age of fourteen I wrote a poem about it and then I burnt it. Because there was nobody I could show it to. And therein you have the source of a lifetime's habit.'

'Habit?'

'Taciturnity,' Cilydd said cheerfully. 'That's why I used to be so silent. My brain was seething with ideas I could communicate to no one except myself. Imagine a youth driven into himself and letting it seep out in convoluted tortured dollops of obscure poetry. And, moreover, Madame Amy More, that's why I'm so loquacious now. At last I've got somebody to talk to and I can't stop.'

He made a quick attempt to kiss her.

'Of course there are other forms of intercourse,' he said.

'John Cilydd,' Amy said. 'Behave yourself and open that door.'

' "Angels ever bright and fair, flying freely through the air, that's what married lovers are." '

He chanted the lines as he opened the door. On the threshold Amy was immediately repulsed by the sour smell of the interior. Cilydd stamped his feet and listened to the sound reverbate through the deserted house.

'Could I have sensed it at the age of fourteen?'

Cilydd spoke in a loud voice as if he were mocking the seriousness of his own enquiry.

'Uncle Ezra Lloyd and all he amounted to. There, but for the grace of God, I would go too. And even if the grace of God didn't exist, I would go just the same because that was what my family, or my grandmother to be more precise, willed for me. Now you see what you've rescued me from, my Amy.'

With a light-hearted imitation of a country greeting, he tapped his great-uncle's study door before opening it.

'Do we have people? Is anyone home?'

Nothing in the study had been moved. Black bookcases with glass doors covered most of two walls. Each shelf was crammed with sombre-looking volumes. The naked edge of a broad marble mantelshelf was hidden by a tasselled border of the same ecclesiastical red plush as the tablecloth. In the damp corners the wallpaper had begun to peel away from the walls and the ancient size contributed its own sickly smell to the odours suspended in the still air.

'Grave goods,' Cilydd said. 'It should have been buried with him.'

He pointed at a high-backed chair upholstered in buttoned black silk.

'That's where he used to sit,' he said. 'Like a king in exile. And I would stand here like a little messenger from the outside world. And he'd always ask the same question. "Do they ask about me?" '

'Where would she be?'

Amy asked about the housekeeper.

'Standing behind me until he dismissed her with one finger. Without lifting his hand from the table.'

He was full of the memory of his great-uncle.

'He went to the States twice in the 1880s. A young man with a burning message. Temperance. The great cities heard his voice. Pittsburgh, Chicago, Philadelphia, Manchester, Liverpool. And he ended up here. Croaking at me twice a week. I was to be his last convert. Even at fourteen I didn't believe a word of it.'

Amy tried to be fair.

'I suppose it was right for his time,' she said. 'All the drunkenness and poverty.'

They wandered down the corridor to the housekeeper's room. There on the table her letters and personal papers had been left in a damp heap around a lamp with a red-tinted globe.

'How can I possibly go through all these?' Cilydd said. 'I'm not legally obliged to. I should just take them out and burn them.'

'There's a foul smell,' Amy said.

'She was mad on cats,' Cilydd said. 'I expect they've left their visiting cards.'

Amy shook her head.

'It's not just that,' she said. 'There's something dead under the floorboards. A dead rat or something. I'm sure of it.'

She continued her inspection of the house with growing distaste. Nothing she saw pleased her. When he bounded up the stairs, she remained at the bottom. She called out.

'Sell it.'

He looked down at her with alarm.

'Get what you can for it,' she said. 'I could never live here.'

For a moment he was transfixed by the finality of her verdict.

'Amy. Amy.'

He invoked her name as he marched about the bedrooms in the hope that she would join him. She remained immovable at the bottom of the stairs. He came down to her, his face bright with a fresh suggestion.

'Suppose we gutted the whole place? From top to bottom?'

Her response was not encouraging.

'Tear up the floorboards. Get rid of the smells. There are five bedrooms up there and room for a new bathroom. "In Xanadu did Kubla Khan" and so forth. The outbuildings are very good. Stables, nice coach-house. Come on, let's go and look at the outbuildings.'

Outside Amy seemed to recover her spirits. In the coach-house she was delighted to discover a governess cart in perfect condition. She fingered the smoothness of a shaft that pointed upwards to the dusty harness on the hooks of the high ceiling. Cilydd was encouraged.

'Five and a half acres,' Cilydd said. 'And the river at the bottom. And an orchard. And a paddock. And a walled garden. It wouldn't take much you know to transform Cae Golau into an island of enchantment. A bower of bliss. With Amy at the centre. A refuge and retreat.'

'Look at that.'

In the grate of the outhouse kitchen Amy was staring at the heaped ash of dead fires and a rivulet of cold candlegrease stuck to the oven door. A cast-iron kettle covered in soot was suspended from a hook in the chimney. On the window-sill near by a paraffin lamp with a cracked glass shade was covered with an unbroken canopy of cobweb.

'I suppose it's better than the house,' Amy said.

'What I'm talking about is an enclosed environment of our own making. Our own private retreat. Away from it all. That's not escapism.'

Amy smiled indulgently.

'It sounds like it,' she said.

'Oh no, the struggle goes on! I agree with you, you know,' he said. 'Quite seriously. We may not be able to save the world, but at least we can do something towards saving Wales. But I've no illusions, my love. One can be just as hard and just as impossible as the other. It's just like poor old Sisyphus's shoulder on the stone. He may never get the rock to the top of the hill, or get his view of

93

the Promised Land, but the poor devil has to keep on trying. But if we had a place like this it would be somewhere where we could retire to, to lick our wounds and regain our strength for the next bout in the never ending contest.'

He took her arm fondly and led her in the direction of the walled garden. A door in the wall, next to a single-storey stone shed, stood half-open, rotting on its hinges. The entire garden was choked with weeds and saplings that had flourished for several seasons. As they stood silently together he tried to take her in his arms and kiss her. She shrugged herself free of his constricting grasp and sauntered towards the orchard. Here the ground on a lower level was water-logged. The ditch was choked with wild irises. The largest apple tree had been blown over in a summer storm. Masses of stony earth still clung to the roots. The branches were covered with a thick green moss and the unripe fruit was tainted even before dropping off. Cilydd came up behind her and placed his arms around her waist.

'I know it looks awful now,' he said. 'But if you gave it your blessing, or waved your wand, or whatever, I would make it worthy of you. Every inch of it.'

With reverential care he nuzzled beyond her mackintosh collar to kiss her neck.

'Stretch,' he said playfully.

'What do you think I am?' Amy said. 'A cat?'

His hands felt for the shape of her body under the thickness of her clothes.

'When you stretch your waist I can picture a centre of grace as well as a centre of gravity.'

He whispered fervently in her ear.

'I can tell you this, here and now, my darling. You fill my thoughts day and night. I can't believe my own good fortune. You've transformed my existence. I still can't believe my luck. I can come home and embrace you every day of my life. It's a miracle. Like your body.'

His hands felt the shape of her breasts, her belly and her thighs.

'I want to learn to worship you to perfection,' he said.

Amy plucked his hands away.

'John Cilydd,' she said with mock reproval. 'You are obsessed with sex. You really are.'

'I'm obsessed with you. Let me hold you. It's so much easier for me to talk when I know you're in my arms.'

'So long as you are a good boy.'

She allowed him to embrace her until his kisses prevented her from breathing.

'Please, Amy. There's a part of you I can never reach. It drives me to distraction.'

'John! Stop will you. Honestly. We have a bed at home. Isn't that enough? Stop. Please. Stop!'

He released her, closed his eyes and raised his arms to shake his hands at the sky.

'I see you whichever way I look.'

He stretched his arms in front of him, miming his own version of blind man's buff. He was pleased when he heard her laugh.

'Your smile. Your skin. Your shape. In every perfect detail. What's the name of that French chap who does nothing but paint his wife getting in and out of the bath. He knows what I'm talking about.'

'Well, I'm a person,' Amy said. 'Not just a body.'

He groaned in the depth of his understanding.

'Oh. I know. I know.'

'I'm not just a thing. I'm me.'

They walked back to the house in careful step. It seemed they were tenderly harnessed together by the delicate thread of their discourse and whatever they said would lead them to a deeper understanding.

'It's never easy for me to talk freely,' Cilydd said. 'I suppose it's to do with the way we've been brought up. All reticence and silence.'

'I know.'

Amy was nodding sympathetically.

'I don't care how pretentious I sound,' Cilydd said. 'So long as you are willing to listen.'

'Of course I am.'

'Millions and millions of us, we live and die inside this slimy envelope of atmosphere like so many ants or woodlice and yet we have this excruciating awareness. Inside this envelope of physical existence now, for me the sexual act has become the supreme sacrament. The very centre of my universe. And that's you of course. A fact, not a philosophy. A presence.'

He released her arm to try and conjure a delicate argument out of the air in front of them.

'How can you put these things into words without distorting them? In my mind they are vital truths but when they come blundering out of my mouth they sound like nothing.'

'Perhaps we shouldn't try and put everything into words.'

Amy made the suggestion in the gentlest way she could.

'You are absolutely right,' he said. 'And yet I've got to say it. Above everything in my life I want to satisfy you, sexually.'

'You do,' Amy said.

She patted the back of his hand comfortingly. He persisted.

'Satisfy you deeply.'

She smiled, but she was embarrassed by his intense scrutiny.

'You do very well,' she said. 'But I don't think women are so passionately and constantly and endlessly interested in that sort of thing. Women's magazines can be a bit misleading you know. They always amaze me when I see them in bulk in the dentist's waiting room. Mind you, even in them, clothes and food and furniture come easily first.'

She shook his arm to make him smile.

'I suppose what it amounts to is I want to lose myself in you,' he said. 'That would be the ultimate consummation. To become part of you.'

Amy shook his arm again consolingly.

'We are two people,' she said. 'Not one.'

He looked disappointed.

'But we become one,' he said.

Amy made an effort to express herself delicately.

'When you become too aggressive I feel I'm like a victim being made use of. When you become too possessive it makes me feel I'm being overpowered. Do you see what I mean?'

He was listening to her as though his life depended on every word.

'I know you don't mean to be aggressive and possessive but the effect sometimes is as if I'm being trampled on. As if what I might think and feel doesn't count at all. Do you understand?'

'Oh, Amy . . .'

For a moment it seemed that his knees would give way and that he would kneel before her in the gravel, weak with a remorse verging on self-contempt. Amy hastened to console him.

'I'm exaggerating of course,' she said. 'But you wanted to know. There's got to be a balance. That's all I'm saying.'

They had arrived at the portico. Cilydd stared at the open door.

'It's what I want most of all,' he said. 'I swear to you. To make you happy. And to know what you are thinking and feeling, if you can bear to tell me.'

'It's time we went,' Amy said. 'We have to pick up little Bedwyr.'

He nodded sagely and locked the door of the house, pocketing the key. There was more he wanted to ask her.

'It's such a crude question,' he said.

'Well, hurry darling, or we'll be late.'

'It will sound stupid. The way I put things. I have so many stupid inhibitions and taboos. And anyway it may be a figment of my overheated imagination rather than any reality. You must tell me anyway. Does contraception spoil it?'

The pained expression on his face would not allow her to take the question lightly.

'Take away the full meaning. The proper effect. Oh God, I don't know what I'm trying to say. But surely it is better to discuss things openly.'

'I don't know,' Amy said. 'I just don't know, do I?'

They tramped together towards the gate in silence. She watched him struggle to lift and close it.

'Amy. Why don't we have a child of our own?'

He leaned against the gate. She considered the question with a studied impartiality that put a distance between them which increased the longer she delayed her answer.

'I'd like to give all my energies to looking after Bedwyr,' Amy said at last. 'At least until he starts school.'

Cilydd weighed her answer.

97

'Perhaps that's my trouble,' he said. 'I'm jealous of my little son.'

'Oh, John Cilydd!'

He smiled.

'He certainly flourishes in the warmth of your affection, bless him. Say "envious" anyway, instead of "jealous".'

'John, you don't need to be. I want to be a good wife to you.'

She allowed him to take her in his arms as he kissed her hungrily. She placed her finger against his lips to restrain his passion and together they leaned against the gate to look back at the deserted house.

'It's not because of what happened to Enid?'

He put the question quietly and held his breath as he waited for her answer. It was a painful subject to bring up. They had both witnessed Enid's death as a direct result of childbirth: his first wife, her best friend.

'I don't think so,' she said. 'As far as I can tell.'

The silence of the countryside brought them closer than any previous attempts to put his thoughts and feelings into words. He held her hand on top of the gate and listened to her breathing. There was something she wanted him to overhear, like a secret.

'When it comes I would like it to be an accident. A discovery. Like stumbling across a treasure. That sounds so silly.'

'No. No. It doesn't.'

'All right then.'

Her voice was louder, calling them to attend to their proper duties.

'Come on or we'll be late.'

He was loath to leave the spot where they had communicated so easily.

'What about the house? Amy. What about it?'

She looked back at Cae Golau. It stood in morose, uncared-for isolation. Her nose wrinkled with particular distaste at the pair of monkey-puzzle trees.

'Do you want me to say what I feel?' she said.

'Of course. Of course.'

She stepped back to sum up the qualities of the site.

'It's a blank place somehow.'

Cilydd squinted uneasily at the property he had inherited from his great-uncle.

'It's a place for old people to retire to, when the struggle's over. A sort of last resting place before the cemetery.'

'But all that could be changed,' Cilydd said.

Amy's condemnation was comprehensive.

'There's no vista,' she said. 'No view. Imagine living on a peninsula without even a glimpse of the sea! It's a damp hollow covered with green mould. Sheltered, of course. But so is the cemetery. And anyway, it would be no good at all for Bedwyr.'

'Why not?'

Cilydd could not understand the objection.

'Absolutely no one around here for him to play with. At least on Marine Terrace we have the sand dunes. The perfect playground for him. And he loves playing with little Clemmie and the other little boys. And later on, I wouldn't want to be out here, by myself all day long, with you in the office and little Bedwyr at school. We have to think of these things.'

'Of course. Of course.'

He looked despondent. Amy took hold of the lapels of his belted raincoat and gave him a friendly shake.

'You're not too disappointed?'

He straightened himself, breathed deeply and smiled at her.

'Of course not,' he said. 'I want you to have exactly what you want. That's all that matters.'

10

LITTLE BEDWYR'S EYES WERE CLOSED. AMY HAD DRAWN THE DARK green curtains of his bedroom in order to protect him from the light. She could observe the world outside through the narrow slit but even as she did so she held her breath to judge whether or not he was asleep. She was tense with awareness of the blare of a brass band on the promenade. There was also the persistent thump of an elephantine waltz being pumped out on a steam organ that could disturb Bedwyr's rest even though it came from a fairground over a mile away on the outskirts of the town. The sounds were brushed against each other in discordant competition by a brisk wind blowing from the sea.

The rash had broken out over his face and arms. In his left hand he clutched a toy sheep from the farmyard she had set out on the side-table, where he could gaze at it without lifting his head from the mound of pillows. The model animals were cast in lead and realistically painted. There were sheep, cows, pigs, horses and miniature carts and waggons with shafts that could be attached to hooks in the horses' flanks. Amy could barely hear his breathing.

'Mam.'

'My little love.'

She responded instantly to the sleepy murmur of his voice.

'What time is the sunlight coming back?'

'Oh my precious.'

She sank to her knees at the side of his bed. He was able to study her dolefully over the collar of his striped pyjamas. She touched his small hand, conscious of the spots. The hand opened, offering her the model sheep. She lifted the warm metal with finger and thumb and leaned over to place it with the rest of the flock, all their heads pointing in solemn stillness towards Bedwyr as if they were waiting for him to recover and start playing with the farmyard again.

'Is Clemmie better?' Bedwyr said.

'Much better.'

Amy tapped the child's hand with her finger.

'His skin is peeling,' she said. 'Little powdery scales. You can blow them away. Like this.'

She lifted his hand and blew on it in an attempt to make him smile.

'Can he come and play with me?'

'The day after tomorrow,' Amy said.

She went on talking to distract him from too intense a pre-occupation with the passage of time.

'When the little cough has gone. When you're feeling stronger. When you've started to eat. Calves-foot jelly. Beef extract. Nice things to make you big and strong. And milk. Lots of milk. And

100

cream. Aunty Nanw will bring us strawberries and we'll all have strawberries and cream.'

'And Clemmie?'

'And Clemmie,' Amy said.

He sucked his tongue in a manner that suggested he had an unpleasant taste in his mouth. Amy took a chance to make him drink. As she held the glass to his lips, Nanw glided quietly into the room. Bedwyr's eyes followed her movements closely and she smiled to reassure him of her unqualified affection before speaking to Amy in her soft but intense way.

'Amy. Tasker's here,' she said. 'He wants to talk to you.'

Nanw smiled winningly again at Bedwyr. The fondness of her expression would easily gainsay any threat to the fragile peace of the sick-room posed by the subdued intensity of her voice.

'What's a bomb, Mam?'

Amy and Nanw glanced at each other in alarm. When she recovered Amy treated the word as representing some figment of an outlandish fairy-tale.

'Who's been talking to you about bombs?'

'Clemmie says they hang down from the sky. And drop in the storm.'

Bedwyr was pleased with the extra attention he had won. His head lay back on the pillow and his eyes grew large as he tried to repeat the effect.

'Dogs bark in the sea,' he said. 'I can hear them.'

'Yes, well that's because you've been ill,' Amy said firmly.

'But you are getting better now. He's much better now, isn't he, Aunty Nanw?'

'Oh yes,' Nanw said. 'Ever so much better.'

'And that means we have to be sensible, when we're better.'

'What's sensible, Mam?'

'It's what good little boys like to be,' Amy said.

Amy moved across the room to use the door to conceal her face from Bedwyr's watchful gaze. Nanw showed she was willing to stay with him while Amy went downstairs.

'Where are you going, Mam?'

Bedwyr's voice trembled querulously at a distance.

'Aunty Nanw's going to keep you company.'

'Don't leave me, Mam.'

'Aunty Nanw's going to tell you a lovely story. About Piggy and the Black Horse.'

Amy pointed hopefully at the farmyard. Bedwyr was satisfied. He sank back on his pillows ready to listen, imbibing his reward for being good.

Downstairs, in the basement kitchen, Tasker Thomas had folded his bulk into the small rocking-chair between the corner of the table and the Triplex grate. He wore a grubby raincoat with a leather belt like a cassock over his cricket shirt, which was open at the neck as if to demonstrate there were more curly red hairs on his chest than on the top of his head. A wrapped sweet dangled despondently between finger and thumb as he rocked himself to and fro in the confined space. When he saw Amy appear on the basement stairs he scrambled to his feet and his round face radiated its customary smile. Her presence alone brought him comfort. For a second it seemed he would offer her the sweet between his fingers. He chuckled boyishly and restored it to the bag he usually carried in his mackintosh pocket ready for distribution among any children he might encounter as he cycled around on pastoral visits.

'How is he? How is the little fellow?'

Tasker raised his red eyebrows in eager anticipation of a good report.

'He's much better,' Amy said.

'Praise the Lord,' Tasker said enthusiastically. 'It just shows what a warm happy home environment can do, and tender nursing.'

Tasker began to make expressive gestures with his hands.

'If only we could irrigate society at large with the tender influence that animates these oases of loving care. That's what I've come to see you about, dear Amy. Mind you it's always a treat for a lonely old bachelor to visit a warm happy home.'

He protested mildly as Amy began to lay afternoon tea on the round table close to the window. The sunlight poured in elongated beams through the glass roof of the lean-to conservatory outside the basement kitchen. He sighed contentedly when Amy made him sit down.

'Such a marvellous atmosphere in this house.'

Tasker raised his head as though to savour a special fragrance in the air.

'Always a refuge and a very present help in trouble.'

Amy listened attentively as she poured water in the teapot. In the oven there were eccles cakes which Nanw had brought with her from the confectioners in Pendraw because she knew Amy and her brother liked them. Amy laid them out on a plate alongside the sponge cake she had made earlier in the afternoon.

'It's such a comfort to come here,' Tasker said. 'You are so kind to me. I don't deserve it. I mean here one may speak one's mind freely, among friends. At a time when mass hysteria can so easily stalk the land. I know I'm probably too sensitive to these things, but I had no alternative but to resign.'

'Resign?'

Amy looked disturbed.

'It seemed to be such a simple matter. At a time of such terrible unemployment and so on, with the world in the state that it is in, I moved that the borough council should ignore the preparations for the Silver Jubilee.'

'Quite right,' Amy said firmly.

'I pointed out that it was no more than a propaganda device by right-wing government to distract the whole country from the fact that millions of people were living on the dole, below subsistence level, and worse than that, a brazen attempt to dazzle the population with militaristic display and imperial bombast. Do you know Amy fach, not one voice was raised in my support. Not one.'

'Oh no.'

Amy mumbled despairingly as she offered Tasker Thomas a hot eccles cake.

'Where were Uncle Gwilym and Uncle Simon?' she said.

'Simon was there and silent,' Tasker said. 'Gwilym was otherwise engaged. "Strangely unavailable", as the poet puts it.'

Tasker made a brave attempt to smile.

'It was all cut and dried of course,' he said. 'It was terribly naïve of me not to know that. And maybe a sin of pride on my part too, thinking I was more highly regarded in the community than was ever in fact the case. At least I can say it has cut me down to a more manageable size. It was all worked out beforehand. Parades and special services of Thanksgiving. Parades led a by a Military Band and the local Territorials. A wonderful mixture. A Jubilee mug and free tea for every child of school age with a New Testament thrown in. And a supper concert for old-aged pensioners and unemployed conducted by H. M. Meredith, the Master of the Workhouse.'

'Him, of course,' Amy said.

She spoke darkly of Eddie Meredith's father as of a man who could never be trusted.

'It brought them all together,' Tasker said ruefully. 'In a way I had quite failed to do. Alderman Llew and Doctor DSO ready to dance hand in hand around the Jubilee Maypole.'

The notion made them both laugh.

'The arch-enemies,' Amy said. 'And just when we thought the awful dead hand grip of these so called Liberals was beginning to slacken.'

'You wouldn't believe it,' Tasker said. 'At the end of the special session they stood up and cheered themselves. Can you imagine it? As if by some mystic process they had voted themselves associate members of the Royal Family. The ingrained servility of centuries. I heard a bell toll in that council chamber. And it tolled for the end of an era in Welsh nonconformity. There was no place for me there any more. So I resigned on the spot. There was nothing else I could do.'

Amy frowned hard.

'I don't know,' she said. 'That's not always wise. Resigning. People need to be led. They can be as stupid as sheep. Especially in Pendraw. We all know that.'

Tasker stopped eating and held his hand to his forehead.

'It's the end of an era for me too,' he said. 'I know I sound foolish and old-fashioned to you and it's a great boon and blessing to me, your sympathy. But I think in the old categories, you see, and until someone supplies me with better ones, it's all I can do. I was meant to serve people. That's what I understand by The Call. But the period of usefulness in this place has come to an end.'

'Oh no,' Amy said. 'You can't say that.'

'Looking back I can see it's been coming to an end for some time. The mysterious tide in the affairs of men. You open your eyes one fine morning and find it has gone out, leaving you stranded on the shore. You see, a man who lives alone has time to think of things like that. Unless he is usefully employed, he sinks into a stagnant pool of self-absorption. I am quite determined, Mrs More, that shall not happen to me.'

Tasker laughed with forced cheerfulness.

'I shall go South,' he said. 'Where I am really needed. Among the working class, employed and unemployed. My friends the miners. There's work to be done there, suffering to be alleviated. A cross to be carried among the people that really count.'

'I thought everyone mattered,' Amy said. 'I thought everyone counted.'

Tasker was pleasantly stimulated by her response.

'Oh they do, they do,' he said. 'But I'm not the man for Pendraw, you see. These are petty bourgeois people well and truly baked into a hard crust of petty bourgeois modes and manners and cast-iron respectability. There's little more I can do for them. Mind you. Mind you . . .'

He raised a warning finger to restrain the impetuous flood of his own volubility.

'There is one thing I must accomplish before I leave. It's the only remedy! Only positive achievement can blot out the strain of failure. And that's why I've come to you, my dear. You are the one person who can help me.'

He was pleased when he saw Amy look puzzled and surprised.

'The hospital, my dear, the hospital! Do you remember how we vowed when poor dear Enid died from what we believed was lack of prompt medical attention, how we vowed that this town would have a hospital of its very own? And now the years have gone by and nothing has been done. Nothing of any real significance. And we know why, don't we? Because the project is still the plaything of sterile party politics. No, worse than that, the sterile internal politics of the only party that counts in this place.'

'It's shameful,' Amy said.

She took Tasker's cup and filled it and pressed him to accept a second slice of the sponge cake. His fingers rose briefly in the air to express the quality of lightness in the yellow cake.

'I have a plan,' he said. 'A little scheme. It's been maturing in my mind for some time. I think now the time has come to put it into practice. And that is where I need your help.'

He smiled benignly and pointed vaguely in an eastward direction.

'I was at Plas Iscoed last month,' he said. 'In connection with my account of the Pithead Baths for the Historical Transactions of our respected denomination. Checking the facts with his lordship and the Honourable Eirwen and putting in a word for more equipment in the ambulance room. A new operating table and instantaneous hot-water apparatus. Killing at least two birds with one stone.'

Tasker chuckled to himself, his spirits fully revived by the recollection of a piece of good work satisfactorily achieved. He became solemn again before making a more personal revelation.

'I don't know whether you know this,' he said. 'But at one time Eirwen and I were engaged to be married.'

Amy made a visible effort to show interest without being too astonished.

'July 1912,' Tasker said. 'Not so very long ago and yet another age, another world. An odd business really. Our mothers were related by marriage. My mother thought I was too unworldly and Eirwen's mother thought she was too plain. So they made up the match. And like dutiful children we went along with it. For a matter of weeks. And then I saw the light, and so did Eirwen I think, and that was it. She went to Florence to study painting and I went to the theological college. But this is all by the way. Last month when I was there we had tea together and we talked about you. I promised I would take you there on a visit. Can you see the shape of my wicked scheme emerging?'

Amy shook her head and looked doubtful.

'She thinks the world of you, Amy,' he said. 'There can be no two ways about that. If you were to appeal for their support, the Pendraw Hospital could be opened in a matter of months not years!'

Tasker stretched out his arms in an expansive gesture.

'Let the children of light be at least as astute as the children of this world,' he said. 'Lord Iscoed is a coal-owner. The wealth of the family is built on the blood and sweat of generations of working people. If there is one thing wealthy coal-owners need these days it is good publicity.'

'But there isn't a coal pit within a hundred miles of Pendraw.'

Tasker wagged his chubby index finger to show how cunning he could be.

'Conspicuous philanthropy,' he said. 'That's what matters. Something for all the newspapers throughout the length and breadth of the land. Next year the General Assembly of our denomination meets in Pendraw. What more fitting occasion for the grand opening with Lord Iscoed and the Honourable Eirwen present, treated like royalty in return for the extent of their munificence? Now then, Mrs More, when shall we visit Plas Iscoed together and set the machinery of our little plot in motion?'

As she pondered Tasker Thomas's proposal, Amy was distracted by the sight of Clemmie's Aunt Menna making signs through the window of the conservatory. The woman's dark blue hat was clamped on her head like a winged helmet. This made the grimaces on her plump pale face stand out with greater clarity. Amy had two doors to open and the second was sagging on its hinges.

'You've got someone with you,' Aunty Menna said.

She mouthed the words with such apologetic emphasis that her discreet whisper was perfectly audible in spite of the salt-laden breeze from the sea.

'I just wanted to ask about little Bedwyr. Our Clemmie will give us no peace until he knows that his little pal is better!'

'Come in,' Amy said. 'The Reverend Tasker Thomas is here. We are just having a cup of tea. Won't you join us?'

Aunty Menna pressed her upper lip hard against her dentures. She would not take tea but she had sufficient matter on her mind to justify entering her neighbour's house. In the kitchen Tasker was on his feet with his arms half extended, suspended between welcome and farewell.

'Dear ladies,' he said. 'I should be going. One is always tempted to linger in this house and take too much advantage of the happy

107

atmosphere. The news is good. The son and heir is better. And so I gather is your little Clemmie. It's such a pleasure to see them playing together. You know, I could sit down and watch them all day. I really could.'

Aunty Menna was studying him with a closeness that clearly made him uncomfortable.

'They are going to have their Jubilee jubilations, then,' she said. 'I'm afraid I knew that's how it would be. It's a nasty little town in many ways, Mr Thomas.'

Tasker squirmed in his long raincoat as he searched in vain for an attitude that would absolve him from any obligations to join in the condemnation of a whole community.

'People talk of Alderman Llew and the shadow of his paw,' Aunty Menna said. 'But there are worse elements than that I can tell you. And the moment anyone blows a trumpet they come out in droves. A whole breed of town loafers. Men who spend most of their time in the pubs when they're not chewing tobacco and spitting into the harbour.'

Tasker had manœuvred himself to the back door which Amy had left open.

'Mrs More,' he said. 'Thank you again for the delicious cake. I shall call back if I may for a brief word with your good husband when he returns from the office.'

Aunty Menna was nodding approvingly.

'These are difficult times,' she said. 'And as my sister Flo says, fair play to her, they can only get more difficult. So we must stick together.'

Tasker waved at them both as he made his way down the path to the door in the wall at the end of the narrow garden. His final salutation was lost in the breeze.

'An exceptional man,' Aunty Menna said as Amy closed the kitchen door.

Her gaze rested appreciatively on the sponge cake which looked all the more delectable for having been already cut. Amy had no difficulty in persuading her to sit.

'A man of principle. There's no telling how much good he will do in this world. It's terrible the way tongues wag in this place. It's as if some people were determined to drag him down. Worse than that, Mrs More. Trample the poor fellow under foot if they had half a chance.'

She held up a slice of cake between her finger and thumb to admire it before slipping it delicately into her mouth.

'This is so good,' she said. 'I must ask you for the recipe. Clemmie always comes home saying what wonderful food he's been enjoying in little Bedwyr's house. My sister Flo says you set such a high standard, Mrs More, it's quite hopeless for us to try and keep up with you. It's such a nice place you have here. And you've made this kitchen so cosy. Everything's always upside down in our place.'

Aunty Menna sighed contentedly. Her thoughts returned to the visitor who had just left them.

'It makes you wonder,' she said, 'where people pick things up. Of course some of the scandal you can trace to its source. But then the embroidery and the lies as it passes from mouth to mouth. It makes you shudder to think of it.'

'What scandal?'

Amy sounded mildly impatient, but Aunty Menna was pleased at having made her ask the question.

'This schoolboy's camp in South Wales. He was supposed to have been in charge. Taking the boys into the sea and bathing with them in the nude. That's the story.'

'Ridiculous,' Amy said. 'And in any case what's wrong with bathing in the nude? People have been doing it for centuries.'

Aunty Menna was not disposed to generalise on the subject.

'The police were called in. That's the story. And we know where it comes from, don't we? Our old friend the Master of the Workhouse. Claims to have heard it first hand from his brilliant son Eddie. But I can just imagine the Alderman giving him the order to spread it thick and thin all through the town. Poor Mr Thomas. I don't know whether he has any idea how much he has to contend with.'

11

MISS EIRWEN'S STUDIO WAS ON THE SECOND FLOOR OF PLAS Iscoed. The windows gave the most extensive views of terraces and gardens that stretched westwards to the edge of an ornamental lake. Beyond the water which sparkled restlessly in the afternoon sunlight, dark shapes of wooded slopes hid the grounds from the outside world. Amy balanced her knee against the cushion of the window-seat as she sipped her last cup of China tea. The remnants of their afternoon tea lay on the trolley behind Miss Eirwen's easel. Miss Eirwen had begun to paint again. She found it easier to talk while she was working. She wore a grey smock with a thick leather belt around her waist and the smock reached to her ankles. Her hair was mostly hidden by a red scarf that threatened to come undone. All her materials, pastels, charcoal, pencil, parchment, pads and water-colours, were set out on tables within easy reach. Her ash walking-stick hung from a vacant easel. She rubbed a smudge of colour off her cheek and smiled at Amy.

'You can see for yourself,' Miss Eirwen said. 'Nothing has changed. I certainly haven't. Except that I'm older of course. And stiffer.'

Her grey eyes shone with the pleasure she took in Amy's presence.

'We can never be other than what we are,' she said. 'I think I've learnt that much. And that seems precious little when you say it. Whatever wealth you enjoy seems to mean a great deal more to others than it does to yourself. Of course it allows me to stay up here all day, playing with my colours and trying to enlarge the tiny talent I possess . . . Listen to me chattering. I suppose it's because I'm so glad to see you.'

She resumed her work with renewed intensity. From time to time she glanced at Amy with the shyness of an excited schoolgirl. She watched her move from the window to put down her cup and saucer on the trolley. Amy behaved as if she were unaware of the close attention Miss Eirwen was paying her.

'The trick is to capture the light,' Miss Eirwen said.

She muttered in a low voice, quite willing that Amy should overhear.

'To catch the moment on the wing. If only I could do it. Since I have little else to do, I should be able to. But it always seems to elude me!'

'You paint very well,' Amy said. 'At least I think so. And so did Leo Galt if it comes to that. And he was an expert.'

Miss Eirwen stopped working. They smiled warmly at each other. Even before she had begun to move, Amy handed her the walking-stick that hung on the empty easel.

'So much has happened to you,' Miss Eirwen said. 'And all I've done is grow older and more arthritic. To think that you are married. To think that you lost your best friend and that now you are mother to her little son. I think that's wonderful, Amy. And you look so well. I always thought it was a small miracle the way your skin took the sun. A peach bloom instead of burning so fair a complexion. You don't mind me making such personal remarks?'

Amy smiled confidently.

'Of course not,' she said.

'I expect I was too possessive, wasn't I? When you were here.'

Miss Eirwen seemed to hold her breath in the silence as she waited for the all important answer.

'I was young and silly,' Amy said. 'You were kindness itself. I didn't deserve such kindness.'

It was the perfect answer. Miss Eirwen was so pleased she looked around as if she were searching for some means to demonstrate her pleasure.

'Will you tell him?' Miss Eirwen said. 'Your husband. About the Garden Cottage. It's yours whenever you want it. A private retreat.'

Amy was slow to answer. Miss Eirwen made an effort to sense her difficulty.

'Politics, is it?' she said.

Without speaking Amy showed that this was indeed part of the problem. Miss Eirwen was happy to exhibit her own brand of unworldly shrewdness.

'Now you tell him that I think that shouldn't stand in his way at all. Tell him I know of at least three left-wing poets in England who spend half their time haunting plutocratic country houses. He writes in Welsh, of course, and in any case our Welsh consciences are that much more sensitive, but you tell him from me that in turbulent times like these he mustn't stop listening to those ancestral voices. Remote or recent, Amy dear, remote or recent. My grandfather was made a lord because he became a coal-owner and a very rich man. But I feel much closer to his grandparents and they were only small-holders, scratching a living from a bleak hillside in Radnorshire. I only hope they didn't suffer from arthritis. But I fear that is more than likely.'

'Just look at Tasker!'

Amy interrupted Miss Eirwen's train of thought as delicately as she could. Through the window they saw Tasker Thomas wheeling an invalid chair across the terrace. The invalid was prepared to enjoy the ride. He wore a flat black hat and a black cloak with a double collar that enveloped his squat form with regal completeness. Only the polished toe-caps of his boots emerged from the hem. White locks hung down beneath his hat and across the arms of the wheelchair an ornate walking-stick lay like a badge of office in temporary disuse. It could be raised at any moment to point out anything that took the passenger's fancy. As they watched they saw Tasker bend down to confide benevolently in the invalid's ear.

'Oh dear,' Miss Eirwen said. 'I hope Tasker won't tell him too much. Sir Prosser has a way of storing the most minute bits of information and making use of them. He even boasts about it to my brother David. Calls it one of the most important elements in his manipulation of hidden power!'

'Do you think he'd be against our Cottage Hospital?' Amy said.

Her obvious anxiety brought a sympathetic smile to Miss Eirwen's pale face.

'I don't think he would deign to concern himself with such a minor matter,' Miss Eirwen said. 'Not unless it happened to be some detail in a wider plan. He fancies himself as a great statesman. An arbiter of the fate of nations. A grey eminence. That sort of thing. That's why my brother David pays him so much attention. That's why he treats this place as a retreat where they can entertain foreign politicians and party leaders and come to secret understandings and unwritten treaties. Sometimes I have to hide away up here for days.'

Miss Eirwen's thin body shook with amusement at the notion. Amy's presence seemed to animate her with a child-like vigour.

'A Cottage Hospital isn't a minor matter,' Amy said sharply. 'If there had been one in Pendraw, Enid might have been alive today!'

'I'm so sorry.'

Miss Eirwen reached out impulsively to touch Amy's hand. She wanted to show how shocked she was by her own thoughtlessness and unseemly levity.

'I'm such a chatterbox today. I seem to want to talk all the time. Please forgive me.'

'He's such a good man,' Amy said.

She was watching the way Tasker held his head to one side and how he smiled as he gave Sir Prosser his undivided attention. Miss Eirwen stared down at the terrace, making an effort to see Tasker Thomas as Amy saw him.

'We were engaged to be married once,' Miss Eirwen said. 'Can you imagine that?'

She adopted a calm analytical tone, prepared to smile at her former self. Amy held herself perfectly still.

'Both of us dominated by our mothers. And now our mothers are gone and we are still here. Apparently unmarked by the experience. Older and wiser I hope. But it seemed the end of the world then. And I suppose it was in a way. The end of one world at least, full of restraints and carefully measured behaviour and domineering mothers. I'm sure you'll never be a domineering mother, will you?'

She was smiling so benevolently, Amy was able to relax. The wheelchair had arrived beneath their window and both Sir Prosser and Tasker were looking up at them as expectantly as two young men. Sir Prosser raised his stick in a gesture of comic command, demanding their presence on the terrace. They could not make out exactly what he was saying but it sounded like a reproof for remaining indoors on such a beautiful autumn afternoon.

'Shall we go down?'

Amy waited for Miss Eirwen to take the lead.

'You go,' Miss Eirwen said. 'But don't let him bully you. You tell him if he says anything that you have my complete support over the Cottage Hospital.'

Amy gasped with pleasure at the emphatic way in which Miss Eirwen spoke.

'Tell him I want to be honourable by deed as well as by title. He loves that sort of silly remark!'

'Won't you come?'

Amy held Miss Eirwen's cold hands as they stood in the doorway of the studio.

'He bullies me,' Miss Eirwen said. 'I'd only spend the rest of the day working out the answers I should have made instead of mumbling like a child and stopping myself from bursting into tears. He really is the most awful bully. I put up with him for David's sake or for old times' sake or whatever, but he takes advantage in the most outrageous fashion. Treats this place as if it were his own. You stand up to him, my dear. And don't let him get under your skin, as they say. That's his speciality.'

She stood in the doorway to watch Amy march purposefully down the corridor. At the top of the staircase she turned to give a little wave. Miss Eirwen was pleased to wave back. Amy tripped gaily down two flights of stairs to the nearest side-door. She found the two men at the south-west corner of the house, studying the painted ceiling of an empty gallery through an open french window. Sir Prosser was pointing out the false perspective with his walking-stick and making ribald comments about the vision of fleshy cherubs and angels in white climbing through a band of curling cloud to a dwindling blue heaven.

'Ah! better a real nightingale than a dumb choir of angels!'

Sir Prosser made the pronouncement in a deliberately resonant voice. He was delighted to see Amy.

'Tell me, Miss Parry, or Mrs More I should say, do pardon me, do you still sing? And where is the Lady of the Manor?'

He raised his stick again to indicate the direction in which he chose to have his chair wheeled. His voice echoed loudly in the quiet and he looked up to see if Miss Eirwen was watching their progress through the studio window.

'What a jumble,' Sir Prosser said. 'What a confusion of styles.

Still what else could you expect from the grandiose illusions of a captain of industry. Mark you I still find it all very impressive. As a mere scholarship boy brought up over a grocer's shop in a narrow black mining valley.'

He held up his stick, so that Tasker and Amy should join him in savouring the sublime stillness of their surroundings. At the sound of a curlew calling in the distance he hunched his shoulders in a grimace of conspiratorial rapture.

'That way! That way!'

He flourished his stick again.

'Follow the path through the golden beech trees to the garden cottage, there's a good fellow.'

Passing through the trees they came across a stone pavilion. The undergrowth of the woodland had been allowed to encroach upon it and the Latin inscription above the portico was mostly hidden by ivy. The wooden seats inside were covered in an unappetising green mould. Sir Prosser was indignant.

' "Perpetual spring and many summers" indeed,' he said. 'A spring clean. That's what it needs. I'll speak to Andrews. Tell me, Mrs More, your husband the poet. Will he like the idea? That's what Eirwen would really like, you know. To see you making use of the Garden Cottage. And in return, my dear, you'd get your Cottage Hospital. Cottage for Cottage. How does that sound?'

He bent his neck back to check whether or not Tasker was smiling at his sally.

'She has promised her complete support,' Amy said.

Tasker was able to express his open delight.

'Has she really?' he said. 'That's wonderful.'

'Unconditional support,' Amy said. 'She said she wanted above all to be honourable by deed as well as by title.'

Sir Prosser was frowning in an attitude of mild unbelief.

'Did she really?' he said. 'Did she really say that?'

'Those were her exact words!'

Amy was resolute.

'Splendid,' Tasker said. 'Absolutely splendid.'

Sir Prosser was irritated by Tasker's enthusiasm.

'I'll tell you this much, reverend friend, you'll be asking too

115

much if you ask the noble coal-owner to withdraw his support for the Company Union and come to terms with the Federation. You mustn't expect too much in this world, no matter what the poets try to tell you. Reality, my friend, is a sequence of open bargains and unspecified understandings. I said as much to the Belgian Ambassador in that very pavilion exactly four years ago. And he understood exactly what I meant. And while we are on the subject of reality, my friend, I'll tell you exactly what I'd do with your unemployed. Ship the lot of them to Canada and Australia and turn one or two of those desolate valleys into reservoirs. Useful and productive reservoirs.'

Tasker waved a finger of reproof.

'Ah,' he said. 'You put on this mask of cynicism. But I know how good you are at heart.'

'Do you? Do you really?'

'I have firm evidence,' Tasker said.

'Have you now?'

'Specific occasions when you put the welfare of your fellow-countrymen before your personal ambition and undoubted urge to self-advancement. Of any politician, my dear Prosser, no one can ask for more. Let me put it like that.'

Sir Prosser was content enough to pretend he had been worsted in the argument. He sighed deeply and stared at a plantation of Douglas firs for consolation.

'What shall we leave behind us?' he said. 'Tell me Mrs More, is there any truth in this strange story I've heard about our old friend Val Gwyn entering a monastery?'

He seemed cheered by Amy's embarrassed silence.

'Now why would he want to do a thing like that?'

He stared at Amy through narrowed eyes forcing her to look away.

'Won't do him any good in Wales you know. We have this violent prejudice against Papists. I don't share it myself of course. But I do know it's a long way from Capel Seion to Châteauneuf du Pape!'

He struck the ground with the walking-stick, delighted at his own wit. He beamed at them both like a naughty child and pointed the stick towards the walled gardens below them.

116

'Forward!' he said. 'To the Garden Cottage. And may your husband sit in it, Mrs More, composing elevating *cywyddau* and modern sonnets. You must never allow him to get bogged down in left-wing dogmatism. You can tell him from me that it's very difficult to set the Communist Manifesto to music. If it wasn't, it would have been done a hundred times over by now and replaced the Te Deum.'

Amy tried to gain Tasker's attention by raising her eyebrows in mock despair at Sir Prosser's overbearing manner: but Tasker was too absorbed in holding the wheelchair steady with all his strength against the gradient to notice.

12

THE TWO LITTLE BOYS WERE ABSORBED IN LOADING A TOY WHEEL-barrow with sand. They wore caps and thick scarves and their efforts were hampered by the overcoats they wore which reached to their feet. Except for Nanw, the women in Amy's basement kitchen sat close to the window so that they could enjoy the sight of Bedwyr and Clemmie and speculate about their unceasing activity. Nanw was in pain after a visit to the dentist. She sat near the fire with a coat and hat on and a large white handkerchief clutched to her cheek. Mrs Annie Rossett was concerned about her. She divided her attention equally between the scene in the sandy garden and the suffering of her friend by the fire, and she managed to do this while continuing to handle her cup and saucer with con-spicuous gentility.

'In their own little world,' Mrs Rossett said. 'So completely innocent.'

She sighed as she spoke as if she were longing for a lost innocence herself. She was a widow and she was childless. She kept house for her disabled brother, the retired minister Nathan Harris, and it was in their house that Amy had lodged when she was an unmarried schoolteacher. Mrs Rossett took pride in their continuing friendship. It had become her custom to call at the

117

house in Marine Terrace in the course of her afternoon walks to the sea and often she accompanied Nanw on her visits. Alongside her at the round table sat Clemmie's Aunty Menna, Amy's neighbour. Aunty Menna was always glad of a chance to escape from her own housework and sit in Amy's kitchen. She behaved like an eager recruit to an exclusive circle and concentrated on formulating pronouncements that the others would be certain to approve of.

'We live in troubled times,' she said. 'I know that much.'

Mrs Rossett was about to agree when she heard Nanw suppress a moan. She leaned back in her chair to express her concern and sympathy. Aunty Menna was obliged to augment her own proposition.

'The poor man comes here with his message of peace and love,' Aunty Menna said. 'And what do the people of Pendraw do? They treat him shamefully.'

She was referring to Tasker Thomas. Her manner grew more assertive as she warmed to her subject. She was expressing what they all felt, but the role of spokeswoman was particularly congenial to a woman confined, as she was wont to complain, for long hours to the solitude of her own kitchen, her sister at school and her nephew too young to chat with.

'We do try to support him,' Aunty Menna said. 'But what can a handful of people do? Against the forces of evil I suppose you could call them. What kind of world will those little boys have to grow up in?'

It was a question they all found easier to ask than to answer. Aunty Menna was encouraged by the silence to ramble on with increasing confidence.

'It wasn't like this when we grew up, was it? I'm sure it wasn't. The biggest tragedy I remember when I was a child was a boy of fourteen being blown off the rigging and drowned in Glaslyn harbour. The whole village was in mourning for weeks.'

Amy offered her a slice of cake and she accepted gratefully.

'I know I shouldn't,' Aunty Menna said. 'I'm putting on so much weight.'

She munched thoughtfully as she craned her neck to follow the boys trundling the little wheelbarrow towards the bedraggled vegetable patch.

'I blame the war,' Aunty Menna said. 'Nothing has been the same since the Great War. It's brought a blight on the world.'

'Peace.'

Mrs Rossett muttered the word consolingly.

'My brother Nathan says that's the only political question that really matters. I learn a lot from him you know.'

She smiled and then shrugged her shoulders to disparage her own intellectual attainment and at the same time reaffirm the profound respect in which she held her brother's. Aunty Menna gulped down her cake. She was eager to talk but apparently torn between seeking enlightenment and pursuit of an unstable train of thought.

'People don't want war do they? Of course they don't. And yet it's what they get. Can anyone explain that to me?'

Amy moved to the new Triplex grate to pour hot water in the teapot. Aunt Menna could not wait for an answer.

'Anything is better than war, I would think,' Aunty Menna said. 'Who wants death and destruction? Who could possibly want it? And think of the generations yet unborn. Who starts it off? That's what I want to know.'

The question hung in the air. Amy was obliged to answer it.

'Power politics,' Amy said.

Aunty Menna repeated the phrase. It was a mysterious concept, but it had to be apprehended. Nanw removed the handkerchief from her mouth to make her own contribution to the discussion.

'Arms,' she said. 'Armaments. Somebody's making money out of it.'

The socket was too painful to allow her to say any more. Mrs Rossett raised a hand delicately to restrain her from causing herself additional suffering.

'Power politics is a male disease!' Amy said. 'I sometimes think that.'

They paid close attention to what she was saying. This obliged her to smile a little if only to indicate that she herself did not take the pronouncements she was about to make with too much seriousness.

'Men are so childish,' she said. 'And so full of fantasies. They have very little understanding of the nature of reality. They are dangerous children, armed to the teeth.'

Nanw was nodding to express her wholehearted agreement.

'Did you see that film?' Amy said. 'What was it called? A boy in the trenches. Wounded. And he's crying for his mother to stop the blood. And the hero tells him not to be a baby. Did you see it?'

The others shook their heads.

'I never go to the pictures,' Mrs Rossett said. 'Do you think I should start? It's the way I was brought up I suppose.'

Modestly she diverted attention from herself to the little boys in the garden.

'Just look at them! Just look.'

Bedwyr and Clemmie stood on either side of the wheelbarrow engaged in solemn discussion about who should wheel and who should shovel. Bedwyr wanted the spade but Clemmie was unwilling to part with it. They faced each other in profile, each reluctant to engage in physical conflict.

'Like little old men,' Aunty Menna said. 'Aren't they sweet?'

Even Nanw was impelled to move briefly to the window and found the strength to smile.

'Bless them,' Mrs Rossett said. 'Bless them both.'

Amy wanted to say more about her visit to the cinema. Mrs Rossett showed herself ready to listen with complete attention.

'It was a frightening film,' Amy said. 'But that wasn't what frightened me most. A cinema organ rose up out of the bowels of the earth and the whole audience started singing. War songs. One war song after another. Oh, I know it was only some form of nostalgia, but it made me shudder. As if this was the only way left for the living to show any respect for the dead. It made me feel quite ill.'

The other women stared at her in awe.

'I suppose I was making too much of a fuss,' Amy said. 'But I was ever so glad to get a breath of sea air on the promenade. This was at Llandudno.'

'It's the penny press,' Mrs Rossett said.

She was happy to pass on a morsel of her brother Nathan's wisdom.

'Instead of being nurtured on the breast of the Sunday School and a healthy diet of hymns and scripture, our modern people are fed on the sweet poisons of the yellow press. My brother Nathan says . . .'

She paused in mid-sentence when she heard a quiet tap on the back door. With surprising alacrity Aunty Menna jumped up to open the door. She looked down to see Clemmie staring up at her through the steel-rimmed spectacles clamped on his head in a way that made his ears stick out. His nostrils looked as wide as his open mouth.

'Bedwyr wants a drink,' he said.

Down the garden Aunty Menna could see Bedwyr was busy reloading the wheelbarrow with his tin spade.

'Does he indeed?' she said.

She stepped back into the kitchen so that the others could hear the conversation between her and her little nephew. She beckoned him in and repeated her question. He looked at her through his glasses with profound suspicion and declined to answer.

'Little Bedwyr wants a drink, does he?'

She turned her head to conceal from him the wink she was giving the women in the kitchen.

'Well now, I wonder why he doesn't come and ask for one himself, Clemmie?'

Clemmie continued to stare upwards at his aunt as he formulated an explanation.

'I'm looking after him,' Clemmie said.

He heard the women in the kitchen laughing. He was pleased with the impression he had made.

'Perhaps he's shy too,' Clemmie said. 'That's possible.'

Aunty Menna could no longer keep a straight face. Her large breasts shook up and down as she doted on her little Clemmie. She spoke obliquely to her audience but the child could hear her easily enough.

'He's barely four,' she said. 'And he's so ready with his tongue. He'll be the death of me, he really will.'

The front door bell rang.

'My goodness,' Mrs Rossett said. 'We are being attacked from the front and the rear.'

121

She placed the tips of her fingers against her mouth to reprove herself for speaking out of turn. Nanw was on her feet mutely offering to go to the door. Amy made her sit down. She removed her apron as she ascended the short flight of stairs from the basement to the ground floor and left it on the steps.

Amy opened the front door. She discovered Eddie Meredith. When the door opened he stood back and spread his arms wide so that the long sheep-skin coat he was wearing spread out like a magician's cloak. He raised his pork-pie hat high in the air and drew Amy's attention to a red sports car with a hard roof in black parked against the wide pavement.

'Well,' Amy said. 'What a stranger.'

Eddie was not put off by the coolness of her welcome. He grinned confidently at Amy and invited her to admire the splendour of his overcoat that reached from his ankles to the high collar that protected the back of his head.

'It's Hungarian,' he said. 'Zoltan Brody gave it to me. Wouldn't take no for an answer.'

He moved closer to the threshold and waited for Amy to notice the red sports car.

'Cost me twenty-five quid,' he said. 'Fourth-hand at least, but in perfect working order, just like its owner. You must let me take you for a spin.'

His dazzling smile was slow to fade.

'What's up?' he said. 'You know I can't bear your disapproval.'

'Do I have to tell you?'

Amy stepped back so that he could enter her house. They could hear the sound of laughter coming up from the basement. Eddie's eyebrows were raised enquiringly. Amy opened the door of the front room. It was unheated and still sparsely furnished. Eddie wanted to show his approval of the new wallpaper in pale green, stamped with a white pattern of alternating leaves and birds.

'It's cold in here,' Amy said. 'You'd better leave that coat on.'

'You're not pleased with me,' he said. 'I've done something terribly wrong. Tell me. What am I guilty of?'

Amy frowned as she considered his elaborate façade of innocence.

'Where else did your father get his information from?'

'My father?'

Eddie raised a weary hand. He could have been taking an oath or making a disavowal of allegiance: anything to distance himself from his obnoxious parent.

'H. M. Meredith,' he said.

He was preparing some form of humorous statement that would demonstrate his critical detachment. Amy did not wait to hear it.

'You supplied him with all the ammunition he needed,' she said. 'And I'm telling you this to your face.'

Eddie inhaled deeply as he began to muster a strenuous denial. Amy stood still with her hand on the doorknob as she completed the process of demolition.

'Moreover,' she said, 'you stayed away at the very time when you could have done something to help Tasker. You conveniently disappeared off the face of the globe.'

Eddie made a sequence of appeasing gestures to show he had an explanation.

'Hetty Remington's aunt,' he said. 'She packed the three of us off on a trip to Antibes. As it turned out, it was a piece of unbeliev-able luck. That's how I met Zoltan.'

Amy was unimpressed. The stony expression on her face seemed designed to show what little value was to be attached to casual encounters enjoyed by the privileged and irresponsible.

'Without him I would never have landed this job in the film business,' Eddie said. 'Twenty pounds a week! A two-year contract!'

'How nice for you,' Amy said. 'I'll go and make the tea.'

'Amy . . .'

Eddie was pleading with her. He followed her to the passage. He became aware of the voices from the basement kitchen. He lowered his voice considerably.

'I've called at an awkward time. You've got company.'

He could not resist raising his eyebrows in mock apprehension at the sound of the women talking. He whispered again.

'Here be dragons!'

'Oh I know we're very boring people,' Amy said. 'Provincial and so on. But we manage. We survive.'

She left him in the passage. He looked trapped. He could have walked out and driven away. Instead he extracted a silver-plated cigarette-case from the inside pocket of his double-breasted jacket and returned to the front room. For want of something better to do, he peered at the books in the new glass-fronted bookcase. They were a mixture of ponderous legal tomes and slim volumes of Welsh poetry including half a dozen copies of Cilydd's most recent collection. Eddie would have opened the bookcase but it was locked. He moved to the bay window and surveyed the view of the harbour. The mountain range in the distance was partially hidden under cloud. The view seemed to give him little satisfaction. He moved about the room, listening intently to the voices downstairs. It was not possible to make out anything they were saying, but the merry tone and the occasional outburst of laughter suggested the women were enjoying each other's company.

His red sports car was the most interesting thing to look at. He smoked and stared, until he turned his head and saw a familiar figure approach down the straight length of the embankment road. John Cilydd carried a briefcase. He held on to his hat and his head was lowered against the breeze from the sea. The unhappy scowl vanished from Eddie's face. He dragged impatiently on his cigarette until Cilydd had come close enough to see him standing in the window. But Cilydd saw nothing except the pavement and his own feet. Eddie extinguished his cigarette in a new ashtray and rushed to open the front door. He was ready to embrace his friend on the threshold.

'Cilydd! You old legal bard. Welcome to your own home!'

Cilydd looked up in astonishment. He needed time to take in the surprise. He noted the exotic sports car and showed that he was amused. He was pleased to see Eddie but resisted his embrace. He placed his hand on Eddie's chest and pushed him inside. He smiled as he listened to Eddie chattering gaily.

'I'm setting up as a Registrar of Domestic Bliss,' Eddie said. 'I'm making a survey with my sensitive antennae and the bell is ringing the top notes in this place I can tell you. How's it going, John Cilydd? Tell me all about it.'

Cilydd stood in the middle of the floor, stretching his arms

slowly and then raising one after the other in a comfortable simula-
tion of Swedish drill. He was clearly pleased to relax in his own
home.

'People are amazing,' he said. 'You wouldn't believe it, but I had
a certain farmer in this afternoon, making his will. I can't name
him obviously but he was pretty prosperous I can tell you that. I
can't imagine how he's ever managed it in times like these. But he
has. Big farm. Big property. He left his wife in the outside office.
"You wait there, Mary" he said. He could have been talking to his
sheep-dog.'

Eddie was ready to chuckle appreciatively. He lay back in the
sofa of the three-piece suite, placed his hands behind his head and
stretched out his legs.

'It was quite a business,' Cilydd said. 'All sorts of provisions for
this and for that. A special bequest for the chapel of course. I was
tempted to scribble in how many prayers for the departed! And
there was an intricate tie-up to stop the husband of a married
daughter getting his hands on any of it. And when we'd finished, I
said "But Mr So-and-so, what about your wife?" He looked quite
surprised.'

As he warmed to his story, Cilydd had begun to act out the
encounter. He drew the knuckle of an index finger against the ends
of an imaginary walrus moustache as he took on the role of the
perplexed farmer. He spoke in a ponderous broad accent.

' "Hum . . . ha . . . yes . . . well! The woman's been a good wife to
me. I'll say that for her. Put down sixty pounds." '

They were still both enjoying the story when Amy pushed the
door open with her knee and carried in a tea-tray. Cilydd offered to
relieve her of her burden but she pointed with her toe towards a
nest of little tables. Cilydd was in an expansive mood.

'I'll light a fire,' he said. 'And can't we offer something a little
stronger to drink? The prodigal's return and so on.'

Amy pressed the tips of her fingers into the side of her mouth.

'Your sister Nanw,' she said.

She pointed meaningfully in the direction of the basement.

'She's been to the dentist. She's in pain still. Mrs Rossett came
with her. And Clemmie's Aunt Menna is there too.'

125

'That's it then,' Cilydd said with a sigh. 'No gin and tonic. If there's one thing I fancy when I get back from the office, it's a gin and tonic. Never mind. Peace and quiet is even more important.'

'You'd better go down and see her,' Amy said.

They exchanged glances. Cilydd resisted the suggestion.

'I'd better stay with her,' Amy said. 'She's in pain, poor thing. I'll tell her you're dealing with a client.'

'You haven't heard all my news.'

In front of Cilydd, Eddie was able to address Amy in the friendliest manner. He was eager to be at least outwardly restored to favour.

'I've landed a job in the film business!'

'No!'

Cilydd was suitably surprised and pleased.

'Twenty pounds a week. Two-year contract.'

'Good Lord!'

'I start off in the Publicity Department. Help out with copy. Then there's small parts and additional dialogue. The trick is to make myself indispensable.'

Amy poured the tea and handed him a cup.

'Your father will be pleased,' she said.

Eddie skated over the comment by working himself up into a state of enthusiasm.

'It's the art form of the future,' he said. 'And I can tell you this, I've got them interested already in a fantastic idea.'

Cilydd was smiling.

'What about your devotion to the theatre?' he said playfully.

Eddie put down his cup and saucer on the small table so that he could gesture expressively in a continental manner.

'Now you listen. I mean this isn't just a social call you know. I tell you this my lovelies, this is a chance to put Wales on the map!'

'Isn't it there already?' Cilydd said.

He was encouraged by a smile of approval from Amy.

'You may laugh,' Eddie said.

He was deeply serious.

'But most of the people at Gaumont British just don't know that Wales exists.'

'Is that something terrible?' Cilydd said.

'Yes it is. These are the people who are going to mould the minds of the future. It's important. It really is. I can tell you this, some of the best poets in England are falling over themselves to get involved in the film business. Honestly.'

'What is your fantastic idea?'

Amy spoke so quietly they both looked at her in surprise. Eddie hesitated.

'Romeo and Juliet of the hills,' he said at last. 'The struggle between two ancient families, over drowning a valley. The struggle between progress and tradition locked into a story of star-crossed lovers . . .'

Cilydd and Amy had both started laughing. Eddie stared at them indignantly. Cilydd held out a hand in a gesture of apology even as his body shook.

'It's not funny,' Eddie said. 'There's big money involved. Or there will be. And all I'm saying, John Cilydd, is that you take a few days off from that office of yours and come with me on a "reccy" as we call it. All expenses paid and a decent fee thrown in. And if you're interested, I know Zoltan would love to have a genuine Welsh poet and national winner in on the script operation. So there you are. It's business I'm talking about as well as the art form of the future.'

He was content at last to have reduced them both to reasonably respectful listeners.

'I know you think I let you down over poor old Tasker. But honestly, if I ever said anything that's been used against him in any way, you must know it was completely unintentional. Being so far away, I had no idea what was going on. I wouldn't want to do my friends anything but good. That's why I'm here now, for God's sake. I wouldn't think of coming home otherwise. Ever.'

He stared at them alternately, a look of triumph on his face.

'Now come on, John Cilydd. What about it?'

Cilydd was shaking his head. With her hands folded in her lap Amy watched them both with sphinx-like impassivity.

'It's a fabulous idea,' Eddie said. 'I know it is.'

'If you want to make a picture about Wales, bring your cameras to Cwm Du or one of the worst hit mining valleys and make a film about that!' Cilydd said. 'Come to Dowlais or Bryn Mawr and make a film about the ruin of a Welsh community. Make a film about despair and degradation. Places where the Labour Exchange has become the only sign of life. And the dignity of those people in the face of adversity and the nice little bourgeois world that wants to forget they exist.'

'My God!'

Eddie sat up.

'You really mean it, don't you?'

'Of course I do.'

With a look of quiet satisfaction on her face Amy offered them more tea and scones. She spoke quietly to her husband.

'John Cilydd,' she said. 'You really ought to go and ask Nanw how she is.'

He shook his head impatiently. He was still too absorbed in a nightmare vision of the distressed valleys even to think about his sister.

'If filming would do any good,' he said. 'It's no substitute for a revolution.'

Amy opened the parlour door. The noises she heard from below suggested an imminent departure. Eddie waved his arms to detain her and to signal that he had been struck with a new idea.

'Listen,' he said. 'Listen. Why not kill two birds with one stone? A valley is a valley is a valley. And practical life is a sequence of well-executed compromises. Who said that? Do you know I think I did! Make *two* films instead of one and halve the expense each way. God! I'm so brilliant! Sometimes I stagger myself.'

Eddie stood up. He walked towards Amy with outstretched arms.

'Mrs More, marvellous Mrs More! Will you let me borrow your brilliant husband for just a couple of days? Three or four at the most. What we need from the technical point of view is two, or even three, valleys adjacent to each other but in two contrasting phases of development. One still unspoilt, the other ravaged by industrial exploitation. One pastoral, no, two pastoral and one or maybe two industrial. Do you see what I'm getting at?'

'I must go down,' Amy said. 'They are leaving, Cilydd. You must come down and say "hello". If they're going, it won't take a minute.'

Eddie was still on the crest of the wave of his own enthusiasm.

'I'll bring old Zoltan along,' he said. 'And Sam of course. Sam spent three months in Hollywood last year and he talks now with the most ridiculous American accent. He was born and bred in Hounslow.'

Cilydd murmured his apologies as he followed Amy out of the room. She closed the door carefully. In the passage she seized his arm. She whispered furiously in his ear.

'He's a poisonous little snake,' she said. 'He doesn't care two hoots about, about what's happening to poor Tasker. You insist on him going to see him.'

The force of her anger took Cilydd by surprise. Amy was too angry to give him time to think.

'And as for going down South with him . . .'

He was shaking his head to show that it was not his intention.

Amy persisted in giving vent to her feelings.

'I can tell you this,' she said. 'If you went, I wouldn't be here when you got back.'

He closed his eyes, disturbed and bewildered by the strength of her reaction.

'Come on,' she said. 'They're leaving.'

He followed her obediently down the stairs.

13

CILYDD WAS SMOKING A CIGARETTE IN THE ENTRANCE TO THE REST tent. He turned his back on the eisteddfod field to watch Amy brushing little Bedwyr's curly hair in the green twilight of the interior. The morning sun was shining after a wet night. In the distance the turnstiles were clicking with increasing regularity as more people ventured in to saunter along the duck-boards laid down over the muddy patches. In the pavilion the first competitions had already begun and everywhere there was an atmosphere of cheerful anticipation. Even the smell of trampled grass inside the tent contributed. Cilydd drew nervously on his cigarette and fingered the half-sheet of notes in his inside pocket.

'Now keep still, there's a good boy,' Amy said.

Bedwyr had bent down to pull up the white socks that hung over his ankles. He straightened obediently as he stood on one of the chairs near a centre tent pole. The handbag in which Amy kept the hairbrush hung open on her arm. She groomed the boy with the intensity of a woman at her devotions. She finished before his patience gave out, so she allowed him to jump down and run to the entrance of the tent without losing the smile of resignation on her face.

'They won't like it,' Cilydd said. 'I know that much.'

Her husband also needed her attention. It was a gesture of comfort when she brushed away traces of dandruff on the shoulder of his jacket. He wore a light brown suit she had chosen for him, a cream shirt and a dark brown bow-tie.

'You just say what you think,' she said. 'That's what you're there for.'

He glanced anxiously at his wristwatch. Amy suggested he set out three chairs near the entrance so that they could sit and observe their corner of the field until the meeting in the Literary Pavilion was due to begin. Bedwyr was fascinated by an area beyond the guy-ropes of the rest tent where a duck-board came to an end and people circulating the field had to take particular care to avoid an isolated patch of mud. The hazard added to the ritual surprise of unexpected encounters with acquaintances and old friends. The little boy was mesmerised by the process: a head would be raised and a mouth would open to release a sound of astonishment. Amy and Cilydd took a more general view. A druidic symbol was stencilled on the gable end of the massive green pavilion and underneath hung 'Y GWIR YN ERBYN Y BYD' – 'THE TRUTH AGAINST THE WORLD'. The thin sound of an early competitor playing a harp wafted towards them on the morning air.

'Perhaps you should have taken him to the beach.'

Cilydd addressed his wife over his son's head. She was entirely sympathetic to his state of unease.

'We'll sit in the back,' she said. 'Bedwyr and I. As quiet as little mice. If he gets restless, we can slip out quite easily. I'll buy him an ice-cream and we'll wander back. It shouldn't take all that long, should it?'

Cilydd folded his arms and looked doubtful.

'I don't know,' he said. 'There'll be rows of would-be critics in there. And I know what they're going to say too.'

'You mustn't worry,' Amy said.

She spoke softly so as not to attract Bedwyr's attention.

'They are such amateurs,' Cilydd said. 'Poetry's just a little hobby for them. It's nothing to do with the real business of living.'

He screwed up his eyes and tilted his face to the sun. Amy wanted to encourage him.

'We'll be there, sitting in the back, ready to cheer you on,' she said. 'Two little mice in the literary lion's den.'

He smiled without opening his eyes. This attracted the attention of a passer-by, a solemnly dressed young man whose head jerked about like a moorhen's as he watched his step in the mud and looked around for someone to accost. He halted in front of them and pointed at Cilydd with his folded newspaper as though he had at last hunted down a suitably significant quarry. His folded mackintosh swung on his arm and his bushy hair stood upright in its own attitude of proclamation.

'John Cilydd More!' he said. 'I'm on my way to listen to you!'

This allowed him to step closer. Early as it was in the day, should he feel so inclined, he could require access to the rest tent. The More family had no right to monopolise it. Bedwyr was intrigued by the visitor's hovering presence. If the eisteddfod lasted long enough, in the end everyone would know everyone else.

'Tell me,' the young man said. 'What do you think of this business of the bards parading in their robes to a mock medieval feast in this millionaire's castle?'

'Rubbish,' Cilydd said grimly. 'Ridiculous rubbish!'

The young man slapped his own legs with his folded newspaper. He was delighted. He had drawn blood on his first question.

'I thought you'd say that!'

There was also the undeniable fact of his own perspicacity to be fleetingly acknowledged. His polished shoes shifted closer.

'I can tell you this,' he said. 'The millionaire won't be there. He left early this morning to take a cure at Baden-Baden.'

He was disappointed by Cilydd's manifest lack of interest in a rare piece of inside information. Jingling the change in his pocket he transferred his attention to Bedwyr. He bent his knees to bring himself more directly into the boy's line of vision and pressed a penny into his small hand. This appeared to give him the right to address Bedwyr in the second person singular in a mock-schoolmasterly manner.

'Now do you know any of your father's verses off by heart yet, my fine lad?'

Bedwyr shrank closer to Amy. Her two rings glittered in the sun as she rested her left hand protectively on his shoulder.

'How about this one?

"The hawk descends
with burning eyes
And where he strikes
The singing dies." '

He chuckled at the alarm on Bedwyr's face. The little boy stared at the gap between the man's front teeth.

'Correct, word for word?'

The young man straightened up in search of Cilydd's approval.

'Alas, yes,' Cilydd said. 'I'm beginning to wish I'd never written it.'

This puzzled his admirer who closed his eyes in a more ambitious effort of reverential recall.

'I wish I could remember it . . . The one about the hero's return. Oh, dear me now, how does it go?'

Cilydd was either unable or unwilling to help him.

' "Who sang away their land and sold their birthright for a tin of soup" . . . no, that can't be right, can it?'

A passer-by tapped the poetry lover on the shoulder. He was

instantly distracted. He raised his folded newspaper in a brief gesture of farewell before engaging himself enthusiastically in a fresh encounter.

'Who was that?' Amy said.

'I can't for the life of me remember his name,' Cilydd said. 'A civil servant of some sort. Born to be anonymously important. Signing bank notes and death warrants with the same illegible flourish. You'll be scratching your head on the scaffold still trying to remember his name before they chop your head off.'

The way Amy laughed made more of an impression on the child than his father's obscure humour. Cilydd was ready to explore the vein further but she drew his attention to the little boy listening in order to discourage him.

'He'll be in there,' Cilydd said. 'In there with the best of them, ready to toss my carcass to the lions.'

'Where are the lions, Mam?'

Amy gave Bedwyr a reassuring hug.

'I can tell you one thing,' Cilydd said. 'I wish old Val was here. He was so lucid on his feet. And he could argue so well without losing his temper or becoming emotional. Do you know I used to dream about being like him and standing up in some great pulpit ready to address the multitude.'

'Oh, never mind about Val,' Amy said. 'You stand on your own feet. After all you are a national winner and this is this year's national eisteddfod. What's the use of all the fuss and bother if puffed-up eisteddfodic personages refuse to listen to one of their best poets?'

She was scrutinising the details of his appearance with a critical eye as she spoke. He seemed overwhelmed with gratitude for her interest and approval.

'I'm not worthy of you, Amy,' he said.

He ignored her warning glance that was meant to make him aware of how closely the child was listening.

'I want to write something good in praise of you,' he said. 'There's hardly a day passes without my having a try. But it's never any good. I get bogged down in the quagmire of my own emotions. And yet I can compose freely enough about other things.'

133

'Well, there you are then,' Amy said.

'You make me re-examine myself,' he said. 'And you make me re-examine the world around me. And I imagine I can see it all in a bright new light.'

'My goodness,' Amy said. 'What more can you ask?'

Cilydd was intent on being serious and on clarifying his thoughts as much for his own benefit as for hers.

'We have to make a better world. That's axiomatic. But in order to do so we mustn't be frightened of the past. We mustn't make a fetish of things that are no longer living and no longer relevant to the task before us.'

'You tell them,' Amy said. 'You make them sit up and take notice.'

Cilydd smiled at her wanly and stretched to touch her hands. She allowed him to hold them briefly before reaching out to stop Bedwyr straying into the mud.

'I was thinking about us,' Cilydd said.

'Oh, us.'

Her tone suggested that this was altogether a lighter topic.

'We manage quite well, don't we?' she said.

He gazed at her longingly. A note of pleading crept into his voice.

'I know I'm your second choice.'

'And I'm your second wife,' Amy said briskly. 'So there you are. That makes things equal. And who has been going on about not getting bogged down in the past?'

Bedwyr was looking up at her, eager to hear her laugh again. She passed her hand fondly over his hair.

'He's so good,' she said. 'Just like she was.'

She smiled at Cilydd before picking up Bedwyr and carrying him across the mud to set him down on the duck-board.

'It must be time,' she said.

She swayed closer to Cilydd as they made their way to the site of the Literature Tent. Bedwyr held her hand and she had to mutter rapidly so that the little boy should not hear his praises too openly sung.

'He really wants to be good,' she said. 'So like her. It's quite remarkable really. I hardly ever have to scold him. Just a touch on the tiller sometimes. It gives you a new faith in the future somehow. The human race *could* improve.'

They loitered at a short distance from the Literature Tent. Except for the total absence of alcohol and mechanical music it was all rather like a bank-holiday fairground. The stands were ranged side by side and bright signs were blazoned above them. The Literature Tent was a rectangular structure of wood and canvas. Most of the audience were already seated inside, but groups lingered at the entrance to enjoy a smoke and a chat. The level of human chatter was loud and yet uncommonly harmonious. Parents were relaxed and children displayed unusual patience. They licked their ice-cream cornets without complaint as their elders stopped to register yet another encounter with people they never expected to see.

'There goes our chairman.'

Cilydd's back straightened as he prepared for his ordeal.

'I'd better go in.'

He fumbled for the notes in his inside pocket. Amy squeezed his arm.

'Don't you worry,' she said. 'You just get up on that bit of stage and tell them what's what. And keep it simple. So that even I can understand.'

'Simple? Yes of course.'

The word only brought him fresh unease. He darted away like a man late for a dental appointment. Amy picked up Bedwyr so that he could see his father search about the side of the tent for access to the speaker's rostrum. He vanished and reappeared, tripping over the guy ropes. Bedwyr and Amy waved but he no longer saw them. She set the little boy down. To get in easily, they would have to wait until the people still lingering and chatting around the entrance decided to move inside. The sun was out and they were in no hurry.

'So here you are then.'

She was startled by the sound of a familiar voice. Bedwyr moved closer to the shade of her protection. With her hand on the little boy's shoulder she turned to see Pen Lewis no more than two yards away, standing in the mud with the bottom of his shabby flannel trousers rolled up. The collar of his open-necked red shirt was turned up and both his hands were plunged into his trouser pockets as if they had been rugby shorts. The normal pallor of his skin was hidden under an outdoor tan. His smile was as challenging as ever. Amy had no way of concealing her surprise and alarm.

'What are you doing here?' she said.

He took his time to answer. The way he kept smiling suggested a bitter taste in his mouth even as he stared at her.

'Well now then,' he said at last. 'Our lads have got a little booth of their own. Outside the city walls. They wouldn't let us inside the sacred precincts. The eisteddfod big-wigs don't really approve of the Unemployed Movement. Sorry for us of course. But they don't want to see us doing anything about it. Have a fag.'

He offered her a cigarette. She refused it with an impatient shake of her head. She glanced toward the entrance to the Literature Tent to see if the people were beginning to move in. Pen Lewis was calm and unhurried. He studied her appearance with open appreciation. He was aware of Bedwyr too, and the way she had unconsciously drawn the little boy to stand in front of her.

'So you gave up your job then?' he said. 'You gave up teaching?'

Amy had to clear her throat before she could answer.

'I had no choice,' she said. 'That's the rule.'

He gazed at the wedding ring on her finger. He was no longer smiling. Amy grew more confident.

'The usual discrimination against married women,' she said. 'In any case, as it happened it was far more important for me to look after little Bedwyr.'

'Oh aye.'

The sound he made was more a resigned acceptance than a comment. For the first time he considered the child as an object of interest in his own right.

'You're a lucky little kid,' Pen said. 'Do you know that?'

'He doesn't understand English,' Amy said. 'Not yet.'

'Aye, but he will, won't he?'

Amy seemed reluctant to accept the inevitable. The boy shrank closer to her when Pen attempted to pat his head. He replaced his hands in his trouser pockets. He stared at Amy with friendly confidentiality.

'You won't be having one of your own then?'

Her cheeks flushed angrily. Her fingers gripped Bedwyr's shoulders so tightly he looked up to see what was disturbing her.

'It's no business of yours,' she said.

'Well no, of course not.'

Pen was grinning happily. Amy turned to take more note of an abrupt commotion at the side of the Literature Tent. A large man with a red rosette in the lapel of his jacket was doing his best to restrain and remonstrate with her husband. Cilydd had his hand on his neck as if he had been stung by a wasp and he was shaking his head vehemently. Nothing would persuade him to return to the rostrum.

'Oh my goodness,' Amy said. 'What's happened?'

She was talking to herself. When he caught sight of her, Cilydd raised his hand and signalled her not to move until he had rejoined her. He ignored the patches of mud to take the shortest distance between the two points.

'What's the matter?' Amy said. 'What happened?'

'Pompous ass!'

Cilydd was still fuming.

'Who?'

'The chairman. Pompous idiot. "Keep it short and sweet, Mr More. Five minutes. That's all I can give you." "In that case," I said, "you can keep them. I won't bother!" '

Cilydd was glowering at Amy, silently urging her at the very least to share his indignation.

'A total mess,' he said. 'Five speakers instead of three! I told them, "You may as well have fifty." Not counting a pompous wordbag of a chairman. All they wanted from me was a note on methods of adjudication. What the devil do I care about the methods of adjudication.'

'Quite right,' Amy said.

It was inadequate. Nothing she could say could equal the enormity of the offence. Phrases from the address he had prepared began to tumble out. All Amy could do was hold on comfortingly to Bedwyr and keep nodding her head to show Cilydd how much she agreed with him. Pen Lewis watched them with the friendly but detached interest of a tourist in a foreign land overhearing a conversation he imagines he can understand.

'I want an eisteddfod which is an integral part of our national being and which we can all look up to and be proud of. A proper celebration of our existence, representative of the whole people. A human response to an inhuman economic and political climate. And what do we have? An antiquarian peep-show in the grip of manipulators from the Liberal establishment. An extravaganza of the petty bourgeoisie.'

'Petty bourgeoisie' was a phrase that Pen Lewis could well understand. Cilydd became aware of his head nodding in vigorous agreement. He was prepared to assume the man in the open-necked shirt had seen the justice of his case.

'He thought he had me trapped in there,' Cilydd said. 'He thought I wouldn't dare walk out. Well, I showed him.'

He was slow to appreciate that Pen could not understand what he was saying.

'This is Pen Lewis,' Amy said in English. 'I don't think you have met before. Pen Lewis from Cwm Du.'

Pen smiled at Cilydd reassuringly. Cilydd's flood of eloquence had suddenly dried up. He had become silent and intense like a man confronted with an encounter he would have preferred not to have occurred at all.

'I've got some idea what you're on about, you know.'

Pen was engagingly cheerful.

'We're on the same side, I know that much. The defence of the oppressed and the exploited.'

He offered Cilydd his hand and grinned as it was taken.

'Dr Livingstone, I presume,' he said.

He was resolved to make Cilydd smile.

'You want to watch out for those wild bards,' he said. 'They're all in the pay of the oppressor. Flunkeys of the system. Imagine them all trooping inside that multi-millionaire's castle. It's obscene, man. That's what it is.'

Pen was grinning happily and John Cilydd was willing to be amused.

'How's old Val Gwyn then?'

Cilydd became silent with an intense effort of recall. What he had to say about Val Gwyn could hardly be condensed into a phrase about the state of his health. Bedwyr had begun to tug urgently at Amy's skirt. She bent down to hear.

'Mam, I want to pee-pee.'

'Oh, my little precious, of course you do.'

With sudden zeal she lifted him into her arms. Both men turned to watch their progress in the direction of the makeshift public conveniences. Pen addressed Cilydd with open-ended benevolence.

'Bards being difficult then?'

Cilydd forced himself to attempt a more objective appraisal of his untidy withdrawal from the symposium on the role of the poet in the modern world.

'Not bards,' he said. 'Big-wigs. Self-important local big-wigs.'

Pen made an amiable attempt at empathy.

'People don't listen, do they?' he said. 'And they don't read either. They just skim over the pages. Like seagulls on the water. They never take it in.'

Cilydd was grateful for a view with which he could feel complete agreement.

'In my opinion you have to work at reading,' Pen said. 'Just like anything else worth doing. Especially what I call philosophical bits. Now I reckon that's one of the many weaknesses of an educational system under capitalism. It doesn't teach people to read properly. Do you know what I mean? To read *into* something, not just skim over the surface.'

'I'm sure that's true,' Cilydd said.

Pen winked mischievously and moved closer to take Cilydd much further into his confidence.

'I tell you what we've been thinking of doing,' he said. 'Dressing up as bards to infiltrate that Yankee's castle. And then kidnap the bugger. Hold him to ransom for forty-eight hours.'

Cilydd was shaking his head.

'Think of the headlines! "Unemployed miners invade multi-millionaire's castle. Ageing American magnate held to ransom." That sort of thing. You can't get anywhere these days you know without publicity stunts. In a capitalist press that's all they take notice of. Otherwise we don't exist, do we? We can march up and down the valleys until our boots wear out and they don't give it half a line. No better than sheep we are to them, roaming the streets without a name or a number. Until the next war comes along and then they'll start calling us the best cannon fodder in the world.'

Pen was greatly warmed by the way Cilydd was ready to agree with him. He was about to say more when a surge of eisteddfod visitors separated them and drove them off the duck-board. Cilydd had to raise his voice.

'He won't be there,' he said.

Pen could not hear what he was saying. When they were re-united he held on to Cilydd's left arm.

'What?'

'I said the millionaire won't be there,' Cilydd said. 'He's cleared out. Gone to Baden-Baden.'

Pen was only momentarily put out.

'Oh well,' he said. 'It was just an idea. You've got to have ideas all the time. Otherwise you go under.'

Once again they were in total agreement.

'The imagination,' Cilydd said.

'That's it exactly! But anchored in Reality. Rooted in History. Historical Necessity. That sort of thing. I used to talk to old Val about it. Very nice chap. But a bit fixated on his own idiosyncratic version of history. I used to try to get him to see the Marxist point of view. Uphill work I can tell you. Maybe because he wasn't a well man to begin with. I've got a feeling you and I could see more eye to eye. Do you know what I mean?'

Pen had to interrupt the flow to acknowledge that Amy and the little boy had found their way back. Amy spoke rapidly to Cilydd in Welsh.

'It's terribly tiring for a little boy to stand about in a place like this. If you're not going to speak we may as well get back to the hotel.'

Pen made an appreciative gesture towards Cilydd.

'I'm working hard on your husband, Mrs More,' he said. 'He's a revolutionary at heart, see. Just like me.'

Amy smiled briefly before looking down at Bedwyr and again addressing Cilydd in Welsh.

'He said he'd like a drink of egg and milk if that was convenient. Can you imagine such innate good manners. I tell you he restores my faith in the human race.'

'All-Welsh rule then, is it?' Pen said.

He spoke amiably enough. Amy quickly apologised.

'I'm sorry,' she said. 'I forgot you didn't understand.'

'There you are, you see. Proves my point, doesn't it? You bring the eisteddfod all the way down here and then you make us feel left out.'

Amy had begun to lead Bedwyr towards the nearest exit from the eisteddfod field. Pen stayed with them and Cilydd was happy to pay him particular attention.

'We feel left out, see,' Pen said. 'No two ways about it. It's as if nobody cares about us. Not even our own kind.'

'It's your heritage just as much as ours,' Cilydd said. 'And I'll say something else. The language is there for the learning.'

'Ah, but is it now? Is it?'

They stood confronting each other on an island of railway sleepers laid out in front of an exit turnstile. Pen was in the mood for debate. Cilydd's notes for the meeting in the Literature Tent lay in his inside pocket, all unused.

'You can't force it down people's throats, see,' Pen said. 'You've got to remember we have a large immigrant population. And why? Solely for economic reasons. Economics come before culture, see. Every time. And more important than that, economics create culture. You've got to hold these elements in proper perspective, see.'

Cilydd raised his hand.

'Language is a living force,' he said. 'It's a shaping agency just as much as economics or politics. That's all I'm saying really. And if you possess average intelligence why not set about learning it?'

Pen laughed with the heartiness of a man determined not to take offence.

'There you are,' Amy said.

She was ready to bring the argument to an end.

'I think we really ought to go,' she said. 'It's quite a way. Bedwyr will be hungry before we get there.'

'Look, I've got to say something!'

Pen looked Cilydd directly in the eye. He had become deeply serious. Amy moved closer to Bedwyr as if he would afford her some protection. The child's pretty head was tilted to one side, his eyes almost closed against the sunlight as he waited to see what the unpredictable stranger would do next.

'We've got to collaborate,' Pen said. 'On the widest possible front. And I'll tell you why. And I'll tell you in plain English. The Fascist tide is rising hour by hour. Now if Fascism gets control of the machinery of State in this country, it will scatter your Labour Party and your Trade Unions like chaff before the wind.'

The force of his conviction compelled them to listen intently.

'And a thing like this.'

Pen waved contemptuously at the eisteddfod field.

'They'd just blow it away. Or turn it into a crypto-Fascist circus. And from what you are saying, that wouldn't be difficult. Do you know there are at least two members of the present government in London who are known sympathisers with Adolf Hitler and that English clown Oswald Mosley.'

Amy was disturbed by the troubled look on her husband's face. She spoke as though to awaken him from a bad dream.

'Rumours like that fly about every day of the week,' she said. 'The penny press lives on them. Scares and rumours.'

Her intervention irritated Pen. He could not be bothered to refute Amy's argument or listen to any recital from her of received wisdom. His voice took on the harshness of a pithead orator and he pointed ominously at Bedwyr.

'You are bringing this kid up in a world where all the nation states are busy turning themselves into war machines. And more than half those machines, more than half, are already controlled by Fascists. Don't forget that.'

When he saw his message had struck home, his mood changed. With a warm smile he offered Cilydd his hand again.

'I don't dabble in politics, see,' he said. 'I live and breathe 'em. Now shall we discuss how we can best help each other? How about it?'

Cilydd nodded willingly.

'Of course,' he said. 'Any time.'

'That's good enough for me. We'll keep in touch. Collaboration and trust. "To arrive at a better state, forged by the actions of free men".'

He walked away, whistling, with his hands in his pockets.

'He's an impressive man,' Cilydd said.

'He's growing up,' Amy said. 'I suppose we could say that much for him.'

She knelt down to make superfluous adjustments to Bedwyr's tunic and trousers. They passed through the turnstiles. A steward offered to rubber-stamp the backs of their hands in case they should wish to return. He made a brief demonstration on the back of his own hand for Bedwyr's benefit. The little boy was fascinated by the purple lettering on the man's skin.

'You don't seem to like him very much,' Cilydd said.

They made their way to the field where the cars were parked, picking their way through pot-holes still filled with water.

'He's the kind of man who makes use of people,' Amy said.

Cilydd considered her verdict in silence. He lifted his son to make their progress easier.

'He made use of Val as much as he could. In some ways he's quite ruthless.'

'But he can be charming?'

He listened carefully for her answer.

'Oh yes,' Amy said. 'I suppose that's true enough.'

14

Lucas Parry spat masterfully into the fire. The tobacco juice sizzled in the flames. There were no women about and he was able to display complete independence of body and spirit before the visitors he could see in the mantelpiece mirror as he struggled with his starched collar and black tie.

'My mother's father was drowned in the pit,' he said. 'And two of her brothers. Fourteen and twelve years old respectively.'

He paid particular attention to Pen Lewis's reflection in the mirror. Pen wore a khaki shirt and a red tie. His arms were folded as he leaned nonchalantly against the Welsh dresser. John Cilydd stood alongside him, nursing his hat in both hands. He was formally dressed in a dark suit and could have been representing a client in a magistrate's court. Their only response to Lucas was respectful silence. It encouraged him to continue. His harsh voice reverberated in the confines of his terrace house.

'Quarryman myself, of course,' he said. 'Granite not slate. Until I earned this limp. No compensation worth mentioning. All I got was a lifetime's disablement. I wonder if you've ever read *The Industrial Revolution in North Wales*, Mr Lewis? It's by A. H. Dodd.'

'Pen,' Pen Lewis said. 'Just call me Pen.'

'It's not written from the worker's point of view, of course,' Lucas Parry said. 'Very few of these academic studies are. But it has some very good things in it, fair play to him.'

He could not be certain Pen was listening. The man's eyes were shifting about as he took unusual interest in his surroundings. The furniture was much too big for the room. A photograph of Amy in her graduation cap and gown was balanced precariously on the end of the crowded mantelpiece. Behind Lucas's high-backed fireside chair, which looked reserved for his exclusive use even when he was not in it, a moon-faced grandfather clock ticked away with stolid regularity as though it enjoyed in perpetuity the right to register the passage of time. The measured pulse was in marked contrast to the irregular grind of traffic passing the front door. The row of labourers' cottages, like the grandfather clock, was a relic of an earlier epoch before Llanelw had burgeoned into a seaside resort.

'This little county is very rich in minerals.'

Lucas was determined to hold their attention.

'I'd go further than that,' he said. 'I could quote you the very words of old Pulford, the original Pulford I mean of course. He

144

used to call the Flintshire miner the most skilled operator of his kind in the world. As far as any form of extraction was concerned. And he had facts and figures to prove it. Relating the hourly pay to profit on a range of minerals. Very interesting to people with any intelligence. Do you know . . .'

Lucas shifted about in the confined space. His raised elbow narrowly missed toppling Amy's photograph frame.

'Pant Pwll Dwr, a small mine mark you, enriched its proprietors by more than one million pounds sterling in twenty years. One million!'

His sallow features froze briefly in a cast of rhetorical indignation. Then they relaxed to display a row of discoloured false teeth.

'I picked that up in the Carnegie Library,' he said. 'At least four months ago.'

'Too small.'

Pen spoke decisively.

'Too small. That's the trouble.'

Both Cilydd and Lucas Parry gazed at him enquiringly, uncertain what he was referring to.

'There is a whole range of extractive industry,' Lucas said. 'And most of the labour is unionised. I can testify to that.'

Pen picked up his khaki haversack, ready to be off.

'The coalfield,' he said. 'The coalfield hereabouts. Too small. That's what I'm saying.'

'I don't follow.'

Lucas would have deemed it impolite to disagree openly with a guest, however temporary, under his own roof.

'I found them tame, to tell you the truth,' Pen said. 'No idea about Lodge politics. Lacking in basic cohesion. No backbone if you want my honest opinion!'

Lucas Parry's face lit up.

'There's a reason for that,' he said. 'And I can give it you in two words. Calvinistic Methodism. Now there you have the key to their condition. The dominant denomination in the locality. And I speak as a dissenting lay-preacher myself. Not much in demand these days but still on the list. Now Calvinistic Methodism in this part of

145

the world has a middle-class outlook because it is governed by a middle-class presbytery. And you remember what the poet Milton said, "New Presbyter is but old Priest writ large".'

Lucas enjoyed displaying the fruits of his learning to younger men who might not have been aware of its range. He reached out modestly for his bowler hat and overcoat on Esther Parry's upright chair. It was also necessary to hoist in place a fireguard before he went out.

'Masses,' Pen said broodingly. 'It's all we've got. To face a government controlled by capitalists and crypto-fascists and the armed might of the State. The masses. And the spearhead is the Unemployed Movement. The workers on the march. From all points of the compass, until we drown the buggers. You can't drown anything with a bloody dripping tap.'

His sudden bellow of laughter seemed indecently loud in their cramped surroundings. He saw the expression of distaste on Lucas's face and clapped his hand over his mouth. He called himself to order.

'Sorry comrade,' Pen said. 'Too much sense of humour. That's my downfall. In fact I'll let you into a secret. The comrades are not too impressed with old Pen's discipline. Puritanical lot. If I didn't have a bit of the gift of the gab, they would have turfed me out a long time ago.'

He winked at them both in turn and placed a finger to his mouth.

'Mum's the word,' he said. 'I'm not criticising anybody. Salt of the earth, the comrades. One and all. I wouldn't swap them for a maharajah's harem. Well now then, comrade More. What's the quickest way to the station?'

He was amused by the look of consternation on Cilydd's face.

'What about the meeting?' Cilydd said.

Lucas Parry bent to look out through the gap in the lace curtains.

'Raining,' he said. 'I'm afraid it's raining.'

'A little rain shouldn't put people off,' Pen said. 'They should be fired by their convictions. That should keep them warm. I can tell you when we marched from Aberdare you could see them coming down the hillsides to join the main stream of the march. Rain pissing down and they kept on coming in their hundreds. No talk of food or shelter. On the march. There wasn't a police force in the country that could stop them.'

There was no room for Lucas to pass between the other two and the table in order to open the street door. With a lordly gesture he invited Cilydd to open it on his behalf. Cilydd hesitated. He touched Pen's arm.

'Tasker will be terribly disappointed,' he said. 'He sees you as a fraternal delegate from South Wales. This is a big meeting for World Peace. It's the biggest effort they've made in this part of the world for years.'

'Just tell him his tame Communist has escaped.'

Pen was determined to be jovial. He squinted at the weather in the streets.

'Spot of rain never did anybody any harm. Ten degrees under at the Lenin School today, I shouldn't wonder. Centigrade, mark you. None of that fahrenheit nonsense.'

'Where will you go?'

Cilydd was plainly concerned for Pen's welfare.

'Don't you worry, boy. I spend half my life in railway station waiting-rooms. It feels like that sometimes.'

'I'll come with you.'

Pen smiled at the sound of Cilydd's impulsive offer. Lucas Parry was disturbed.

'They'll be expecting us, John Cilydd,' he said. 'Amy and Esther and Miss Prydderch. They'll be waiting. Professor Gwilym will be there too. I understand his wife is not well enough to attend.'

He turned to address Pen more forcefully.

'Mr Lewis,' he said. 'This is an important meeting. This is an example of United Front. That's what you want, isn't it? If I understand you correctly? Peace is the vital issue.'

Pen took his time to answer. He raised his fist in a gesture of resolve.

'All these capitalist governments spending every penny they've got on armaments. Right?'

Lucas nodded understandingly.

147

'For what? For bloody mass slaughter, that's for what. And who'll be the first ones to catch it?'

Pen tapped his own chest.

'The workers. The poor bloody workers. And while the storehouses of the world are full to overflowing, famine and hunger are on the march. And who are the starving? Who are the hungry?'

He tapped his chest again.

'The poor bloody workers. And what can stop it? Not a dripping tap, comrade, I can tell you that much. Only the mass might of the international working class on the march. Now which way is the station?'

'I'll take you in the car.'

Cilydd spoke as though his mind had been made up to accompany Pen.

'Where do you want to go?'

Lucas Parry had not finished.

'Now listen a minute,' he said. 'Surely peace means peace. Doing away with war as an instrument of policy. Stopping the Arms Race. Suppressing the armaments industry. Beating swords into ploughshares and so on.'

Pen looked at him pityingly.

'Bourgeois pacifism,' he said. 'Look comrade, I haven't got time to argue. You read J. Stalin's Report to the Seventeenth Congress. It's all down there in black and white and plain English. "Bourgeois pacifism is living its last hours", man. Expiring like a stranded whale on the beach of history.'

He turned to Cilydd.

'Okay,' he said. 'You can give me a lift to the station. Then you can come back and take our friend here to the meeting. I wouldn't want to get you into trouble with the ladies.'

Lucas Parry stood in the small doorway of his house, staring alternately at the rain-laden clouds and the mysterious figure in the car. Pen sat in the passenger seat, nursing his khaki haversack, huddled snugly inside his long overcoat. He lifted his hand as the car moved off in a long awaited signal of farewell to which Lucas responded with great animation.

'So that's where your missus was brought up.'

Pen murmured the comment as if he were thinking aloud. Cilydd seemed not to have heard him. He was concentrating on driving through the wet streets. There were many crossings, no settled priority and few policemen on point duty. The shops were already lit up and the wet pavements shone with reflected light. Late shoppers scrambled across the streets with their heads down, darting from one shop to another. More than once Cilydd was obliged to brake suddenly to allow women burdened with parcels to pass the bonnet of his car.

'Funny dream I had last night,' Pen said. 'Women in high-heeled shoes and men in bowler hats dancing between the trenches. And all the bullets passing between their legs.'

He could see how hard Cilydd was straining to catch any words he might choose to utter and at the same time drive with proper care. He shook with quiet laughter inside his overcoat.

A paper seller stood under the wooden canopy at the entrance to the railway station. He was barely five foot tall and the great bundle of papers under his arm appeared to be on the point of dropping one after the other on to the wet cobbles. The little man called out his wares in a falsetto that easily pierced the noise of traffic. Then his face tilted upwards and he yawned like a cat. Cilydd held out a threepenny bit. With no other customer in view the little man took his time to find the change. Cilydd presented Pen with the newspaper.

'I know it's rubbish,' he said apologetically. 'Just something to read on the train.'

The paper seller overhead him.

'Rubbish,' he said. 'I don't sell rubbish. What you've got there is good value for money.'

He shouted the word 'Echo' with renewed vigour as they left him.

'I'll get the ticket,' Cilydd said. 'Where do you want to go?'

Pen laughed good-humouredly.

'One way. South.'

Cilydd was reluctant to leave him. On the draughty platform they made their way to the station buffet. The sight of pies and sandwiches displayed under glass domes was enough to make Pen hungry. They occupied a tile-topped table next to the grimy window that gave a view of interminable railway tracks. A porter lugged a train of empty luggage trolleys across a deserted platform. The iron wheels rumbled like a protracted warning. The noise stopped as arbitrarily as it had started. Being inside looking out as he munched his way through two pork pies seemed enough to keep Pen wholly contented. Cilydd was sipping hot tea with some caution. Pen grinned as he saw the worried look on Cilydd's face.

'Tight little thing, the family,' he said.

Cilydd's eyebrows raised in a mute plea for further enlightenment.

'Nothing personal,' Pen said. 'But when it's tied in with bourgeois individualism, the knot is very tight. Very tight indeed. If I had the brains I wouldn't mind writing something about it.'

'What about your family?'

Cilydd asked the question with polite diffidence.

'Minimal.'

Pen lit a cigarette and inhaled deeply.

'Just as well. I've got a room in my sister's house. She can't make her mind up whether to be proud of me or be ashamed of me. It's quite laughable really. Depends on the tide in the affairs of men as it happens to lap around the doorsteps of Trealaw Street. She hates it when I'm carted off to prison. My brother-in-law is a bit like your father-in-law. Or is he your uncle-in-law? Didn't they bring up Amy? Him and his wife?'

Cilydd nodded.

'Well they made a decent job of it. She's a top-class woman.'

Pen drew on his cigarette.

'You'd better be getting back to them,' he said. 'Or they'll be mad at you too.'

Cilydd pressed forward against the table to show his overriding concern was for Pen.

'Where will you sleep tonight?' he said.

Pen appeared to have given no thought at all to the question.

'If I get down at Wrexham, I'll doss down in Rhos,' he said. 'Couple of comrades there will put me up anytime. You don't need to worry. It's not a bad old life, you know, working for the Party and the Unemployed Movement. At least you feel you're doing something. Helping history along. Giving it a bit of a shove here and there.'

He pointed at the clock behind the counter that had the black letters LMS stamped on its white face.

'You'd better get moving. I'll be fine in here with this evening rag and a packet of fags.'

Cilydd stood up, one hand in his pocket.

'Will you take a pound note, Pen?' he said. 'As a contribution to your expenses.'

Pen took his time to consider the offer.

'Aye,' he said. 'All right then.'

Cilydd was eager to commit himself further.

'Listen,' he said. 'If you think there's anything I can do, as a lawyer or whatever, don't hesitate to let me know.'

Pen looked pleased.

'I might take you up on that, comrade.'

He spoke light-heartedly. Cilydd became more intense than ever.

'When I see the way things are going, it makes me want to help,' he said. 'Send for me if you need me.'

Pen raised his thumb approvingly before they shook hands.

'It's worth thinking about quite seriously,' he said. 'We need lawyers at this stage of the struggle. We need every lawyer we can get.'

15

THE HONOURABLE EIRWEN OWENS WAS NOT ACCUSTOMED TO wearing a hat for prolonged periods of time or to carrying a bouquet of long-stemmed red roses. She looked around in the new hospital corridor echoing with people's voices and when she saw Amy moving towards her, her pale face grimaced involuntarily before she smiled. Her hip was giving her pain. She had no stick and she needed support. With barely a word spoken, Amy relieved her of the bouquet so that she could lean heavily on her arm. Having Amy so close to her restored Miss Eirwen's flagging spirits.

'It's all very splendid. But a trifle wearing.'

She gripped Amy's arm tightly.

'Everyone is so grateful,' Amy said. 'They know that without your help all this would never have been possible.'

Miss Eirwen stared at Amy with melancholy intensity.

'I was thinking,' she said. 'It must be five years since you first came to Plas Iscoed. Or even longer. You were only a girl then. Ready to challenge the world of course. Do you know I was quite frightened of you.'

It was a public occasion and it was appropriate that they should smile together. Miss Eirwen was protected from her own shyness. She could speak more freely, perhaps, than if they had been completely alone. Opening the new hospital was an occasion for general rejoicing. They stood back to read a brass plaque above the mahogany frame of partition doors. The words 'Enid Prydderch More Ward' were etched in bold capitals. An ecstatic voice behind them obliged them both to turn around.

'The fulfilment of a dream! What else can one call it?'

Sali Prydderch clasped and unclasped her hands and lifted them towards the plaque. Her large eyes were brimming with tears.

'A children's ward. How appropriate. How utterly appropriate. "Even here, virtue hath her rewards and mortality her tears".'

Miss Eirwen was mildly embarrassed by the quotation. She could only assume Miss Prydderch was expressing some personal form of gratitude. She nodded graciously and gave a smile of muted approval.

'And the name "Prydderch" left in,' Sali said. 'I'm so pleased about that. Not just for myself I may add. More for other members of dear Enid's family not able to be present. Absent friends should we call them?'

The question was addressed to Amy. It was sufficient to allow her to attach herself to Amy and Miss Eirwen for an informal inspection of the ward. The three nurses, with starched cuffs, collar and caps, had already disposed themselves alongside empty beds somewhat in the manner of shop assistants waiting for opening time. The most senior approached Miss Eirwen ready to make smiling response to any question. Miss Eirwen had little to say as she limped forward leaning on Amy's arm. Sali Prydderch followed close behind them in the manner of a lady-in-waiting whose stylish clothes outshone the dowdy correctness of the Honourable Eirwen.

There were twelve iron bedsteads with white sheets and red blankets evenly spaced out, six on either side of the long well-lit and well-ventilated room. The walls were tiled in brown as far as the window ledges and the rest distempered green. Essential furniture was parked in a single line from the elaborated fireplace to the partition doors. A rocking horse and a model castle established that the ward was intended for children. Sali Prydderch paused to admire a large bowl of cut flowers. The senior nurse was glad to explain how flowers would be removed overnight but returned during the day to make the place more cheerful. She pointed out the larger lockers for the long-term patients who would have day clothes to wear and be encouraged to move about.

Miss Eirwen was drawn to a large coloured reproduction of Holman Hunt's *The Light of the World* hung over the empty fireplace. She pretended to look at it as she talked to Amy.

'I was so looking forward to meeting your husband,' she said.

'He should have been here,' Amy said.

She turned around as though she expected Cilydd to appear at any moment.

'I imagine he's shy,' Eirwen said. 'I just wonder whether he disapproves of us. My brother and me. Coal-owners and that sort of thing.'

She paused so that Amy could react to such a frank appraisal of a situation they both needed to confront. Amy was embarrassed.

'He should be here,' was all she could say.

'He didn't want the Garden Cottage,' Miss Eirwen said.

'He takes his legal practice so seriously.'

Amy was over-anxious to explain.

'He wants to build it up. And of course he is interested in social legislation and industrial relations and that sort of thing. That's why he's not here now. There was a case in South Wales he had to attend to. He rushes around so much. He hardly has any time at all for poetry these days. You could almost say he's given it up. He makes jokes about it. "The Muse doesn't live here any more", and that sort of thing. So I expect he thinks it would be a mistake to sit in the Garden Cottage all day and wait for the Muse to visit him.'

Amy placed her fingers against her burning cheek. Miss Eirwen smiled at her consolingly.

'At any rate you and I can discuss these things calmly together,' she said. 'It is distressing. Terribly distressing. And I don't think all these amalgamations have helped. They just widen the gulf between master and men in the most inhuman way. Mind you it was never easy in the coalfield. I'm the last one to agree with Sir Prosser P. on anything, but he was born down there and he insists that in spite of the chapels and the choirs and all the social props and so on, primitive barbaric instincts are only just below the surface.'

Amy was frowning at the closed door in the reproduction of Holman Hunt. The brambles and the ivy suggested it would never open and the expression on the face of the man wearing the crown of thorns was irredeemably gloomy.

'They're just below the surface everywhere,' Amy said.

She spoke casually enough but the remark was sufficient to reduce Miss Eirwen to uncomfortable silence. Tasker Thomas had appeared in the entrance to the ward and he was waving both hands to gain their attention. In honour of the occasion he was wearing a clerical collar and a perfectly pressed grey suit. He was restless with pleasure and responsibility. He waved also to Sali Prydderch and the senior nurse and made them understand that the Honourable Eirwen Owens was the object of his particular concern. As he waited for her he tugged a briar pipe out of his pocket and fingered it for some obscure form of talismanic reassurance. When Eirwen was close enough to address he pushed it back urgently into his pocket. He took half a step backwards before he spoke.

'I don't want to rush you, dear lady,' he said. 'But the photographer is waiting. And there's a place reserved for you, Eirwen. Next to your brother, David. Our two chief benefactors,

Lord Iscoed and his most excellent sister, the Honourable Eirwen Owens. This is an occasion when titles really mean something, if they ever mean anything at all.'

She barely smiled. Tasker steeled himself to remain cheerful. He veered about, glancing at his watch, shifting to the corridor window to squint up at the high cloud and blue sky and then reassembling himself in the position of escort and making an effort at self-restraint as though recalling some vestigial memory of her disapproval of his innate exuberance.

'Amy can tell you, my dear Eirwen, what a glorious day this is for our little community. And what a key role you have played in the achievement. The mere example of your generosity has brought the opposing factions of this town together. They are all here today to honour you. And this photograph, you see, will be a record of the triumph for posterity.'

He was encouraged by Amy's smile and her sympathetic attitude. He wanted to reach out and grasp them both but a gesture of shaking invisible arms had to suffice. He beamed at them and his voice boomed benevolently in the corridor as they made their way to the staircase. Sali Prydderch followed at a respectful distance, well able to hear and approve of everything Tasker was saying.

'It is consoling you know,' he said. 'And reviving. It should go without saying and yet it has to be said. Humanity can always learn when the right example is set. We can improve our minds and our actions, step by step. We are capable of learning the inestimable benefits of co-operation.'

Miss Eirwen raised a feeble hand to protect herself from the sound of his voice and his waves of enthusiasm. She muttered her protest.

'If there's one thing I can't bear, it's having my photograph taken.'

With childlike glee Tasker translated her reticence into exemplary modesty.

'I know, I know,' he said. 'You do good by stealth and that's always been your way. I've always admired your quietness – no, I mean quietude in the spiritual sense – being such a noisy chap myself. But this time you would be doing a special grace by appearing in person. And setting a seal, we can hope, we can hope, on a new era of co-operation and goodwill.'

The chairs had already been set in two rows in front of the pillared portico. The photographer's long chin jerked spasmodically in and out of his butterfly collar as he shifted his heavy tripod about in the search for the most telling point of view to adopt. Lord Iscoed was already seated in the central chair. His protruding eyes and bristling black moustache were also in motion as he made a detailed scan of the proceedings. The movement of an eyebrow approved or disapproved of the positions the assembling dignitaries were adopting and they seemed to accept his authority without question: except for his sister.

'Do you think Amy, Mrs More, could sit next to me? Or at least stand behind me?'

When Amy gently released his sister's arm and showed a determination to withdraw, Lord Iscoed's long teeth appeared beneath his moustache in a brief smile of approval. Then he began to concentrate on settling an expression on his face that would reflect his dedication to public benefaction. The aged Alderman Llew sitting on his right looked subdued but still aggrieved from a sense of insufficient attention. His old adversary in Liberal counsels, 'Doctor DSO', seated somewhere to the Honourable Eirwen's right, was quite capable of taking too much credit even in the fraction of a second the official opening was being recorded for posterity.

The guests and the ad hoc choir under H. M. Meredith's direction were waiting with subdued impatience for the photography to be completed. Refreshments were laid out in the dining-room of the new Cottage Hospital. Amy was concerned to see that Tasker Thomas was not left out of the main photograph. She acknowledged a brief greeting from Cilydd's Uncle Gwilym and his nervous wife before putting her hand in the small of Tasker's back and pushing him forward. He became self-conscious and laughed so loudly that Lord Iscoed's frown directed him to a marginal position on the edge of the back row. Amy withdrew to a safe distance. She was startled when Eddie Meredith came up behind her. He was wearing crêpe-soled shoes and carrying his own Kodak camera.

'Where's the poet?' he said. 'Our National Winner. The least he could do would be to write an ode to celebrate this auspicious occasion.'

She was reluctant to answer him.

'The funeral of the hatchet,' Eddie said. 'Quite an impressive subject. And a happy ending, that's always important.'

He pointed his Kodak and studied the scene through the cube-shaped viewfinder.

'I've taken one or two of old Tasker,' he said. 'All by himself on the steps. Doesn't he look positively elegant?'

'He should be sitting right in the middle,' Amy said. 'But for him, this would never have happened. It's time people realised that.'

'I agree. I agree.'

Eddie was anxious to please her. He was encouraged by a faint smile on her face.

'What happened to your famous film?' she said.

He was not put out by her question. He waved a free hand as he lined up a picture that would show the photographer at work.

'It fell through. That's how it is in the film business. Everything seems to be taking shape and then suddenly the bubble bursts. Usually lack of finance.'

Amy had turned to watch a drift of cloud dragging its shadow across the dark blue waters of the bay. Sunlight glittered on the walls of a ruined castle on a rock that stood between the mountain range to the east and the great expanse of water.

'Just how rich are they?'

Amy observed him with scientific calm. She could have been studying the metamorphosis of a tadpole into a frog. Merely the casual way his question slipped out proclaimed he had reached a stage of development when the genus spent time speculating on the extent of the wealth of more well-to-do specimens. Eddie was shifting backwards to frame her in the foreground of the view she had been looking at. The brass buttons of his double-breasted blazer flashed in the sun as he moved.

157

'They're both very rich, aren't they?' he said. 'And I hear he's prominent at Geneva. Big at the League, as they say. And what about her? Passionately devoted to the Arts. Do you think you could introduce me?'

'What on earth for?'

'She's devoted to you from all I hear.'

Amy blushed angrily. She saw the choir was assembling to be photographed. H. M. Meredith was waving in their direction.

'Your father is calling you,' Amy said.

Eddie raised a hand to restrain his father's impatience.

'There's a definite market for shorts,' he said. 'This document-ary business is going to make a lot of difference. A new trend. All it needs is reliable funding.'

'You mustn't keep your father waiting,' Amy said. 'Always remember, virtue is its own reward.'

Eddie stepped back and held out his arms like a player penalised, pleading his innocence before the referee.

'What have I done?' he said. 'Why should you . . .? What . . .?'

He broke off when he saw Miss Sali Prydderch was advancing decorously towards them to talk to Amy. He bowed briefly to her before hurrying off to carry out his father's orders and photograph the members of the choir.

'Amy! Isn't this a perfect site for a hospital! Just look at that view.'

Sali Prydderch made gestures of appreciation. Looking westward they could see the mouth of the harbour guarded by its own isolated outcrop of black rock. The centre of the town, almost two miles away, was hidden by the gorse-covered summit of a rounded hill. Under this hill the main road from the town wound up a narrow gorge which framed, in the furthest distance, a sunlit view in sharp outline of the last hotels and boarding houses at the west end of the promenade.

'I'm so happy about it all,' Sali Prydderch said. 'In such a strange way it was a thrill to see the children's ward named after dear Enid. I just wonder, is that why John Cilydd stayed away? He's such a sensitive person. Old memories. Old pain. Who can tell what goes on in a poet's mind?'

158

Her voice trailed off as she hesitated to become more explicit. She sighed deeply to fill the silence.

'It's the past,' she said. 'Always the past. And all the patterns it keeps on weaving inside our poor little heads. Constantly weaving.'

She moved closer to Amy, eager for some response.

'I'm so glad for Tasker,' she said. 'This is really his triumph. Over all obstacles. Don't you agree?'

Amy nodded.

'It's a stony path,' Sali Prydderch said. 'The path of reconciliation. Sometimes I think it can only lead to the Cross. Do you know what I mean? And yet, why should it? Why can't people learn to be reasonable?'

It was a question they both found impossible to answer.

'I imagine Eirwen Owens came instinctively to his rescue.'

Sali Prydderch was bent on uncovering an explanation for the success they were celebrating. She could see Amy's eyebrows were raised.

'Well they were engaged once, weren't they? We can't help detecting it, can we? The pattern of the past. One can muse over it for ever. Why are you smiling?'

'I was just thinking,' Amy said.

'Thinking what?'

'If we spend too much time musing over the past, we could get run over by the future when we're not looking.'

16

AT THE WHEEL OF THE BATTERED STANDARD SALOON, PEN LEWIS was singing. In the passenger seat Cilydd glanced nervously over his shoulder to reassure himself that the two vehicles behind still had them in sight. The stout man on the back seat was asleep. On his lap he nursed a polished leather attaché case on which his bowler hat lay in solemn state. He was dressed well enough to be on his way to a wedding and the expression on his plump pock-marked face suggested quiet content. His white hair was waved at oratorical length and black eyebrows above the closed lids were also visible platform assets.

'Nim asleep?'

Cilydd nodded.

'It's my voice, mun. Did I ever tell you I was a boy soprano?

> "And many a gilded tower
> And many a palace steep
> Shall crumble in that hour
> When Labour wa-hakes from sle-heep
> When Labour wakes from sleep!"'

Nimrod Thomas snorted briefly, sniffed and opened his eyes.

'Are we there then?'

He frowned at the unfamiliar landscape he saw through the side-window. The noise of the car's faulty exhaust startled two cart horses grazing near the road. They lumbered away through the gorse bushes towards the sand dunes.

'Are all the horses that big around here?'

He yawned and rubbed the end of his nose. Pen was in high spirits.

'This is the frozen north, Nim Tom,' he said. 'Only slate and sin left between you and the Pole. Better put your hat on!'

It was a serious mission and Nimrod Thomas could not allow himself to approve of Pen Lewis's levity. It was also difficult for him to twist his stout frame with any semblance of dignity to peer through the oval back window.

'Are the lads still with us?' he said.

'All present and correct,' Pen said. 'Will Hops has been sick on the side of the road three times. And Archie his butty got lost for quarter of an hour in Dolgelly. And there was trouble with the petrol pump on Ronnie's taxi. Otherwise we're okay, Mr Chairman.'

'This is a serious undertaking,' Nimrod said.

'Of course it is.'

'I shall require each man to sign for the half-crown he receives to cover the day's expenses the moment we arrive at our destination.'

He tapped the lid of his attaché case with a blunt forefinger.

'First thing,' he said.

'Right,' Pen said briskly. 'You're in charge Nim Tom. The Joint Lodge Chairman.'

'And don't you forget it.'

Nimrod Thomas relaxed a little. It had been necessary to make some demonstration of authority so that John Cilydd More fully understood the intricacies of their relationship. Cilydd craned his neck to look upwards on the landward side. He called out as soon as he caught a glimpse of the new hospital up on the hillside.

'There it is! Now take the first turning on your right.'

Pen slowed down so that the other two cars could catch up with him.

'Bit of an eyesore,' Cilydd said.

He seemed increasingly nervous.

'Best thing to do with a red brick monstrosity, built on a site like that. Convert it into a hospital. Best thing to do with it. At least those with a bed near a window will have a view.'

Pen chuckled as he watched the other two cars draw nearer in the driving mirror.

'Lads look as if they're having a high old time,' he said.

'This is a serious occasion,' Nim Thomas said sternly.

'Quite right, Nim Tom,' Pen said obediently.

The Chairman of the Joint Lodge Committee gave the hospital on the hill his critical attention.

'Very nice,' he said. 'But a bit small. You know there's nothing I would enjoy more than opening one of those myself. If it was a bit bigger.'

Pen slapped the palm of his hand on the steering wheel.

'By damn, Nim Tom, that's just what you will be doing come the Revolution! When the day of the working class dawns, that's what you'll be doing all day. Opening schools and hospitals, declaring this and that open and the missus alongside you collecting bouquets from pretty little girls.'

The other two cars drew up behind them and a delegate from each came forward to receive solemnly enunciated final instructions from Nimrod Thomas through the car window.

The shorter man was carrying a miner's safety lamp and he held it up as if he were searching for a path in the dark. Pen winked mischievously at Cilydd.

'Now then,' Nimrod said. 'This is a serious occasion, not a Sunday-School outing. And we are not picketing. Is that clearly understood. We are a deputation.'

He tapped his attaché case again.

'I have here a letter addressed to Lord Iscoed requesting the favour of a brief interview.'

'Where's the evidence then?'

The thin delegate's face was racked with suspicion. He drew his white muffler tighter around his neck until he was in danger of choking himself.

'We've got documentary evidence to prove that the scab Union and the Non-Pols are being subsidised on a weekly basis by Hendrerhys Colliery Company. A subsidiary of Amalgamated Holdings. And who's the Chairman of Amalgamated Holdings? Lord Iscoed. And the chief shareholder? His sister.'

He recited his litany close to Cilydd's face in order that his stranger in their midst should not be in doubt of his grasp of the issues involved.

'Now cool down, Will Hops,' Nimrod Thomas said.

Archie swung his symbolic lamp.

'We'll drag the bugger out, string him up and watch him swing in the wind.'

'Now listen to me,' Nimrod said. 'Mr John Cilydd More, who is a respected solicitor in this district and a national eisteddfod winner, will deliver this note of mine to his lordship. We'll do nothing to disturb their ceremonies up there. Only wait patiently by the gate.'

' "The rich man in his castle, the poor man at his gate".'

Archie was prepared to chant ironically.

'That's not a castle,' Nimrod said. 'That's a hospital. And we must respect it as such. All we are doing is requesting the favour of an interview. When we get it, we troop in there in an orderly fashion and put the case before him.'

'What if he says "No"?'

Will Hops grimaced as if his suspicions were giving him indigestion. Nimrod was slow to answer.

'So much the better,' Pen said. 'That will expose him for what he is. We seize the initiative. Be ready to turn the situation to our advantage as best we can. Let the dynamic of theory transform wild adventure into policy.'

Archie stared at Pen admiringly.

'Who said that?' he said.

Nimrod raised his fist.

'Decorum,' he said. 'That's what I want from each and every one of you. Perfect decorum. We are civilised working-class leaders. Not a bunch of wild Indians.'

The cars drove up the hill in noisy low gear. Pen was able to lean towards Cilydd and speak without being overheard by Nimrod.

'Nervous?'

Cilydd stared ahead gloomily.

'Not so much for me,' he said. 'It's the least I can do. People have just got to be made aware of what it's like down there.'

'Stop worrying, man,' Pen said. 'You worry too much. Live for the day and let the dialectic take care of history.'

'I don't think you should have come,' Cilydd said. 'You're still bound over to keep the peace. You could be had for contempt and goodness knows what. Look, if there's any trouble, which I certainly hope there won't be, you keep well out of sight.'

Pen's laugh rang out above the noise of the engine.

'Nothing to lose,' he said. 'Except my claims.'

The Standard bounced untidily on the grass verge outside the hospital gates. Pen could not resist a brief cheerful blast on the horn. The other two cars drawing up behind him responded.

'Now that's enough of that!' Nimrod Thomas said.

The men were stretching themselves with exaggerated movements to show how stiff they had become after the long journey. Pen gave a hand to help Nimrod out of the back of the car. It emerged he was wearing spats with his Sunday suit. Pen brushed his shoulders with the care of a valet and then reached in the car for his bowler and attaché case. In the drive Cilydd encountered Amy and Sali Prydderch. Sali smiled vacantly to demonstrate generalised goodwill. Her presence seemed to reinforce Cilydd's confidence in himself. He was ready to embrace his wife and apologised for his unusually dishevelled appearance.

'What on earth is all this?' Amy said.

'Such a collection of old crocks. I thought we'd never make it,' he said.

He seemed to expect Amy to respond with pleasure. Instead she stepped closer to sniff his breath.

'Where have you been?' she said. 'What's all this?'

Cilydd spread out his hands in a generous gesture.

'A deputation,' he said. 'What else?'

The men had formed up in a line outside the gate. Nimrod Thomas was preparing to advance towards them. He suffered from emphysema and his approach up the slope was slow.

'These are federation men,' Cilydd said. 'Don't be misled by their light-hearted manner. All that comes from courage in adversity. And comradeship of course. Steady comradeship.'

Sali Prydderch made an effort to share in a detached admiration for representatives of the mining community. Amy had caught sight of Pen Lewis. He raised a thumb in cheerful greeting.

'Whose idea was this?'

Amy spoke so sharply that Sali Prydderch turned away. In front of the pillared portico most of the leading citizens had moved away. Miss Eirwen was a lonely figure among the empty chairs. She waved diffidently when she saw that Sali had noticed her. Sali was resolved to be helpful.

'Amy,' she said. 'I'm sure Eirwen Owens is trying to gain your attention.'

Amy glanced quickly over her shoulder.

'She needs someone to lean on,' Amy said. 'Could you possibly lend her your arm for a moment? I'll be there as quickly as I can.'

She had little time to give vent to her anger, as she turned to Cilydd.

'Pen Lewis,' she said. 'I might have known. I suppose you realise he's making use of you.'

'Amy,' he said. 'It's so terrible down there. A whole people condemned. Our people.'

'You don't have to tell me.'

There was no time to say any more. She was confronted by Nimrod Thomas. His chubby fingers were already in the act of lifting his bowler hat. Cilydd was slow to introduce him. Pen Lewis took up a sideways stance to introduce the Joint Lodge Chairman to Amy.

'Mr Nimrod Thomas,' he said. 'Chairman of the Joint Lodges and of the Institute Committee. Rank and file member of the EC of the SWMF and so forth. To see Lord Iscoed, Chairman of Amalgamated Holdings. Nim, this is Mrs More, wife of our good comrade and fellow traveller on life's dusty road. Now Nim here is a fluent Welsh speaker, Mrs More.'

Nimrod smiled engagingly at Amy and offered her his hand. She was obliged to take it so that he could shake hers with prolonged cordiality.

'Your husband is a good man, Mrs More,' he said. 'He has taken up compensation cases other lawyers wouldn't look at. Including my own. With little success up to date. But that's no reason for not keeping on trying.'

The other members of the deputation were becoming restive outside the gates.

'Come on Nim Tom. Get on with it.'

He breathed heavily as he turned to administer a rebuke. Pen Lewis relieved him of the attaché case he was carrying and held it horizontally ready for Nim to open.

'We'll have none of that, Will Hops! We've got an excellent case and we're not going to spoil it by being unreasonable.'

'Open it then.'

Will Hops pointed at the attaché case. Some of the others echoed the word 'unreasonable' in imitative chorus. It was clearly a favourite expression with Nimrod. He took the teasing in good part.

'I apologise for the boys, Mrs More,' he said. 'They've not been out much lately. The fresh air has gone to their heads.'

The attaché case opened with a satisfying click. He extracted an envelope which he handed solemnly to Cilydd.

'If you would deliver this to Lord Iscoed . . . perhaps it would be

165

in order for me to sit on one of those chairs and do a bit of accounts.'

He held up a blue sack of coins and a note-book which each man would be required to sign in receipt of the daily allowance.

'I shall occupy myself until we are summoned. I shall wait patiently.'

Inside the building, Cilydd and Amy could hear the reverberation of animated chatter mingle with the clatter of plates in the Dining Hall where refreshments were being served. Amy attacked her husband in an agitated undertone.

'This is absolutely mad,' she said. 'You realise that don't you?'

'Don't worry, Amy. Everything will be all right. Nimrod is one of the most responsible and respected . . .'

'You're not responsible,' Amy said. 'Allowing yourself to be manipulated in this way. And what are the Prydderchs going to think? On this day of all days. On the very day a ward is named after poor Enid. You were conspicuous by your absence. You realise that?'

'We should have been here two hours ago,' Cilydd said. 'The petrol pump went on one of the cars.'

'It's Pen Lewis, making use of you. This Lodge Chairman or whatever he is, is only a front. It's the Communists behind this. Can't you see that?'

'Of course I can. But Communists can be right sometimes. In fact they are very often these days.'

His blithe manner irritated her so much, she could think of nothing else to say. Tasker Thomas had noticed their unobtrusive presence at the entrance to the Dining Hall. With his arms outstretched in welcome he was moving towards them. It gave Amy fresh ammunition.

'It will spoil everything for poor Tasker. You realise that. He'll get the blame. After all the work he's put into getting this place finished. Honestly, I could kill that Pen Lewis. And you are a fool to listen to him.'

'It was my idea,' Cilydd said.

He grinned at her as Tasker's large hands landed on his shoulders.

' "That which was lost is found".'

Tasker's enthusiasm was renewed by the sight of Cilydd.

'Eirwen is longing to meet you,' he said. ' "Where is he", she said, "this poet husband of Amy's? Where does he hide?" I think she's enjoying it all you know. In her heart of hearts. Shy person though she is. And so is David. Fair play to him, underneath that stern exterior, he's a man with a tender heart.'

Tasker spoke with the conviction of a man yearning to believe what he is saying.

'He's brought a deputation with him from Hendrerhys Collieries,' Amy said.

'Has he?'

Tasker looked astonished before looking pleased.

'Has he really?'

'You know Nimrod Thomas,' Cilydd said. 'He knows you. He's leading the deputation.'

Tasker demonstrated an infinite degree of pleasure by holding his mouth wide open.

'Old Nim! Where is he? Where is the dear old fellow? A man for binding the wounds if ever I saw one. You know, he and I . . .'

Tasker wriggled as he tried to condense what should have been a lengthy history.

'We managed to put a spoke into one of those proposed Government Labour Camps.'

He began to laugh as he attempted to imitate the bass rumble of Nimrod Thomas's voice.

' "This isn't Nazi Germany, my friend. We don't want no Labour Camps and we don't want no Blackleg Barracks".'

Amy became impatient.

'They are waiting outside,' she said. 'They want to speak to Lord Iscoed.'

It was only now the potential awkwardness of the situation seemed to dawn on Tasker. His jaw fell as he turned to ascertain the whereabouts of the coal-owner. He saw him engaged in private discussion with Alderman Llew who was attended by his closest supporters. Doctor DSO was also in the offing holding a plate and pushing crumbs of cake about with his finger-tips as he waited his

167

turn to gain his Lordship's ear. He could also see Miss Eirwen sitting somewhat apart gazing glumly into the middle distance as she gave ear to Sali Prydderch's attempt to sustain an interesting conversation.

'I have to hand him this letter,' Cilydd said.

'Yes. Yes, I see.'

Tasker stared at the cheap envelope and pondered the problem. Miss Eirwen caught sight of Amy. Her face lit up as she raised a limp hand to attract her attention. Amy had to introduce her husband. His reluctance to approach could be attributed to shyness. Miss Eirwen compelled herself to offer her hand so that he could shake it.

'I read your book of poems with great pleasure,' she said. 'It was so kind of Amy to send me a copy.'

The effort of sustaining such a public compliment made her blush. She looked down at her feet. Her voice became barely audible.

'My Welsh isn't as good as it should be,' she said. 'But I made the effort. I could see there was much artistry involved. Technique perhaps is the word. I always admire technique.'

Tasker leaned forward eagerly to catch her words. When it was clear she had completed her statement he patted Cilydd cordially on the back.

'There you are,' Tasker said. 'A poet always has his audience. Silent, scattered but discriminating.'

He closed his eyes and prepared to recite.

'The hawk descends
With burning eyes . . .'

Cilydd raised the letter.

'Would you excuse me,' he said. 'I have a letter for your brother.'

'David is over there.'

There was a note of relief in Miss Eirwen's voice. She was being surrounded with too much attention.

When Cilydd held the letter out, Lord Iscoed paused in his discourse to gaze at the envelope with intense suspicion. Alderman

168

Llew did not move as he watched Iscoed scan the contents. He stroked his small white beard and waited expectantly for his lordship's reaction.

'I can't possibly see him now,' Lord Iscoed said.

His protruding eyes glared at Cilydd.

'Them,' Cilydd said.

'Them, even more so,' Lord Iscoed said. 'Out of the question. Utterly ridiculous.'

People near them had stopped talking to listen. The silence grew. From quite different directions, Eddie Meredith and his father H. M. Meredith, became aware of it. Both began to shift as unobtrusively as they could toward the heart of the encounter.

'They are outside,' Cilydd said. 'Waiting.'

Lord Iscoed's inclination was clearly to dismiss him. Banish him from his presence. Cilydd's face was very pale, but he stood his ground.

'Outside? Here?'

Cilydd nodded. Tasker Thomas transferred himself from paying attention to Miss Eirwen to stand at Cilydd's side. He smiled at both parties to show how glad he would be to do anything he could to help.

'One can't possibly receive deputations from all and sundry at any time of the day or night,' Lord Iscoed said.

He raised his voice in a bid for sympathetic attention. Murmurs of approval came from both the Alderman and the doctor and their immediate supporters.

'There is a machinery that deals with such matters,' Lord Iscoed said. 'Constitutional machinery. Established by written agreements. Between owners and workforce. Capital and labour. Management and men. Or whatever you like to call it.'

Lord Iscoed was soothed by the support he was getting and by his own statesmanlike performance. He was able to smile and look around with the calm confidence of a victor in debate.

'Shall I tell them that?' Cilydd said.

'By all means.'

Lord Iscoed smiled again. To Tasker at least the smile suggested that here was a man strong enough to dispense benevolence with

169

justice. He was encouraged to speak. He took Cilydd by the shoulder and steered him closer to Lord Iscoed in order to participate in a more intimate exchange.

'It's old Nim,' Tasker said. 'You remember Nimrod Thomas, David? In his frock-coat. And the business about the widow's free coal in the autumn of 1926?'

Lord Iscoed glared at Tasker. He resented his intervention. At the same time he restrained himself and remained silent, conscious of their exposure to public scrutiny. Tasker began to whisper with the dedicated intensity of a trainer bringing his lips as close as possible to a champion's ear.

'You were splendid then, David. Over the widow's coal. Your magnanimity made a deep impression. It was all of a piece somehow with all your other good works. Why not have a brief word with old Nim? Nim by himself. He's come all this way. In the name of the "brotherhood of man".'

Lord Iscoed's eye movements suggested he was already engaged in making fresh projections and calculations.

'So that old Nim won't have to go back empty handed,' Tasker said. 'With absolutely nothing to report. Such a humiliation in the eyes of his fellows. Such a defeat for moderate leadership. With the extreme men always waiting their chance. Lurking there in the wings. Remember the verse about the children of this world and the children of light.'

Mention of the verse made Lord Iscoed frown. He refrained from comment. Instead he took out a small gold watch from his waistcoat pocket and consulted it as if it were a compass.

'Ten minutes,' he said. 'I'll give him ten minutes. You can tell him that. And no more. In the small consulting room. If the hospital authorities have no objection.'

Tasker squeezed Cilydd's shoulder. As they hurried towards the entrance they could hear the excited clatter break out behind them as the people in the Dining Hall became more widely aware of what was going on. Nimrod Thomas lumbered slowly to his feet. Tasker embraced him with enthusiasm and Nimrod took hold of his bowler hat to make sure it did not fall off.

'Nimrod Thomas,' Tasker said. 'Straight as steel.'

'And just as stiff,' Nimrod said.

'Fellow workers all.'

Tasker raised his free arm to greet the deputation with the phrase Nimrod himself always used.

'All right then.'

Pen Lewis stepped forward. He drew impatiently on his cigarette.

'What's the verdict? Let's hear it.'

'He's willing to see the chairman alone,' Cilydd said. 'For ten minutes.'

'Ten minutes.'

Members of the deputation repeated the phrase with increasing indignation.

'Good God! Ten minutes! It's a calculated insult. That's what it is, lads.'

'Look at the hypocrisy of it!'

Will Hops waved a fist at the hospital.

'The great philanthropist. The big League of Nations man! The apostle of peace among the nations, *myn uffern i*, and the rights of free speech and religious liberty. Pumping money into the Scab Union to undermine working-class unity and keep us miners down on starvation level. I'll tell you what we ought to do. Go in there and grab the bugger and hold him to ransom.'

'Now steady on Will,' Pen Lewis said. 'What we need from this, lads, more than anything else is maximum publicity. Right? We've got Jack here to take a few pictures, if he can, and to write a full report for the *Miners Monthly*, and the *Worker*, and any damn paper that will take it. So we behave like lambs, see? And get his bloody lordship to show himself in the worst possible light. Get it? We want the world to see his face when Nim presents him with the most damning collection of evidence that proves he's as guilty as hell.'

Pen put his hand under his chin.

'Right up to here. Pumping money into the Scabs' Union and lying to the Federation, time and time again.'

Pen turned to face Tasker Thomas.

'We want to see your pal Iscoed hung from his own gibbet and

171

twisting slowly in the breeze. And that's going to take a lot longer than ten minutes, Reverend Thomas.'

There was a pained expression on Tasker's face. He appealed to Nimrod.

'I wrote to Sir Prosser Pierce,' he said. 'About the use of inexperienced youth on the coal face. Deafened by the noise of the machines. And the roof cracking over their heads and so on. He's taking it up with the Home Office.'

'Prosser Pierce,' Pen Lewis said. 'There's another one in the pay of the owners. And your pal in there. Prosser Pierce and Iscoed are hand in glove.'

Tasker pressed his hands together, pleading with Pen and the stony-faced members of the deputation.

'We have to try,' he said. 'There must be goodwill.'

He pointed at the miner's lamps Will and Archie were carrying.

'You know . . . "better to light a candle than stand still cursing the dark".'

'Tonnage and yardage, man,' Pen Lewis said. 'That's what's in the dark. Wages and profits, see. It's the built-in conflict of the capitalist system. Your trouble is you've never learnt to understand economics. Now then, Nim, you show his lordship all the evidence. And take your time about it. As soon as they see their chance, the lads will come in and blockade the door. You'll have a lot more than ten minutes, so don't hurry. And Jack will be there with his Brownie. We'll have a few snaps with a bit of luck.'

Amy appeared suddenly in the doorway. Her eyes were screwed up against the bright light. She beckoned urgently to Cilydd. He was intent on listening to Pen and reluctant to move. She stood behind him and spoke fiercely in his ear.

'They've sent for the police,' she said.

At the sound of the word 'police' the men stopped talking and turned to listen to her.

'From Glaslyn and Pendraw. And the Alderman wants reinforcements from further afield. He says with these Communist monkeys from the South all you can expect is trouble.'

Nimrod Thomas's back straightened and he addressed Amy sternly.

172

'This is an official Joint Lodges Deputation. Union business. Customs and conditions. Black-leg labour. Management misdemeanours. Nothing to do with politics.'

Cautiously John Cilydd drew Amy and Pen Lewis to one side.

'You've got to get out of here,' Cilydd said to Pen.

Pen began to tick off the strength of their position on his fingers.

'It's all there,' he said. 'In Nim's little case. Copies of correspondence. Copies of Scab Union spy reports. Hotel bills. Thank you very much sir. It's all there! We've got him!'

'If you stay here they'll get you,' Cilydd said. 'That's the point. Bound over. And still on bail. You'll spoil the picture, Pen.'

'The publicity,' Pen said. 'We need every ounce of it.'

He looked at Amy ready to give her work to do.

'Couldn't you get somebody from the local papers?' he said. 'Who's in there altogether? Stuffing themselves on Pendraw pancakes?'

'If you are involved it will be the wrong kind of publicity,' Cilydd said. 'Moscow gold and hired agitator all over again. And apart from that do you want to go down for four or five months? That old lion in there is Chairman of the Bench. You let me handle this. I know this territory.'

Pen's lips were stretched in silent dissent. Cilydd was enjoying the exercise of authority.

'Amy, where have you left the car?'

'It's by the back entrance,' she said. 'Behind the kitchens.'

'Take this man and hide him somewhere. Glanrafon. No. Better Uncle Lloyd's house. Cae Golau. That will do.'

He hurried her up as she hesitated.

'Just walk straight through the building,' he said. 'Spirit him away.'

17

OUTSIDE THE BACK DOOR A SPARROW FLEW OVER A HEAP OF RUBBISH thrown out of the house. It perched momentarily on the edge of a mildewed boot without laces that must have belonged to

Cilydd's great-uncle. At the sound of Amy's approach, the sparrow's tail perked up. He gave her a sharp malevolent glance before taking off for the safety of the highest branches of a sycamore tree. Amy had changed into older clothes. She wore a straw hat and a brown apron in front of a yellow dress buttoned down the front. She carried a basket on her arm. The food in it was covered with a starched white napkin. She moved through the band of sunshine that fell across the dark scullery from the open door. She surveyed the dirt and the damp green walls with distaste and disapproval before she saw a piece of a cigarette packet on the wooden draining board. A note was written in indelible purple ink. She examined it closely. It read, 'Come into the garden, AM' with a large exclamation mark. Amy turned it over more than once as if some additional significance belonged to the soft cardboard itself and the way it had been flattened out when he licked the butt of indelible pencil before writing the message.

Without hurrying, she walked past the stable and coach-house under the row of sycamore trees that thrust out of the hedge at irregular intervals marking the wide but stony lane that led to the orchard and the walled kitchen garden. These lay in a sheltered hollow behind Cae Golau which tilted gently towards the south. Through the framed doorway Amy could see quite plainly the path Pen Lewis had taken through the high grass to the further end of the overgrown garden. She adjusted the basket on her arm as she hesitated to cross from the shade of the sycamores and the single-storey garden outhouse into an area so totally exposed to the sunlight. Weeds grew everywhere in such flowering profusion that they had taken on a beauty of their own. In the driest corner a colony of charlock had settled and its yellow blossom shone in competition with the richer gold of ragwort which had taken root in what used to be an asparagus bed. The quiet of the afternoon was alive with the insidious murmur of bees and insects. Just inside the garden door in the last area of shade, a rank growth of red poppies leaned out across the path. Pen had trodden on the lower blooms. They gave out an unpleasing narcotic smell that made Amy wrinkle up her nose. She stared with hypnotic stillness at the texture of a piece of sacking in the window of the outhouse next to the garden door. It had been stuffed into the broken pane several seasons ago and was bleached into a fragility that would crumble at a touch.

She trod carefully in Pen's footsteps. The earth was uneven and in places the grass grew higher than her waist. When her basket brushed against the dry heads of a dogsfoot a few seeds sprinkled on the white napkin covering the food. She stepped aside to avoid a dark patch of nettle before she caught her first glimpse of the man lying in the long grass with his hands behind his head and his eyes closed. He was so relaxed he appeared completely at one with the haphazard fecundity of the garden itself. His shirt was open to the waist so that the white strength of his body could bathe in the warm air. Among the fibrous roots of the grasses bent over by his long legs, ants were working, apparently not too disorientated by an alien presence. They went about their business with a minute urgency that reinforced his immobility. She watched them crawl over the rough material of his trouser leg, devoted to their labour, heedless of danger, bound together by an overriding concern for the perpetuation of their miniature brown race. Through the transparent wall of grass beyond Pen's black hair she could see the purple flower of an orchid in bloom.

'You've found time to change. That's good.'

The sound of his voice startled her. There was a smile of approval on his face although his eyes still appeared to be closed. He was too comfortable to move. No breeze of any consequence could reach his bare skin. Amy blushed as she became conscious of her pretty straw hat. Her legs were bare and her feet protected by sandals with wooden soles. She knelt down to spread the white napkin on the ground. For the first time he moved. He reached out in an attempt to touch her arm. The straw hat tilted back as she lowered her head to extract the beef sandwiches and the cake and place them with particular care on the white cloth. There was tea in a thermos flask, milk in a medicine bottle and sugar in a mustard tin.

'You should eat something,' Amy said. 'I'll go over to Glanrafon to see if there is any news.'

He sat up and began to attack the sandwiches with evident enjoyment. She allowed herself to glance at him eating when he surveyed their strange surroundings. Concentrating on maintaining a steady hand, she poured him a cup of tea. He accepted it while his mouth was still crammed full. He shaded his eyes to stare at her and deep dimples of contentment appeared in his cheeks.

'This is what paradise is like,' he said. 'Farm bread, farm butter. The sun shining on the weeds. Nobody working. Lovely.'

He had succeeded in making Amy smile.

'Come on now, Amy. Have something to eat.'

He took a particular pleasure in using her name. She shook her head slowly. He chewed steadily as he gazed about him through eyelids narrowed to protect his eyes from the naked light. High above the landscape, he watched a buzzard circle on a current of air, its heraldic black and white markings clearly visible against a blue firmament tinted with bright silver.

'Quartering,' Pen said. 'That's what he's doing. On the day shift. Looking for prey. And we take it as a symbol of freedom. Fair enough. Above ground as opposed to underground, isn't it? Last February we had a stay-down in Hendrerhys. Some of the lads were down there for over a week. Singing hymns in the dark and chasing rats.'

'Why did you come?'

Amy spoke in a low voice. She made their isolation in the deserted garden an invitation to speak the truth.

'It was his idea,' Pen said. 'Not mine. Hidden urges to dabble in higher strategy. He's a deep one, is your husband.'

Amy sank back on her heels. She stared at her fingers in her lap. In their bent immobility they were like unspoken questions.

'He's fascinated by me,' Pen said. 'By my life I mean. He wants to know everything about the life of the pit and about my life and about how the two are related. I go gabbling on and he listens to every damn little thing I say. "What are you doing?" I say to him. "Writing an epic poem about colliers or what?" "Why not," he says. "I could do worse." Talk like hell we do. Surprising what we've got in common.'

Pen grinned as he stuffed his mouth with another piece of cake.

'We swop bourgeois guilt complexes for proletarian wisdom,' Pen said. 'Homespun varieties. Fair exchange.'

176

He stopped speaking long enough for them both to become conscious of the small world that immediately surrounded them. They watched the ants working. With a stem of grass Pen became momentarily absorbed in trying to divert their path. Nothing he did could interrupted their single-minded activity for long.

'What do we say to each other?'

The question was bold enough, but he looked uncharacteristically shy.

'Why did he bring you here?' Amy said.

Her despairing whisper compelled him to attempt a wider view of their situation.

'Circumstances,' he said. 'I've told you before. We are all made by circumstances. The forces that shape our society shape us. I am what my society makes me. Bloody hell, could anything be more true than in my case? Because I can see that, I have no objection. I revel in it! And that's why I offer myself to be used by the force that will reshape that society and improve it beyond all recognition. That's why I cheerfully hand over the keys of my future to the Party. For me, nothing could be easier.'

Amy's eyes were enlarged with a frank admiration she no longer attempted to conceal.

'How many times have you been in prison?' she said.

'I've lost count,' he said.

He made a flamboyant gesture.

'I'm a jailbird,' he said. 'Disgraceful, isn't it? It's a wonder I haven't been cut out of chapel.'

'How many times?'

'Honestly I hardly remember. You mean, since . . .?'

With unexpected delicacy he refrained from defining the period since they had been lovers.

'It's part of the political process,' he said. 'And none of it your fault, my lovely. A bit of bound over here and breaking sureties there. Nothing serious see. Three months was the worst.'

'It's what he admires,' Amy said. 'Your sacrifice.'

'That's a bit of a bourgeois way of looking at it,' Pen said. 'Prisons are of our own making. You're only truly free when you feel you're helping to shape the future.'

'I've tried my best.'

Amy's blue eyes were glistening with tears. Her hand groped out blindly for a broad blade of grass to tug at. In the silence they could hear the shrill buzz of a honey-bee temporarily trapped under the broken glass of a cold-frame rotting against the brick wall. The frame had been broken long enough for an ash sapling to grow out of it and cast a shadow almost to the height of the wall.

'He doesn't really know me,' Amy said. 'In a way it's Enid he's still married to. But I want to do my best for him.'

'Well, damn, of course you do.'

He paid her such close and sympathetic attention that her whole being enlarged itself and became the chief growth and flower of the neglected garden. When she raised her head he studied the parallel tracks of tears coursing down her cheeks. Moved by tenderness, he shifted close enough to check their flow and then caress the smoothness of her cheek with the side of his finger.

'Now what's the comic song?'

He searched for the words as a form of appropriate incantation.

'Wonderful Amy? Wonderful. Wonderful. That's what you are, see? Wonderful.'

With great care he began to unbutton her frock. She watched his fingers like a child who observes with pleasurable fear the details of a delicate ritual. From the far distance came the shrill whistle of a shepherd and his faint angry cry as he reprimanded the dog he was exercising. Overcome with alarm, Amy seized Pen's hand and held it still. He showed how calm and patient he could be.

'I dreamt about you,' he said. 'Wasn't much else I could do was there? Just that and hope. Going over the little we've been allowed to enjoy. And hoping to have it again.'

She tried to push his hands away: but his persistent skill transformed her small protests into reluctant forms of collaboration. His hands slid along her skin as though they were relearning the landscape of her body with a blind adoration.

'I dreamt about you too.'

Her whispered confession was the end of words. Their mouths were given up to fervent kissing. They embraced each other with a strange combination of rage and desperation. Their bodies fought

178

on the warm ground with uninhibited strength to win back the reality of a union they had so long been obliged only to dream about. The place where they lay became their abode of love, as much part of them as they were part of each other. The sun's rays dried the sweat on their naked bodies as it dried the grass on which they lay exhausted with the effort of possessing each other. After such exercise they could have no more secrets from one another. The naked truth was the only fit expression of the unity they had achieved. Staring at the blue distance of the sky, Amy stretched out her hand to feel his body alongside her.

'If this were a dream,' she said, 'I would never want to wake up. Only sleep for ever.'

Pen did not speak. He leaned over her body to admire and stroke and kiss it. The yellow dress still clung to her elbows. Where his hand moved across her shoulders and her breasts, light moved and caused her damp skin to gleam. As his kissing wandered down her body she held his head in her hands and demanded a more explicit communication.

'Pen, listen,' she said. 'How can I come to you?'

He stared at the light shining in her eyes and sighed. It was a question to which he could give no satisfactory answer.

'I know I was wrong,' Amy said. 'I've made a mistake. I know that. And you are entitled to punish me for it. Of course you are. But if it's true, if it's true we are two halves of one whole, surely we have to be together?'

He remained silent. He searched through the pockets of his jacket for a packet of cigarettes. In the distance they heard the shepherd whistle again. The cry carried on the wind suggested encouragement and approval. All Pen found in his pockets was the necktie he had worn in order to appear a respected member of the deputation waiting upon the chairman of Amalgamated Holdings. He pulled the red tie out to its full length before starting to roll it up into a tight ball. Amy began to dress with jerky self-conscious movements. She looked around at the overgrown garden as if she were calling to mind her old dislike of the place.

Pen spoke at last.

'You have to let the wave of time carry you along,' he said.

179

'What's that supposed to mean?'

Like a harassed housewife, Amy busied herself with folding the napkin and putting the tea things away in the basket.

'In the larger context,' Pen said. 'In terms of the revolutionary crisis, what we want for ourselves doesn't matter all that much any more.'

Amy's laugh was a nervous reaction.

'Oh my goodness,' she said. 'I had no idea you were so important.'

'Not me!'

Pen spoke with explosive emphasis.

'Us then,' Amy said.

She struggled to sound self-possessed. On her feet she began to brush her dress and shake the creases out of her brown apron.

'Go on,' she said. 'Tell me more.'

'There is nothing more,' Pen said. 'We have to subordinate our personal whims and wishes to the overriding need of the revolution and the Party.'

'So you wouldn't want me to leave Cilydd in case the Party needed him,' Amy said. 'Is that it?'

He shook his head angrily.

'It's not that simple,' he said. 'That's all I'm saying. Anyway this situation was never of my making. And what about that kid? Little Bedwyr? At one time you were prepared to sacrifice everything for him.'

'You do want to punish me,' she said.

'Good God, no,' he said.

Amy stood above him, the basket on her arm.

'That's why you came up here with your deputation. That's why you came. To make me suffer.'

Angrily he reached out to take her arm and bend it so that she was forced to go down on her knees. She cried out with pain. The basket toppled over.

'You bully,' she said. 'Call yourself a socialist.'

To comfort her he tried to envelop her in his arms as if she were a child hurt. Clumsily he covered her distorted face with kisses.

'You are all I ever wanted,' he said, 'in this world or the next. You. You.'

Only his hands, his limbs, the strength of his body seemed capable of saying the things he longed to say. She struggled in his arms to assert her independence. The breathless protests she managed to make only fuelled his desperate aggression.

'You don't want me,' she said. 'You don't want me.'

The skill and patience he had shown before evaporated like something that had never been. He used all his strength so that the relationship of their bodies became a grotesque violent mockery of the shape of love. Her nails dug into his shoulders. Spittle flowed from the corner of her mouth. Her neck and thighs were bruised. Nothing would assuage the torment of his emotions except possessing her again. When it came, the act of mating was brutal and brief. Her fists battered weakly against his face and chest until he fell away from her groaning her name with what sounded like confused despair. She shifted as far from him as she could to dress herself. With her back turned and through her angry sobs she examined herself, showing her disgust at her condition. He lay face downwards in the grass as still as a corpse on a battlefield, one arm stretched out for help that would never come. While she was picking up the things from the basket, she heard from the direction of the house the birdlike voice of a little boy piping out a question to whoever was accompanying him.

'Oh, my God . . .'

The desperation in her voice made Pen look up. Her arm shot out towards him in an absurdly dramatic gesture.

'You must hide,' she said. 'In the garden shed. Do you hear me?'

Obsessed with the state of her dress she hurried towards the garden doorway. Near the poppies she made a last effort to repair her appearance and restore herself to a state of outward composure. She stood still with her head thrust forward in an attempt to identify the sounds of sporadic conversation outside the house. The man spoke as loudly as he could in country fashion to reassure anyone that might be listening that he was going about his lawful occasions. He encouraged the child to ask the most naïve questions so that he could give grandfatherly replies that would demonstrate disinterested good humour spiced with weathered wisdom.

'Is Mr Lloyd gone to heaven, grandfather?'

Amy heard this question clearly enough as she walked towards the house in the shadow of the sycamore trees. The little boy's head was tilted right back as he looked at the molecatcher's weathered face ready to absorb the nuance of expression along with the answer.

'Nothing could be more certain,' the molecatcher said.

The twinkle in his small eyes belied the solemnity in his voice. One bowed leg was stretched forward to demonstrate to his grandson and anyone else who cared to watch that this was the way a working man rested before taking out his tobacco box from his waistcoat pocket to provide himself with a well-earned plug to chew.

'A man of unquestionable virtues,' he said.

He had already noted Amy's approach, but it was part of his rustic etiquette not to betray this fact until she was close enough to greet with appropriate courtesy.

'Those are the kind who are chosen,' he said. 'No question about that. Good afternoon, Mrs More. I saw the car in the lane.'

Amy stood at some distance not confident enough of her appearance to subject herself to the molecatcher's keen scrutiny. There was no reason either why he should begin to make guesses about the contents of the basket on her arm.

'Good afternoon, Robert Thomas.'

Her voice was that of a benevolent schoolteacher. The molecatcher immediately drew her attention to his grandson.

'This is little Bobi,' he said. 'My daughter's son. We have called at the suggestion of your good husband. He asked me to take a look at the place with a view to ridding it of rats and any other vermin.'

Amy remained statuesque and silent as he waited for her reaction to a piece of information that was also a creditable licence for his intrusion.

'I bring the boy with me on these occasions,' Robert Thomas said. 'To Glanrafon and Ponciau, that is. We are never too young to learn. Or too old for that matter.'

His shoulders shook with silent laughter once he was sure that a smile had dawned on Amy's shaded face.

182

'This is little Bedwyr's mother,' Robert Thomas said. 'You've seen little Bedwyr, haven't you, Bobi? Playing at Glanrafon Stores. You've even played with him on occasion. Isn't that a fact?'

'It's not really convenient today, Robert Thomas,' Amy said. 'I expect my husband will be along with some strangers any minute.'

The molecatcher had already raised his hand to indicate that he and his grandson would vanish with all speed and think no less of Amy or her husband for a minor inconvenience that after all would be put to good use on his next professional visit.

'When next you call at the shop, Robert Thomas,' Amy said. 'I will leave the key with my sister-in-law.'

'Excellent, Mrs More.'

Amy remained standing in the shadow of the sycamores until the molecatcher and his grandson had passed out of sight and out of earshot.

18

WITH HER HANDS CLASPED BEHIND HER BACK, AMY WAS SHOWING lively interest in the series of water-colours on the parlour walls of the Garden Cottage at Plas Iscoed. Miss Eirwen was less patient with her own efforts.

'How can one compete with nature!'

She muttered to herself as she limped towards the bay window. The cottage was unoccupied and the air was stale. She struggled to open a window. In the drive immediately below the steep bank which was covered with St John's wort, her uniformed chauffeur, Griffiths, was waiting patiently alongside the Daimler. He looked up at her expectantly. Her gesture indicated that she did not require his help.

'Would you like to see upstairs?'

Her pictures hung on every available space. Amy looked at each one politely as they made their way upstairs. Eirwen leaned on her arm and laughed both at her work and at her disability.

'You wouldn't have to put up with all these,' she said. 'There are far too many. I don't know where else to hang them, that's the trouble.'

The water-colours on the stairs were mostly studies of Eirwen's favourite flowers: anemonies, lilies, chrysanthemums. The attempts to paint corners of the terraces and gardens and parklands surrounding Plas Iscoed were less successful and relegated to the darker corners.

'It's very dry,' Eirwen said. 'Which is rather good considering the climate and the long period it has to stand completely empty. But it needs living in, like any other house. There are really only three bedrooms and that small room for the maid next to the bathroom. Do you have a nanny for the little boy?'

Amy laughed and shook her head.

'I do ask the most ridiculous question, don't I? You could have whoever you wanted to stay. It would be rather nice to have lively and artistic people making use of the place. But all that would be entirely up to your husband. If he needed peace and quiet for his creative work he could have it here, for as long as he liked.'

Eirwen continued to talk more rapidly as if to relieve Amy of any obligation to express gratitude.

'I mean what else is the place good for? I thought once, you know, of moving in here myself and turning the Plas over to some kind of educational venture. But when it became obvious I was going to become some sort of a cripple it meant I needed more room rather than less. And I excuse myself on the grounds that at least my needs and my rather helpless condition do at least provide employment for people who might very well otherwise be unemployed.'

She paused to invite comment. Amy remained judiciously silent.

'One has to justify one's privileges,' Miss Eirwen said. 'Well, at least I do. There have to be good works, of one kind or another, and there has to be patronage of the arts.'

In the bathroom she raised her walking-stick to break an ancient cobweb above the window. A wasp was trapped at the bottom of the white bath tub. It wiped its front legs against each other as though it was aware of the hopelessness of its position. For a moment they watched it with detached interest. In the profound silence they heard a snatch of music from the string quartet playing in the sunken garden.

'Perhaps you want to join in the festivities?'

'Oh, no.'

Amy was quick to reassure her.

'It's more interesting here,' she said.

They moved across the landing to the front bedroom. There were dead flies on the dust sheet that covered the double bed. Amy opened the window, removed the dust sheet and shook it in the mild breeze. The chauffeur looked up. He had lit a cigarette which he concealed from view in his fist. Beyond the trees, Amy could see the tops of the tents pitched on the central lawn and flags fluttering from the poles. At the far end of the lake she could see the boat-house with its white façade in imitation of a Greek temple. Viewed from the manor-house, or from the Garden Cottage, it was a focal point in the landscape.

'You know we have detectives in the house,' Miss Eirwen said. 'From Scotland Yard.'

She smiled at Amy's nervousness.

'They're guarding the Frenchmen,' Miss Eirwen said. 'David was keen for them to come and witness this League of Nations Union Rally. I suppose it does some good. We must believe that, surely?'

She waited for Amy to show her agreement.

'David tells me the French are acutely worried about this business in Spain. He says they are absolutely determined the war should not spread. And our government agrees with the French. Sir Prosser says intervening in Spain would be like lighting a match above a powder keg.'

Miss Eirwen breathed deeply as she took in the peaceful scene. The music of Haydn wafted towards them on the summer air.

'Another European war in my lifetime is something too awful to contemplate,' she said. 'I know that much at least.'

Amy's hands clenched nervously inside the pockets of her blazer. She turned to study the water-colours on the pale walls of the sparsely furnished bedroom.

'He does his best.'

185

She could hear Miss Eirwen's pleading openly for her brother.

'There is a world-wide depression and that can't be poor David's fault. Do you know there was a time when our family was regarded as almost the ideal employer. That's why he was so hurt when those men turned up at the hospital. Public memory is so frighteningly short. We were the very first you know to institute pit-head baths. And when David had his twenty-first, the miners themselves ran a special train excursion to bring their families up here to the celebrations in the village. It rained all day and the field was an absolute quagmire, but they sang like angels.'

In the silence it became apparent that her fond recollections had made little impression on Amy.

'I know the conditions in the South are terrible and distressing. All the unemployment is dreadful. I know that. But it was very unfair to David to have to face an accusing deputation on the very day he was opening a hospital. And I said as much to Tasker. It was so discourteous.'

'It wasn't Tasker's fault,' Amy said.

Her defence sounded lame and half-hearted.

'He's so emotional about everything,' Eirwen said. 'And he seems totally unaware of how much he gets on David's nerves. And mine if it came to that.'

'He's a good man.'

Amy's protest sounded both sulky and inadequate.

'Oh, of course he is,' Eirwen said. 'But he brings all these things on himself. Bobbing about trying to reconcile this and reconcile that. People resent it you see. And of course Prosser P. thinks it's all a great joke. "Who does old Tasker think he is?" He said this to me as if it were all my fault. "The Gandhi of Wales?"'

She saw Amy bite her lower lip.

'We must be frank with each other,' she said. 'But we mustn't let these things come between us either, must we?'

She reached out her cold hand. Amy was obliged to take it.

'There is so much good we can do,' Eirwen said. 'If we work together. It's wrong to make exaggerated promises and so on, but I feel closer to you than I do to almost anyone. Even David. Nothing would give me greater happiness than knowing that you are making use of this place. In any way you like. And to see that little boy playing here. It would bring the whole place back to life. Speak seriously to that husband of yours. Will you promise? I know he's carried away by his sympathy for the poor and so on. But he is a poet. Sooner or later he will have to pause and give his Muse a chance. And where better than here?'

Together they turned to admire the view. The ordered landscape, the music, the expanse of blue sky and the curve of fleecy clouds had a visible effect on the behaviour of the guests at the Fête. The extent of the grounds easily absorbed their numbers so that groups could emerge with trays of afternoon tea from the refreshment tents and look out for sheltered retreats with the measured care of temporary proprietors. The cars and buses that had brought them were totally hidden among the trees that also hid the long entrance drives.

'I would so love to paint this scene,' Miss Eirwen said. 'There is nothing more difficult than placing figures in a sunlit landscape. Nothing. Anyhow, I'm not very good at doing figures. It's all very well to be impressionistic with blobs and nobs. But I would love to be able to record all this like one of the Dutch masters. Can you imagine anything more ridiculous?'

'You mustn't blame Tasker,' Amy said. 'Really you musn't.'

Miss Eirwen smiled at her affectionately and patted the back of her hand.

'Very well, my dear. All is forgiven and forgotten. If that's what you want.'

Amy pressed her advantage.

'I think it would be wonderful if he could stay here for a while.'

The initial idea seemed to have little appeal.

'He needs time to think,' Amy said. 'I think he's reached some kind of a crossroads in his life. He needs time to stand back and reassess.'

Amy gestured urgently as she made the effort to express herself.

'He's been battered by those people at Pendraw. I mean that. Literally battered. It's a horrid little town in many ways. The last place on earth for an idealist, for a reformer, for a sensitive man like Tasker. He needs a rest. He really does. Perhaps they would appreciate him more if they knew he was highly thought of at Plas Iscoed.'

Miss Eirwen closed her eyes, possibly to blot out the vision of Tasker Thomas ensconced in the Garden Cottage.

'He'd be lecturing me all day,' she said. 'Every chance he could get. I don't think I could stand it.'

'I know he sets tremendous store on your judgement of things,' Amy said. 'I think he is suffering from a sense of failure. What he needs is a chance to achieve something.'

'That's true of everyone, surely?'

Both took refuge in silence. The desire for warmth and understanding remained, but it appeared that nothing they could think of saying would bring them any closer. They could only turn their attention to the extensive view through the window.

'Just look at that!'

Miss Eirwen pointed at a small procession led by her brother David pushing Sir Prosser Pierce's wheelchair. As a concession to late summer Sir Prosser wore a panama hat with a curved brim. They were followed by two elegant figures prepared to pay Sir Prosser the maximum diplomatic attention. They were bare-headed and their glassy brilliantined hair caught the sunlight as they bent forward to catch Sir Prosser's jovial remarks.

'My goodness,' Eirwen said. 'Did you ever see a man so puffed up with self-importance?'

It was a deliberate irreverence.

'And here come the detectives guarding the Frenchmen. Two plain-clothes policemen. My goodness what a subject. If only I could keep them still for a few minutes I would love to try it.'

Amy was responding with a sympathetic smile. It was enough to encourage Eirwen to further rapid appraisal.

'It's like a royal progress, isn't it? And he's simply dying for everyone to know that he is in conference with two diplomats from Paris. And David is so patient with him. I suppose politicians are important. They make decisions that affect all our lives. But I do wish Sir Prosser wouldn't be quite so pompous about it.'

The wheelchair had arrived at the ornamental bridge which crossed a small stream at the point where it flowed into the lake.

188

Here Sir Prosser could see and be seen. He raised his walking-stick to point at a boat with a red sail that had emerged from the white façade of the boat-house.

'"French Diplomats with Bodyguards",' Eirwen said. 'The title alone would be enough to get the picture hung in the Academy. "Politician in Wheelchair" wouldn't be quite so catchy. Oh, dear. Figures are so difficult. If I had a camera it might help. But that would be inadequate. One is always too far away or too near.'

She was slow to realise that Amy had become restless.

'Shall we go back to the house?' she said. 'We could see a great deal more from my studio window.'

The figure in the boat was attaching banners to the mast. There were words printed on them but they could not be read while the banners only twisted in the breeze. Guests were moving towards the side of the lake. The man was struggling so hard to stretch out the strips of cloth, his boat was threatening to capsize. Momentarily the word 'SPAIN' became legible before collapsing as the boat veered about.

'Oh no.'

Amy groaned.

'What is it?'

Miss Eirwen was immediately suspicious. From his wheelchair on the bridge, Sir Prosser was waving his stick in an imperious manner. He plainly objected to the boat and whatever it represented. Lord Iscoed was beckoning to the two plain-clothes men. The boat was close enough to the shore for Amy to believe she recognised the man who had triumphantly unrolled one of his slogans. It read 'AID FOR SPAIN NOW!'

'I must go to him.'

Amy muttered to herself. Miss Eirwen tried to restrain her.

'Is it your husband, Amy? Is it?'

'They'll arrest him.'

From the outbuildings behind Plas Iscoed, dogs had begun to bark. Amy turned on her heel and fled from the bedroom. In the drive she was confronted by Griffiths, Miss Eirwen's chauffeur. For a moment it seemed as though he thought she was escaping and that it was his duty to catch her. His stance was resentful and hostile. At the best of times, being the servant of an ailing spinster was an irksome condition for so masculine a man. He would have been glad to capture Amy and subject her to some form of unbending authority. She squeezed past the Daimler and began to run. A path through the trees brought her quickly to the edge of the lake. She saw Pen Lewis wearing her husband's second-best Homburg hat and distributing leaflets so lavishly among the guests that some of them were littering the ground. Marching purposefully forward she saw he was also wearing John Cilydd's grey suit. It was buttoned tightly around his powerful frame. She found it easy to elbow her way through people so intent on behaving themselves in spite of their growing curiosity. Even as the two plain-clothes men were advancing, she took hold of Pen's arm.

'Mr Lewis,' she said. 'Would you come with me? The Honour-able Eirwen Owens wants to speak with you.'

She spoke loudly enough for anyone nearby to hear the invitation. The plain-clothes men hesitated. They turned to wait for Lord Iscoed to trundle Sir Prosser's wheelchair in their direction. The two Frenchmen stood on the bridge, puzzled and intrigued by what they saw of native behaviour. Pen was ready to face the opposition. The Homburg hat was tilted back and he was prepared to bawl out with the cheerful largesse of a fairground barker. Amy pinched his arm as hard as she could. She began to steer him in the direction of the Plas.

'Miss Eirwen is waiting,' she said. 'We mustn't keep her.'

Pen looked back, reluctant to lose an opportunity to confront the class enemy. Amy whispered fiercely between her teeth.

'Walk, you bastard.'

He was so surprised at her vehemence she was able to lead him easily through the sunken garden. Here the quartet had stopped playing to enjoy their well-earned tea. They were absorbed in their own conversations and plainly unaware of anything untoward. Pen waved an arm to gain their attention.

'Flunkey Fascism,' he said. 'Play your little tunes while the Spanish Republic is being murdered!'

Their looks of alarm brought him only momentary satisfaction. Amy pushed him hard in the direction of a narrow path through a maze of clipped evergreen hedges. They emerged behind a refreshment tent to confront a row of indoor servants and women from the estate. They stood with their sleeves rolled up, washing dishes in enamelled basins. Pen began to distribute the leaflets he had left among them. Amy snatched the bundle from his hand and slapped them down angrily on the nearest table. He grinned at her, finally reconciled to the retreat she was imposing on him.

'Where's John Cilydd?'

Amy could have been an anxious mother seeking the whereabouts of her erring son. Pen winked at her mischievously.

'With the girls, where else?'

'What girls?'

'Margot and Hetty. Margot has joined the Party. I'm not sure about Hetty. But they're both on picket duty. Outside the West Lodge. Carrying a massive great banner between them, "Save the Spanish Republic". Never saw anything like those two. They seem to know everything. They know exactly who's on the side of the Fascists. And your pal, Sir Prosser, is one of them.'

'He's not my pal,' Amy said angrily.

'What's he doing living here then? Using it like his private retreat. The evil little gnome has openly declared for a quick Fascist victory.'

From the terrace, Pen began to show some interest in the big house.

'So this is it,' he said. 'Where's the old bird herself? Gone into hiding?'

As he spoke the Daimler drew up in front of a wooden ramp that covered half the shallow flight of stairs from the pillared portico of the main entrance to the level of the first terrace. Griffiths pressed the horn. A butler and a footman emerged to assist Miss Eirwen out of the car. Once outside she stood still as though she expected Amy to join her. When Amy failed to move she accepted the butler's arm to help her up the ramp. Pen nudged Amy.

'Thought you were going to introduce me,' he said.

She stood still, occupied with her own thoughts. He made an effort to guess what they were.

'Cooked your goose, then, have I?'

'Don't talk rubbish.'

She marched him beyond the hexagon-shaped library out of view of the house. Beyond the outbuildings on the south-west side, Amy's little car was parked under the beech trees. As they climbed in, she turned to look back at the house for the last time.

'I came to argue a case for Tasker Thomas,' she said. 'You've just about ruined that.'

Pen began to unbutton the waistcoat he was wearing. He breathed out dramatically.

'Whew,' he said. 'That's better.'

He tried to be sympathetic as he saw the troubled look on Amy's face.

'You don't want help from people like that, girl,' he said. 'Not when you know which side they are on. They've got blood on their hands.'

'She's just a lonely spinster,' Amy said. 'That's all. She doesn't care about politics.'

'She lives on the profits,' Pen said. 'First the blood of the Welsh miners and now the blood of the Spanish people. My God, you've got to be blind, deaf and dumb not to see it. Think of their Prime Minister sending off that slinky bastard Halifax to drink Mussolini's health in Rome. I tell you the buggers are hand in glove with Rome and Berlin. It's what Wes Hicks calls the Invisible Axis.'

The car jerked forward. Amy drove along the drive towards the West Lodge. Pen sat back with his thumbs in the armholes of Cilydd's waistcoat, well pleased with his argument and his adventure. He sat up with surprise when Amy turned off the main drive into a track leading to a plantation. Where she drew up, the young saplings were surrounded by chicken wire to protect them from the sharp teeth of the squirrels. She switched off the engine and turned to look at him squarely. Her silence made him uneasy. He smiled at her.

'What's up?' he said.

'Pretty pleased with yourself.'

There was little rebuke in the way she spoke.

'I'm curious to know how you will react to a piece of

information I have and no one else has. You will be the very first to know. I'm pregnant.'

They were surrounded by the quiet of the countryside. There was no dwelling-place anywhere within view. At the end of a short tunnel of trees they could see black cattle move like a mirage as they grazed waves of rich grass. The field was distanced by its own heat haze and yet the silence was so deep they could hear the crisp rhythm of the cropping. No wind reached them through the trees and the birds were silent. Pen's lips moved positively enough, but his voice seemed to die in his throat.

'Is it mine?'

His hand stole shyly along the back of the seat until his fingers touched her shoulder. Her answer disturbed him.

'Do you want it to be?' she said.

He rubbed his forehead hard. He muttered like an adult who tries to answer an impossibly simple question from a child.

'Well of course,' he said. 'Of course.'

'This is a wonderful place to be innocent,' Amy said. 'Whatever innocence means. Like the Garden of Eden. I think she did want to leave it all to me. It wouldn't be much use without innocence as well.'

Pen's head was shaking in mute protest. She had him at such a disadvantage. Amy smiled and stretched her arms.

'You don't have to negotiate with me, comrade. You just say what you want and you can have it.'

'Oh, Amy . . .'

Overcome by emotion he embraced her. She made no resistance, but her passivity soon made him realise how closely he was under observation.

'You tear me to pieces,' he said. 'Do you know that? You shatter me.'

He brushed his lips urgently across her forehead. 'Oh damn . . . oh damn . . .'

'It's your choice.' Amy spoke quietly. 'If you want me still, I'll give it all up. Even Bedwyr.'

He made a noise like an animal in pain.

'I'll do whatever you want, Pen. I'll join the Party. And you can do whatever you have to do. A hunger march or whatever. I'll take my share of the load if it's what you want.'

Amy's voice was quiet and utterly beguiling. He burst out in raucous protest against so much sweetness.

'Why the hell did you marry him? Why? Can you tell me that?'

Amy remained calm.

'You can always analyse these things when it's too late. Or you think you can. Selfishness is the simple answer. But of course that's the simple answer to everything.'

'You're not selfish,' Pen said. 'And I'm not either.'

'He rescued me from the classroom. He offered me security. If you're born poor that's something you long for. I wanted to look after Bedwyr. I wanted to love him and care for him for Enid's sake. And I was afraid of you. Afraid of poverty. Afraid of life.'

They both bowed their heads in silence. Any sound they heard was no more than the reverberation of their inner uncertainties. They had little comfort to offer each other. He reached out to grasp her hand and then let it go.

'You think you have the strength to twist the sinews of history and all the time you are just a bloody victim.'

He slumped back helplessly in the passenger seat. Amy stared at the pallor of his skin. He looked physically ill.

'What is it?' she said.

'I'm thinking of him,' Pen said. 'He depends so completely on you. What would become of him?'

Amy leaned forward resting her hands and her chin on the steering wheel. Her lips were stretched but she was not smiling.

'He's such a vulnerable creature,' Pen said. 'Now there's innocence if you like. He wants to join the Party. I told him to hold his horses. He couldn't understand why. I said he'd be more use to us as a lawyer. He's so vulnerable. Such an awful mixture of intelligence and innocence or ignorance, whichever is the right word.'

'So you've made your choice.'

She spoke in a low voice devoid of praise or censure. He reacted as though she had inflicted on him the most painful wound. He rolled about in his seat unable to escape his agony.

'Just give me time,' he said. 'That's all I ask.'

'That's the one thing I haven't got to give,' Amy said.

She pressed the self-starter and reversed the car back to the drive.

19

THE MIST IMPOSED ITS OWN SILENCE ON GLANRAFON STORES AS IT did on the surrounding countryside. It hung outside the kitchen window, pale and envious of the warmth inside. Aunty Bessie was making pastry and the operation took up half the scrubbed surface of the kitchen table. Mrs Lloyd sat in her high-backed chair at the other end of the table with her felt cap on her head. Her chapped fingers twitched in the lap of her apron as her eye followed the muffled action of Bessie's glass rolling-pin. The weather had immobilised her like an infirmity and she was fretting at her own inactivity. Nanw emerged from the scullery with a basket on her arm and the lower half of her face swathed in a thick woollen scarf. She glanced meaningfully at Amy who stood in her hat and coat near the passageway to the shop as if she would never sit down in Glanrafon kitchen without having been specifically invited to do so.

'Where are you going?'

The grandmother's question was muttered like an accusation. Nanw was ready with her answer.

'To look for eggs. Amy, will you come with me?'

Together they passed through the shop which was closed for the half-day. Across the yard that was bisected by a private road they could make out the shape of Robert Thomas the molecatcher in the doorway of Uncle Tryfan's workshop. In the granary above, Bedwyr and Clemmie had acquired a new playmate. Bobi, the molecatcher's grandson, was jumping on and off the ancient weighing machine. It creaked and clattered while the other two made a busy pretence of weighing him. Every sound that was made was distinct but isolated in the cold mist. Even the clang of a hammer on the anvil of the smithy, only a hundred yards down the road was robbed of its customary reverberation. Robert Thomas was diverting Uncle Tryfan with gnomic pronouncements. Amy stood still to listen and smile.

'Hedges move in the mist.'

Robert was intrigued by the portentous sound of his own voice. Uncle Tryfan had a small lamp lit on his work-bench. He clutched one of Bobi's boots against his leather apron. A row of hob-nails in his mouth glittered like iconistic embellishments of his beatific smile as he listened to the molecatcher indulge his fancy.

'And there are certain rocks that can move in the mist,' Robert Thomas said. 'Transport their substance from the top to the bottom of the hill like pregnant women on their way to market. I suppose you would call that rank superstition, Tryfan Lloyd. As an orthodox man.'

Nanw plucked at Amy's sleeve impatiently.

'Listen to him,' she said. 'That man will say anything, in or out of liquor.'

The boys in the granary were laughing. The sound was high-pitched and excited. Momentarily it commanded Robert Thomas's attention.

'Children!' he said. 'What an empty place this world would be without them, Tryfan Lloyd.'

'Clemmie's getting over-excited,' Amy said. 'He's such a nervous child. Frightened of his own shadow. And then something comes over him and he gets wild and silly.'

Nanw had more serious matters she wanted to discuss. Looking for eggs was no more than a pretext to leave the house so that they could talk more freely. Between the blank gable of the stone outbuildings and the Dutch barn the soggy ground was partially hidden by scattered hay. On the slope ahead the black branches of an oak and an ash loomed alongside each other out of the mist making stark contrary signals.

'The thing is one has to think of the future.'

Nanw closed her mouth abruptly, alarmed at the loudness of her voice in the surrounding quiet. In the shadows of the barn she whispered.

'She hasn't made a will, has she?'

She seemed hopeful that Amy could enlighten her. This was her brother's wife and her brother was a qualified solicitor. There could be few things that Cilydd would not confide in his wife.

'Not as far as I know,' Amy said.

She took hold of the worn rungs of the ladder leaning against the highest section of hay.

'Well she should, shouldn't she?'

Nanw was making an appeal for Amy's support.

'It's not just me being fussy. That's what he'd say if I mentioned the matter. But the thing is I live here, day in, day out, and I see things he never sees.'

'Of course you do.'

It was mild encouragement but Nanw seized on it eagerly.

'What will happen when she goes? She can't live for ever. Nobody can. She's not well. I can see that. And yet everything goes on as though she were going to be here for ever.'

Amy had moved up the ladder until she could sit on a rung and look down at Nanw with her chin in her hand.

'She owns everything,' Nanw said. 'I don't care so much about myself, but what about Aunty Bessie? And what about Uncle Tryfan? I mean Simon and Gwilym are so jealous of each other they'll tear the place apart when she's gone.'

Nanw plainly longed for her sister-in-law to share the extent of her disquiet and foreboding. The degree of sympathy Amy was showing was too detached.

'John Cilydd should do something about it,' Nanw said. 'After all it's his inheritance as well. And little Bedwyr. Won't you make him talk to her?'

Amy nodded. It was no more than a sign that she would do her best.

'Nanw,' she said. 'Didn't you ever think of getting married?'

The question was gently put. Nanw responded with a sour smile.

'I was born to be an old maid,' Nanw said. 'Tied to this place. Tethered to the Post Office section.'

Amy showed more intense concern.

197

'Wasn't there anyone?' she said.

With the empty basket on her arm, Nanw snatched at a handful of hay in which to cradle any eggs they might find.

'Oh yes, there was someone.'

She muttered her confession.

'What happened to him?'

Amy's eyes were large with curiosity.

'He was killed in the war,' Nanw said. 'Not that it would have made all that much difference, if it's marriage you're talking about. He would never have married me. I just wasn't smart enough. He was very ambitious.'

'Men.'

The word seemed a stop-gap rather than a categorical condemnation, while Amy considered how much sympathetic interest was still called for. The young man in question had been dead for at least eighteen years. She contented herself with an acceptable generalisation.

'Such selfish creatures.'

She shifted up the ladder to a plateau of loose hay. The scent was a memory of summer: an invitation to warm oblivion. Here a human being as much as a small animal could hibernate until the cold mist rolled away. Climbing the ladder to bring her head on a level with Amy's, Nanw found her brother's wife curled in a posture that was almost embryonic. The expression on her face was secretive and enclosed. Her question slipped out.

'Amy. Are you . . .?'

It was so tentative and tactful that Amy could only smile lazily and nod. Sooner or later her secret would become common knowledge. There could be no good reason for withholding it from Nanw.

'Does he know? Of course he does.'

Amy smiled enigmatically. Nanw gripped the sides of the ladder more tightly. Early knowledge of such matters was among the few female prerogatives. It was a fact that she could savour and appreciate the longer it remained hidden in her heart and she was grateful to Amy for giving it to her. Amy yawned and stretched herself.

'We ought to be looking for nests,' she said. 'Not making them.'

They plodded about in the hay looking for holes large enough to provide a stray hen with a nest. Amy gave a cry of triumph when she uncovered a clutch of six eggs, brown, clean and recently laid. She was setting them carefully in Nanw's basket, when the blanket of silence was torn by a childish howl from the direction of the granary.

'Bother,' Amy said.

They listened to the ominous wail.

'You can't leave them alone for five minutes. Honestly, who'd want to be a mother?'

She dropped the basket in the hay and climbed down the ladder. Nanw followed her more slowly. Robert Thomas saw them pass with a smile on his weather-beaten face as though life had taught him childish misfortunes and misdemeanours were equally better left to women. Nanw steadied herself with her hand against the wall as she climbed the slippery stone steps to the granary. She heard Amy's rebuke before she saw what had happened. Clemmie's nose was bleeding, but it was Bobi who was crying. Bedwyr's arm stretched out of his sleeve as he plied Amy with a sequence of breathless explanations.

'Bobi, he dropped the weight on his foot Clemmie I told him to lookout he was jumping too much Bobi he show me and Clemmie how strong his father was I said "Look out" and Clemmie knocked his nose on the iron . . .'

'Hush now.'

Firmly Amy stemmed the flow of Bedwyr's confused account. While she and Nanw were cleaning up Clemmie's nose and comforting Bobi, Robert Thomas appeared in the open doorway of the granary. He chewed contentedly at his plug of Amlwch tobacco as he observed the women's efforts. He leaned over the low parapet at the top of the steps to launch a brown ellipse of saliva on its trajectory. It landed in front of a Rhode Island Red cockerel and obliged the bird to pause briefly in its task of printing monotonous hieroglyphics in the band of smooth silt between the road and the cobbled forecourt of the shop. He enjoyed the vantage point at the top of the steps and the alternative views it gave him of the interior and exterior worlds. In this weather they were equally mysterious.

199

'Eyes in the mist,' Robert Thomas said. 'That's what we need in this old world of ours. To pick out the dangers ahead. "So that there shall be no more revenge or inflicting of wounds, nor love of warfare except the War of the Lamb".'

'Bobi has hurt his foot, Robert Thomas,' Nanw said.

She spoke sternly as though the accident were in some measure the molecatcher's fault. The full headlights of an approaching vehicle had captured his attention. The motor car was advancing in cautious low gear. When the driver blew the horn the sound was like the forlorn bellow of a calf lost in the mist.

'"Who is it we see coming from Edom and both his hands covered with blood?"'

'Robert Thomas,' Nanw said. 'You would be better employed keeping an eye on the children instead of trying to grind the air with your endless phrases.'

The molecatcher grinned cheerfully and turned his head to spit again into the mist. His keen eye was now able to identify the motor car.

'Here comes the man in this world I most want to talk to,' he said. 'The man of law and the son and heir so to speak if one may use the expression, crossing the threshold of the mist in his shining chariot.'

He waddled down the damp stone steps stamping his steel heels with practised caution. He watched John Cilydd park his car on the forecourt in front of the shop. He was so anxious to consult him that he made short work of the customary formal compliments.

'If there was time, John Cilydd More, I would like to put before you one or two things I have heard and one or two things I have seen.'

'What is worrying you, Robert Thomas?'

Cilydd frowned as he removed his leather gloves. The mole-catcher was quickly sensitive to his preoccupied state.

'You came safely through the fog.'

He slipped in the solicitous enquiry in a way that suggested he was aware of having omitted to make it initially.

'As you see . . .'

'And I am thankful for it,' Robert Thomas said.

200

It was a polite preliminary before he launched his appeal for advice.

'I was dealing with the vermin around Cae Golau and I encountered two men. And twice this week I have encountered these same two bold men on other land with their survey instruments. In my opinion they were paid agents of the English Air Ministry in London. They ignored me of course. I was something low in the ditch up to his ankles in water. But none the less a being with intelligence. Perhaps a little higher than a beast if a lot lower than an angel. A common man, but a man who has heard and felt the message of peace brought by our respected and reverend Tasker Thomas. Shall the pleasant places be laid waste and the dwellings of them who seek peace reduced to the haunts of the wild fox and the owl.'

'Come to the point, Robert Thomas.'

The molecatcher's mouth hung open momentarily, he was so taken aback by Cilydd's unusual brusqueness. He heard the footsteps of Amy and Nanw on the granary steps.

'My seven and a half acres,' he said. 'Hardly big enough to make a vineyard for Naboth, John Cilydd More, but it's my bit of land and it helps me as one of the lowly of this world to bolster my bit of self-esteem. But it lies in a strategic place. What should I do when the alien government rolls up in its juggernauts and demands to take it from me?'

'Compulsory purchase.'

Cilydd repeated the phrase as though he were dismissing a case. He wanted urgently to talk to Amy. She had heard enough to show more sympathy for the molecatcher's problem.

'John Cilydd,' she said. 'Is that all? Robert Thomas has been worrying about it for days.'

'It's the kind of world we're living in,' Cilydd said. 'We are all victims.'

His Uncle Tryfan had appeared in the doorway of his workshop. It always gave him special pleasure to see his nephew arrive at his old home. They had an understanding. They shared a repertoire of jokes and reminiscences that contrived never to wear out however often they were repeated. He raised Bobi's boot to gain John Cilydd's attention.

'So you've come then,' Uncle Tryfan said. 'In spite of the fog. Would you call this spawning weather? Listen. Robert Thomas wants to consult you urgently on a legal matter.'

'Excuse me. I must have a word with my wife.'

He led Amy away from the others until they and the buildings were hidden in the mist.

'Amy. Listen.'

He spoke in a low excited voice. The things on his mind far transcended local concerns in their importance.

'Pen Lewis has gone to Spain. This card came to the office this morning. Posted from Perpignan ten days ago.'

He held out the card. She did not take it.

'It's amazing really,' he said. 'How some men can take action without any hesitation at all. In Cardiff during the riot case everyone was going on about the anti-Fascist crusade. The time and place to make a stand. A moment that had to be seized to turn the tide of history and all that sort of stuff. Everyone except Pen. All he said to me was "You can't go, comrade. You've got responsibilities. Wife and child and so on." He just slipped away without saying anything to his sister. To fight. You can't help admiring a man like that.'

'It's a war.'

She spoke so quietly he could barely hear her.

'Of course it's a war. It's a crusade. It's the only decent crusade there's ever been. At last the Fascist tide has been stemmed. So far and no further. And from now on it has to be rolled back.'

'A crusade?' Amy said.

She quickened her step. He held out his hand to hold her back.

'Machines don't go on crusades,' she said. 'You know that. They mutilate and destroy. They bring death everywhere and leave the world dead. You know that.'

Cilydd's enthusiasm would not be dimmed.

'Oh but this is different . . .'

His voice rose in his attempt to call her back.

'Of course you have to destroy, before you can rebuild. But it will be a new society, Amy, and a better cleaner world. I hate war as much as you do but what other answer is there? How else can we stop them?'

She walked on as he waited for her to answer, until her figure was lost in the mist.

20

A MY PAUSED FOR BREATH AT THE TOP OF THE FLIGHT OF STAIRS. From the room at the end of the corridor came the strains of Rachmaninov's second piano concerto being played on the gramophone. The romantic surge transcended the worn condition of the record. Connie Clayton smiled understandingly as she waited for Amy.

'Miss Margot,' she said in a hushed respectful tone. 'She says music helps her to get better quickly.'

Through the window on the third floor of 43 Culpepper Place, Amy gazed down at the heaps of soiled snow piled against the iron railings. Two muffled figures on the pavement made their way with uneven circumspection. When they stopped they looked as inanimate as carved posts. The afternoon sun shone in concentric circles of pale fire that consumed the centre of the bare treetops. Outside the dazzle the intricacies of twigs and branches appeared glued to the cold air.

'You look so well, Amy. You look a picture of health I must say.'

Connie Clayton breathed her admiration like a husky article of faith: the figure of a pregnant young woman had to be an affirmation of the supremacy of life. No sequence of words or phrases could hope to do justice to the condition. Amy's coat was open. In the sixth month she carried her pregnancy high. She wore no make-up and in the winter light from the window her skin showed Botticelli smoothness.

'A picture of health.'

Amy followed Connie down the passage and watched her tap her knuckle coyly on the door. Margot Gromont was in bed. A fire blazed in the grate and the room was as warm as an oven. Margot's hair hung over her right eye as she consulted one of the books strewn over her bed. The gramophone needle stuck in a groove and

Margot waved her pencil in its direction urging anyone near to take the thing off.

'It's supposed to help me write,' she said. 'I don't think it does one bit. I'm so lacking in basic discipline.'

Connie Clayton had begun to tidy the room. There were cups and glasses and trays that needed collecting. The hearth needed sweeping. Margot's attempts at writing left the room in a state of chronic disorder.

'Miss Margot,' Connie said. 'I'm not sure you are well enough to be trying to write. The doctor said you should rest you know. Influenza can be very undermining. I remember that terrible Spanish 'flu at the end of the war. It was fearful. Really fearful.'

'Now don't fuss, Connie dear. I'm not ill at all. This is just a subterfuge to give me peace and quiet to finish this report. If that's what I'm going to call it. Now you just leave Amy and me in peace so that we can have a quiet chat. We have some vitally important things to talk about. Haven't we, Amy?'

She smiled as engagingly as she could at Amy who stood as far away as possible from the fire and from the bed, apparently uncertain still of the wisdom of her visit. Connie paused at the door, nursing a tray of dirty cups and glasses.

'Any news of Master Nigel?' she said anxiously.

Margot burst out laughing. This induced a spasm of coughing which left her lying exhausted against her hill of pillows.

'You won't believe this.'

She raised a feeble arm in Amy's direction as she struggled to recover her breath.

'It ought to appeal to you all the same. He's supposed to be driving an ambulance so I can't tell you how he got involved, but the thing is he was in an aeroplane and they were transporting the pregnant wife of some government minister to a hospital in Barcelona for special treatment. It was a pretty rickety affair and they were losing height, so the pilot ordered poor old Nigel to bale out. There in the middle of nowhere. I don't know whether his parachute opened, but he landed in rather a smelly lake!'

Margot pressed her hands against her ribs to prevent a further outburst of painful laughter. Connie responded with fresh outrage although she had heard the story before.

'I don't know what will become of us I'm sure,' Connie said.

'I don't know what it is about Nigel,' Margot said thoughtfully. 'He has his way of rushing bull-headed at things. No finesse I suppose that's what it amounts to. I mean would you believe it, in Albacete he was run over by a donkey!'

This time Connie Clayton permitted herself a faint smile.

'I must get on,' she said.

She glided gracefully from the room. Margot sat up and gazed eagerly at Amy.

'I'm so glad you came,' she said.

Her long jaw hung down and her eyes glowed with excitement and triumph.

'I couldn't believe my eyes,' Margot said. 'There must have been at least two thousand men in the church. There was a platform where the altar used to be and someone was playing a piano on it. Terribly out of tune. And there he was blowing his trumpet for all he was worth, playing "All through the Night" if you please. You should have seen him. He was in wonderful shape. He was in his element.'

Margot reined in her enthusiasm in order to observe the impact of her information on Amy.

'The British and American Battalion headquarters. We've got to win, Amy. We've simply got to. It's a painful process. Of course it is. The whole contingent was due to move into the line within the next couple of days. He gave me this note for you. I promised I'd see it delivered even if I had to go all the way to Pendraw myself. And then as luck had it, Connie told me you were coming to London.'

Margot scrabbled untidily through her papers and books to find Pen Lewis's note. When she held it out, Amy seemed reluctant to accept it. The blue envelope was stained with greasy fingerprints. Margot watched Amy tear it open. The letter was brief enough.

Dear Amy,
Just a line out of the line to say I'm okay and thinking about you. You could have knocked me down with a feather when I bumped into

Comrade Margot in Tarazona. She's a good sort and her heart is in the right place. The whole world has got to understand that we must win the anti-Fascist struggle. We've got to give Franco, Hitler and Mussolini and their capitalist chums one-way tickets to Hell. Keep your chin up and do what you can for the Cause. When this is over I'll answer for any of my responsibilities, Amy. You know what I mean. Salud.

Pen

'Can I see it?'

Margot could strain her curiosity no longer. Amy handed her the piece of paper. Margot scanned it quickly.

'He's right you know,' she said. 'We've got to wake up this country as it's never been woken up before. He's a wonderful man, Amy. An absolute hero. Do you know what I think? When the time comes we've got to dismantle the old order. And that includes the British Empire, my dear. It will be a painful process. No one denies that. But it will be worth it to get rid of capitalism and the twin evils of war and unemployment for ever. And when we come to build a new socialist world, it will be men like Pen Lewis who will take the lead. The selfless ones. The true heroes.'

She waited for some response from Amy.

'Don't you believe me?' Margot said.

Amy moved to the window. She sat down in the chair in front of Margot's writing table.

'I don't know what to believe,' she said.

Margot waved her hands enthusiastically over the papers scattered on her bed.

'It's all perfectly clear to me,' she said. 'That's why I'm trying to write my autobiography. I mean I'm the offspring of what used to be called the ruling class. All my life I've made it my business to try and understand the workings of history. I mean that's why I read PPE at Oxford, for God's sake. If I can explain myself to myself, then that will help a lot of other people to understand what's happening. That's the way I see it. Of course it's a damned sight easier to explain the past than predict the future. I realise that. But if freedom and progress and liberty and fraternity and equality etcetera, etcetera mean anything, fascism and militarism must be stopped. And the horrid paradox is that they can only be stopped by the armed struggle of the workers, throughout the world. And that's the truth of it.'

Margot slapped her hand confidently on the cover of the largest notebook on her bed. She lowered her chin and contemplated the figure of Amy looking through the window.

'You're a big anti-war person, aren't you?' Margot said. 'I was too. When I was fifteen one of my uncles asked me what I was going to do with my life, "Put an end to war", I said. And I meant it too. Of course he just laughed. He didn't even realise my father had been killed in the Great War. And all those young men.'

Margot sank back into her pillows momentarily absorbed in a vision of sadness and loss.

'The meaning of life.'

She murmured to herself pulling long strands of hair through the corner of her mouth.

'We create life, we women. It's men that destroy it. Any fool can see that. That is certainly something that has to change. Old Hetty Rem is absolutely right there. The males have made such a mess of the world since the days of the patriarchs it really is time the ladies had a go. And with machines taking over warfare and hard labour that day cannot be all that far distant. But today the struggle!'

Suddenly overwhelmed with the urge to adventure, Margot jumped out of bed. The yellow pyjamas she was wearing were wide at the ankles and they flapped excitedly as she marched to where Amy sat by the window. The sun was lower in the sky. The oblique light flooded through the window and bathed Amy's head in a golden glow. Margot grasped her by the shoulder.

'We mustn't be afraid,' she said. 'I'm absolutely convinced of that. We have to venture everything. Risk it all. There's no other way.'

Amy looked eager to share so much enthusiastic conviction.

'Why don't you come with me to Paris?' Margot said. 'I'm off tomorrow wet or fine.'

'You're ill,' Amy said.

'Am I hell.'

Margot laughed and pranced gaily around the room.

'Mind over matter,' she said. 'I just wanted a bit of peace and quiet to write. I justify my selfishness by the ends not the means. Action and reflection. Advance and retreat. Ebb and flow. Menstrual cycles. Capture it all on paper and make sense of the process. Do you see what I mean? Social forms. We have to analyse the process. If it's beyond the wit of woman to create the better social shapes then what's the point of talking about socialism? Everything's got to change and a terrible new beauty will be born. Why don't you come?'

Amy turned in her wrists to indicate her pregnant condition. She was smiling, obviously cheered by Margot's high spirits.

'So what?' Margot said. 'You can take that lump with you any-where. Mistress of your own situation, not the slave of circum-stance. Arise ye women and ye workers! I'll take you to hear Thorez orating in the Butte Chaumont. Hear the workers sing.'

Margot began to sing lustily herself.

> 'C'est la lutte finale
> Unisons à demain
> L'international sera
> Le genre humain!'

They began laughing together.

'It would be fun,' Amy said.

'Of course it would. Freedom is making tunnels through the all-encompassing pressure of circumstance.'

Margot was pleased with the notion that had occurred to her.

'Should I put that down? Should I? Circumstance is a substance. That's it! Designed to keep us in our appointed place. Like mud worms wriggling from the cradle to the grave. If you're properly conscious you should make new shapes. Open fresh tunnels.'

Margot rushed to her notebook and began to scribble. Amy watched her with a certain envious amusement.

'What could I do?' Amy said. 'With my schoolgirl French. I'd be petrified.'

'Thousands of things,' Margot said.

Her gestures were positive but unspecific.

'There aren't enough hours in the day or pennies in the bank to spend on this inexhaustible cause. And he might turn up there too. In the Place du Combat. The great Pen. They think he's too valuable for cannon fodder. Battalion commissar and then back to Britain for a speaking tour. He's being groomed for stardom, as they say in the pictures. I'm pretty sure of it.'

Amy was clearly impressed by the extent of Margot's understanding of the complexities of the situation. Margot for her part was thoughtfully contemplating Amy's pregnant condition.

'Tell me,' she said. 'Is it Pen's?'

In such an atmosphere of forthright frankness, nothing but the truth seemed appropriate. Amy nodded.

'Not that it matters,' Margot said. 'In the new society it will be motherhood that counts. But the thing is, he was quite obviously gone on you. It was quite touching really. To see a grown man like that, an absolute hero of labour, blush like a schoolboy. I never saw a chap who more deserved a bit of consolation. Gosh, it opens up such a range of possibilities. After all, what are we? Fully paid-up members of the human race or just child-bearing chattels? Gosh. Look who's down there! Cousin Nigel, returned from the wars.'

Margot pressed against the window to wave down at the figure in the street. Nigel was solidly wrapped in scarves and a leather jacket but his head was bare. His fair hair stood out like frozen straw. Even at a distance they could read a look of alarm on his red face.

'We don't do enough,' Margot said.

She began to search in the large wardrobe for clothes to wear.

'I know enough to understand that. I keep my ears open at the dinner table. I know it's our ruling class that invented this Non-Intervention thing and then pretended it was what the French Socialists wanted. And they try to make people laugh at us. But what I say is if they exercised a fraction of the power they hold, Hitler need never have been allowed back in the Rhineland. All that scares them is the idea of Bolshevik Revolution. They'll do anything, absolutely anything to avoid that. Oh my God, I'd like to exterminate the lot of them. Including my uncle.'

They heard Nigel's heavy tread in the corridor outside. He pushed open the door without knocking. He gave no greeting.

'Talk about the blood of the martyrs!' he said. 'One hell of a mess. On the Jarama. Head on clash between the Moors and the International Brigade. The Saklatvala Battalion cut down from four hundred to less than a hundred. Pen Lewis has been killed.'

'Oh, God.'

Margot fell against the bed. She could not take her eyes off Amy. Nigel put the tips of his fingers in his mouth to blow on them. The silence in the room grew heavier the longer it was maintained. There was nothing to say. The flames crackled in the grate. Amy rose slowly to her feet. Margot struggled for breath.

'Amy. Amy. Where are you going?'

Amy pressed the palm of her hand against the bedroom door.

'Home,' she said. 'Where else?'

21

'THERE SHE IS! LOOK!'

Nanw tugged urgently at her brother's sleeve. She pointed across the deserted promenade in the direction of the Pavilion. The dome was glittering in the spring sunshine. Small clouds made the sky more immense than ever. The tide was almost as far out as the horizon. Stretches of shallow water reflected the cold blue of the sky. Amy was standing by the low wall above the sunken gardens watching children on tricycles chasing each other around the empty bandstand. A winter overcoat emphasised her pregnancy. The children rang their bicycle bells and the sound was like the twitter of starlings.

'What are you going to do, John Cilydd?'

Nanw could not contain her curiosity. Her voice was tinged with a disapproval which seemed to include the length and breadth of Llanelw Promenade. It stretched for two miles from the new bridge over the estuary to the sandhills in the east. Any structures erected on it, or connected with it, like the Pavilion with its octagonal centre dome built in ferro-concrete, or the open-air theatre, or the swimming pool, or the amphitheatre or the tennis courts and bowling greens, were wholly dedicated to entertainment and to diverting the attention of the working class if not the entire human race from the harsh nature of reality.

'Eddie Meredith says there is something between them.'

Nanw's voice was dark with suspicion. There was no knowing the number of rules her sister-in-law might have broken. Her behaviour had become hopelessly unpredictable and egocentric. She was no longer the woman Nanw had once believed she could always rely on. She had taken to wandering alone in places like amusement parks, watching the varieties of ways in which idle and frivolous people while away their time.

'I told Nain she'd gone to Llanelw to look after Esther Parry,' Nanw said. 'I had to say something. She kept on asking about her.'

She looked up at her brother as though she were longing for some sign of approval. It was not forthcoming.

'Of course this isn't the proper time to talk about it. But there never is a proper time for some things it appears. I don't know whether you've thought about it or not John Cilydd, but it really is time Nain made her will. If she hasn't done it already, that is.'

Cilydd was staring at Amy across the width of the promenade.

'I know politics and so on are very important,' Nanw said. 'I'm not a complete fool. But work and business have to be attended to. It would be a very odd state of affairs if everybody wandered off to take part in this or that campaign. This or that movement. Some of us have to stay at home and work. Day in and day out without a word of thanks from anybody.'

Abruptly her brother left her side. She watched him march steadily across the expanse of promenade. When he reached Amy's side, she showed no surprise at his presence. Her hands were deep in her coat pockets and the tip of her nose red with cold.

'They've put up his picture,' Cilydd said.

He took out a clean handkerchief and dabbed at the dewdrop on the end of her nose.

'In the Institute Library. In a heavy frame. It's not very clear. Enlargement of a snap in uniform taken when they were out of the line. But they've written very nicely on it, "supreme sacrifice" and so on.'

Amy's eyes continued to follow the circular motion of the children on their cycles. She shivered with cold. Cilydd placed a protective arm over her shoulder.

'What are you thinking about?' he said.

She answered quite easily.

'Enid,' she said. 'I was thinking about Enid.'

He squeezed her shoulder.

'You've nothing to worry about,' he said. 'I'm sure of it!'

'We were sitting down there once in the summer. The band was playing and there were people everywhere and she was eating ice-cream and laughing. I said, "Enid, what's the joke? Why are you laughing?" She looked at me with those big blue eyes of hers and she said, "I was just thinking we are all made out of that love which fashioned the world." She waved her ice-cream cone around to include everybody. I had no idea what she was talking about. I just watched the people and the kids whizzing around. I still don't understand. But I can hear her voice as clear as a bell.'

She looked at Cilydd. He took her arm and together they walked along the empty promenade.